To my family, with love

THE GOOD TEACHER

Rachel Sargeant grew up in Lincolnshire. She spent several years living in Germany where she taught English and she now lives in Gloucestershire with her husband and children. She is a previous winner of *Writing Magazine*'s Crime Short Story competition, and her writing has appeared in *My Weekly*. She has published three novels and her most recent, *The Perfect Neighbours*, became a top ten Kindle bestseller.

@RachelSargeant3
www.rachelsargeant.co.uk

Also by Rachel Sargeant

The Perfect Neighbours

THE GOOD TEACHER

RACHEL SARGEANT

First published in hardback as *Long Time Waiting*

KILLER READS
A division of HarperCollins*Publishers*
www.harpercollins.co.uk

KillerReads
an imprint of HarperCollins*Publishers* Ltd
1 London Bridge Street
London SE1 9GF

www.harpercollins.co.uk

This paperback edition 2019

First published in Great Britain as *Long Time Waiting* by Robert Hale Ltd 2010

A catalogue record for this book
is available from the British Library

ISBN: 978-0-00-832723-1

Set in Minion by
Palimpsest Book Production Limited, Falkirk, Stirlingshire

Printed and bound by CPI Group (UK) Ltd, Croydon, CR0 4YY

Chapter One

Her back aches like hell. She tries for the hundredth time to read her watch but can't see her wrist, no matter how far she cranes her neck. The hot metal handcuffs cut into her arm and send pain searing up to her shoulder. It might be broken, but fractures are worse than this; she knows that. Her body has taken a pummelling but the bruises will heal.

She shifts her buttocks, peeling the thick pyjama trousers from her clammy thighs. She's in the lounge on a kitchen chair, old with paint splatters, the remnants of previous decorating forays. White speckles from several ceilings, large splodges of powder-blue bathroom sheen, and buttercup, pink and cherry from the nursery project. Happy days long gone. She's never had to sit for so long in this chair. She usually perches on its hard edge long enough to force down a couple of cream crackers and a cup of camomile tea. Even the leisurely Sunday breakfasts are a thing of the past.

Reg Kenny weaves across the lane, taking care not to stray off the tarmac. Not that it would matter much – although the thick grass verge is soaked in dew, the ground below is rock hard. As he pedals, he feels sweat on his forehead. It's going to be another scorcher. Doreen doesn't know what she's missing and he isn't going to tell her. His early morning cycle rides are his only escape from the infernal woman. And besides he has his little detour ahead of him. He pedals faster at the thought of what lies ahead and breathes harder, taking in the country freshness.

The chance to freewheel downhill fuels his good humour. The riotous hedgerows rushing by, the morning birds in full voice, the warm air on his face. And the sun glinting through the trees that line the road – his road – through Martle Top, the one little bit of countryside between Penbury and the motorway. The car parked in the lay-by annoyed him earlier. The thoughtlessness of some people: radio blaring, passenger door wide open, driver probably stopped for a pee in the ditch. Just as well Reg didn't see him. He'd have given him a piece of his mind. Still, he's nearly there now. His stomach flutters and there's a delicious prickle through his shoulders. He's like this every time. The first few days he thought it was guilt, but he knows now it's the thrill of anticipation.

Raging thirst replaces the hunger pangs. Her forehead throbs and it's hard to swallow. She tries not to panic.

If only the curtains were open a crack, the postman might have spotted her through the window and called the police. After the sharp thwack of the letterbox, she heard his "This Is Me" whistling fade away down the gravel path. She tried to call out but, with the tape over her mouth, she only managed a pathetic humming sound that had no hope of reaching the man chirping off into the warm June morning. She hates those curtains now, garish with the broad daylight behind them. Their peach colour makes the room loud and stuffy, hurting her eyes and aggravating her headache. A clashing backdrop for the vase of dark red roses on the table, their pungent perfume tainting what precious clean air she has left. A familiar wave of nausea threatens, but she fights it off.

Reg chains his bike to the railings and walks briskly into the Little Chef. Why should he feel guilty?

Doreen's fault. She shouldn't have withdrawn her services. A grown man has his needs.

The chain digs into her ribcage whenever she arches her back, forcing her to slump into the seat. The carriage clock ticks behind her. Oh for a clock that chimes. At least she'd be able to count off the hours. She daren't rock round to face the mantelpiece. If she topples over, she'll bang her already-raw face into the hard floor. And it isn't just herself to think about. She has to keep pain to a minimum; she might have to wait all day.

To deaden the ache in her neck, she rests her heavy arms on the chair and moves her knees apart, easing the pressure on the handcuffs around her ankles. But now it's even harder to hold her bladder, so she squeezes her legs together again. If she wants to avoid wetting herself, she'll have to accept the intermittent burning sensation up her calves.

Reg swings his leg over the saddle and sets off home replete. He deserved his cooked breakfast. That puny porridge Doreen serves up since he retired wouldn't keep a toddler fed.

He gets off his bike again. The hill's getting steeper. He used to be able to cycle up it. Better not tell Doreen. She'll say he's past it. Men of his age can't expect to do so much. Stupid woman.

"*It's just gone five past eight on Mids FM and on the line now is Carole in Brigham. Hi, Carole*," a radio shouts, polluting Reg's country air. That bloody car in the lay-by is still there. No driver or passenger about. What on earth are they playing at? A crude thought creeps into Reg's mind and he smiles. He pushes the bike across the road, quickening his pace.

He peers through the open passenger door. Well, there's no one at it on the back seat. Hardly surprising. That shrieking radio would put anyone off. Reg lays his bike in the long grass. They must be in the ditch or the field beyond. You've got to admire their stamina. They've been down there longer than it's taken him to ravish his Olympic Breakfast with extra mushrooms. With the stealth of a marine commando, he moves towards the ditch. Perhaps he'll share this one with Doreen. It might put her in the mood for some how's your fath—

"Father God in Heaven," he gasps and stands stock-still, the taste of bile mounting in his mouth. His eyes fix on the glint of metal and the shiny patch of red seeping through the grass. In the next instant, stomach heaving, he's back on his bike, tackling the rest of the hill from the saddle.

The milkman came at about 6.30 a.m. – at least she assumes it was 6.30 a.m. because that's when he always comes. His chinking of bottles is often the first sound she hears on waking. This morning, frozen by the enormity of her situation, she didn't think to call out to him until she heard the clanking, whirring sounds of his aged milk float dying away as it left. Hers is the only house in the street that still has milk delivered.

The final spin of the washing machine behind the closed kitchen door filled the silence after that. Then time became vast and empty until the whistling postman. The mail usually arrives before 8 a.m. despite changes at the Post Office, so that must make it about 9 a.m. now.

There's a distant crunching outside. More steps follow and grow louder as they trip their way up the gravel. It must be Linda. Of course, it's nine o'clock. Linda and Dean will have dropped the children off at school and then come to pick her up, as arranged. She pictures Linda teetering up the path, her broad feet forced into tiny sandals.

In the background a car engine rumbles. She's amazed that she can hear it above her hammering heart. Dean will be waiting in the car. She hears a light tapping on the front door glass. Linda's false fingernails. She forms the words "Linda, help" at the back of her mouth, trying to force them through the heavy adhesive that clamps her jaws together.

"Gaby, are you in there?" Linda's voice invades the house through the opened letterbox. "Are you going to let me in?"

With all her might, she gulps out one more "Help". The sound reverberates in her ears and, for a moment, she thinks it's reached the front door. The letterbox snaps shut and footsteps move around the house towards the lounge window. She rocks against the chains, causing two of the chair legs to lift and then slam down with a muffled thud on the carpet.

"Dean, she must have forgotten." Linda's voice is directed away from the house. "I've put their milk in the bushes otherwise it'll be honking in this heat." Linda's jerky steps return past the front door and recede down the path, the sound of gravel scattering in their wake.

Gaby struggles to catch her breath as a car door closes and the car speeds away. Tears prick her eyes. Her best hope of rescue will be joining the Penbury ring road without her. Crying makes her head throb, but she weeps on. The fight flowing out of her.

Reg – ice-numb now despite the heat – tries to lean his bike against the potting shed but it slips, clattering to the ground. The noise brings Doreen to the back door.

"Where the heck have you been all this time?" She squints at him. "You look peaky, a bit like your porridge looked before I chucked it. I suppose you want me to get you something else now?"

"Whisky," Reg gasps.

What time is it now? Exhaustion giving way to panic again. How long can she survive without a drink? It's been hours and her lips feel like crumbling plaster. Gaby makes another effort to calm down by breathing in through her nose and letting the air slowly reach her lungs. She clutches at any passing thought to occupy her aching mind. The letters on the doormat. She likes getting letters, even if most are mailshots. Her thoughts wander to the postman. She blinks back tears again, regretting that she's never really looked at him before and wondering whether there'll ever be another chance.

A car pulls up outside the gate. The engine stops and a door slams. Heavy shoes trudge along the gravel accompanied by faint crackling voices like a radio. She breathes in sharply, preparing to hum out as before, but this time ready for disappointment.

"Yes, sarge. If there's no reply, we'll force entry," a calm voice says on the other side of the front door.

Gaby's breathing quickens and she can hardly believe her ears. She's in some other world, unable to move. Seized by terror, suddenly afraid to end her familiar incarceration after so many hours. But then her survival instinct takes hold and she presses against the chains, rocking back and forth, willing herself closer to the window. After hearing three sharp knocks at the door, she crashes to the carpet. Shattering pain spreads across the side of her face. Everything numbs and darkness comes.

Chapter Two

I scramble up the metal staircase inside the south entrance to Penbury Police HQ. Late. Should have taken the car instead of waiting for the bus, but I was flustered enough without getting behind a hot, sticky steering wheel. I try taking the steps two at a time, but the thick woollen tights drag on my knees. Unseasonal legs, and slow, but ladder-free at least. I tried my best with my mother's honey blush tights, but the minute I tore open the packet and the two bits of beige nylon flopped down, I knew they were designed for an underfed tenyearold. And that was before their accident.

I up my pace and clamp my shoulder bag to my side – my one act of rebellion against Mum's restyling efforts.

"Now all you need is a briefcase," she trilled at the end of our shopping session.

"But I have to be approachable, Mum – a friendly face serving the whole community."

"Really, Pippa, darling, you sound like that rather grand lady officer they keep interviewing on the local news."

I swelled with pride when Mum made that comparison. I haven't met Superintendent Chattan yet, but I'll settle for having half the poise the woman exudes in her television appearances.

At the top of the stairs I slow down, trying to get my breathing under control. My bag's heavy, too much fodder inside. Pink lipstick from Mum, change for the bus home, tissues, sweets, apples, the Penbury CID Induction Pack and a small handmade card in joined-up writing: *Good Luck, Sis. Love Jamie.*

Rushing along the narrow corridor past the glass-panelled general office, I tell myself I'm not all that late, but I catch sight of four heads already barricaded behind high in-trays and jumbles of phone consoles and computer screens. I break into a trot and wonder which workstation mine will be. What if my new colleagues don't rate me? Being late on day one isn't the best way to win them over. They might not speak to me – I hate silences. Hopefully I'll be out on the road most of the time.

I touch the buttons on my jacket. Too formal? Another idea of my mother's. *Now you don't have to wear that ghastly uniform anymore.* After trouble with toothpaste spatters, I had to change out of her pink lace blouse selection into a royal blue T-shirt, an old favourite. It looks good with the jacket – so long as I don't undo the buttons to reveal its full glory. If the weather forecast is anything to go by, I'll have to boil.

Through the chipped double doors, across the stairwell and into the corridor beyond, I reach a line of varnished wooden doors, each bearing a nameplate. I stop before the first one: *Detective Inspector Liz Bagley*. I re-check my jacket buttons.

I'm about to knock when the door flies open and two unsmiling figures appear. One I recognize as Mike Matthews, the sergeant from my interview panel. But it's the woman with him who seems more familiar. A mass of dark hair, toned face and full red lips. DI Bagley or Cher?

"You're late, DC Adams," she says. A small woman, she has to tilt her head to meet my eye. Her black curls quiver. The fierce northern accent is pure Rottweiler.

"I'm sorry, I …" I wrack my brain for a plausible explanation that doesn't involve Colgate or laddered tights. "I, ma'am, well, I …"

Bagley steps through the door and forces me aside, barking her orders at high speed. "There's been a murder and an assault. Almost certainly connected. You go with DS Matthews. He's your supervising officer. He's meeting Forensics at the assault scene."

She breezes past, short strides, high boots, dancing gingham skirt, and stops at the far end of the corridor to lob Matthews an afterthought. "I'll be on Martle Top, but try and manage without me."

"Yes, ma'am," he calls. When the wired-glass fire doors bang shut behind her, he mutters, "Ride 'em, cowboy."

I grin but Matthews's face hardens. "The car's in the yard," he says and sets off. I rush after him.

We reach the car and he manoeuvres it out of a tight space and is soon moving at speed along the street outside the police station. He hasn't spoken since the corridor and gives no indication of remembering me from the interview. At the time, he didn't make much of an impression on me either. His questions were about simple textbook scenarios. I'd been awestruck by the other interviewer, DCI James Hendersen, a booming bear of a man determined to trick me with a heavy cross-examination. Matthews appeared meek in comparison.

As DS Matthews drives through the drab industrial part of town, I study him out of the corner of my eye: smart trousers, crisp, short-sleeved shirt and tie. Most of the young detectives I've met who made the move from PC to DC swap one uniform for another, namely jeans and a leather jacket. He must have a "dress to impress" mother like mine, or maybe he has a wife.

After a while, I break the silence. "Where are we going?"

"To the attempted kidnap scene."

"Oh, right. Good," I say, trying to sound on the ball. When Matthews doesn't elaborate, I add, "Where is that exactly?"

"A house in Southside." He touches the brake to give the car in front time to turn off.

"Who's been kidnapped?" I ask. "Is it a siege situation?"

"I don't think we'd put you through a siege on day one."

I feel myself reddening and the silence returns. He seemed innocuous at the interview. What little I can remember of him was of someone sympathetic, about my age, on my side. Perhaps he isn't as young as I first thought. There's a slight furrowing on his forehead as he concentrates on the driving but the rest of his face is line-free. In his late twenties? Five years my senior at most. He's clean-shaven – the sort of man Mum would approve of, except for the haircut, if you can call it that. Wild Afro extends as far as his shirt collar. It puts me in mind of my father's photographs of touring Jamaican musicians in his early days with the Midlandia Symphonic. Odd that Matthews takes care over the rest of his appearance but has hair left over from the 1970s.

He turns the steering wheel to take a left and catches me looking. I cover my embarrassment by asking another question. "Have the kidnappers been arrested?"

"They tied up a Mrs Gaby Brock in her own home and scarpered. Uniform found her." He moves out past a parked car.

"Who reported it?" I ask, gaining confidence. I seem to have persuaded him to brief me about the case.

"No one." He flicks the indicator and turns left again, yanking down the sun visor against the head-on sunlight. We're in a residential district – rows of tight terraces with postage-stamp front gardens.

"How did we know to look for her?" I choose the word "we" carefully. I can't bring myself to say "uniform", not ready to detach myself from my former colleagues.

"Because her husband was found murdered this morning in a ditch at Martle Top, close to his own car, by a pensioner on his bicycle. Stabbed in the chest. Knife by the body." He looks at me, apparently hoping for some sign of revulsion.

He's read me right. As my stomach muscles clench, I make a desperate attempt at humour. "It sounds like an Agatha Christie to me."

I realize my mistake even before all the words are out. Matthews takes his eyes off the road and looks me full in the face. "You what?"

My mouth still not shut, more words tumble out. "In many of her novels, the murderer sets up the scene. You can tell—"

Matthews touches the brakes, nudging us both against our seat belts. "Agatha Christie. Now I've heard everything. Don't tell me I'm working with Miss Marple for the next six months," he says, not smiling.

"It was a joke." Don't detectives have a sense of humour? I'm suddenly homesick for the camaraderie of uniform. Getting through the day with easy banter and Sergeant Conway treating us like favourite nieces and nephews.

Matthews puts the car into gear and continues at a slower pace. We enter a leafy residential area that I recognize as Southside, so named when the town was little more than a village. These days it would be more aptly called Eastside, the town having sprawled out below it.

"This isn't a joke," he says angrily. "Know the facts before you laugh about it. These are real-life victims. Gaby Brock was found lying on the floor, shackled to a chair in her own lounge. There was a chain round her legs and across her chest. Her wrists were handcuffed to the chair legs. The keys for the padlocks were in the pocket of the pyjamas she was wearing when uniform got there. And before you get any other fanciful ideas, she couldn't have snapped the cuffs shut on her own arms and then pocketed the keys."

"Has the victim been able to say anything?" I try to make my voice sound brisk and efficient.

"They were asleep when two men burst in, gave them both a beating, made her husband tie her up and then dragged him out of the house. It appears they took him to Martle Top in his own car and knifed him. Sounds like drugs to me. Shades of the Easter Day shooting in Briggham."

I've heard of the Briggham case. It's said to have all the hallmarks of a gangland contract. I feel a twinge of excitement at the thought of what this new case might involve, but decide against quipping to Matthews that he needs to know *his* facts before judging it to be drugs-related. Somehow I don't think he'd see the funny side.

He switches off the engine as we pull up across a driveway in a short road of newish detached houses, their dull frontages enhanced by conifers and flowering shrubs. Several hydrangeas are in full bloom at the house in front of us. Someone has stuck a pint of milk under one. But what sets this house apart from its neighbours is the blue and white *Police Do Not Cross* tape all round its perimeter and a police officer, whom I don't know, standing outside the open front door. When she sees Matthews, she lets us step under the tape without question.

From the doorstep we can see that the house is alive with scenes of crime staff in their white forensic suits, looking through waste bins, checking drawers, and examining carpets with an E-vac. One of the forensic scientists in the hallway looks up and raises his hand in a latex glove. "Long time, no see, Mike."

"Hello, Dave," DS Matthews calls as he slips on his forensic suit. "Didn't expect to be working with you again. I thought your team had moved to Briggham."

"We have. Got put on to this job by the ACC himself."

"Somehow that doesn't surprise me," Matthews replies.

"It does me. I'd expected separate teams here and at Martle Top to avoid crosscontamination, but not the cavalry."

"Depends who the senior investigating officer is," Matthews says.

"Who?"

"Liz Bagley."

Dave grins. "Is it true what they say about her?"

"What do you think?" Matthews replies. "She's persuaded the assistant chief constable to cough up the staff, hasn't she?"

"Inspector Bagley?" Dave leers. "Expect a Shagley more like."

Both men laugh but stop when they remember I'm there. Matthews glowers at me and I brace myself for another tongue-lashing, but he just asks me to put on coveralls and check on progress upstairs.

Once suited up, I enter the house and walk up the narrow, carpeted staircase. The bathroom is at the top of the stairs, tidy and ordinary. Apart from a plastic cup on the washbasin containing two toothbrushes and a tube of paste, and two dry towels hanging over the bath, the bathroom suite is clean and free of clutter. I lift the lid on the wicker laundry basket even though the kidnappers are unlikely to have stopped off to do the washing. The basket is about a third full of what looks like pale tops and white underwear – quite unlike the overflowing colour riot of my linen bin. I let the lid fall and turn to the wall-mounted cabinet. Inside is a neat arrangement of cut-price shampoo, shaving foam and razor, full-coverage foundation, concealer and a powder compact. The only person I've known with such an immaculate bathroom cabinet (but without the make-up) is my father after he left my mother and before he married Joanne. I close the cabinet and head into a bedroom.

Chapter Three

Across town Bartholomew Hedges climbs down his ladder. He can't work. He tells himself it's the heat, but knows it isn't. The fair weather is his friend, kind for completing the exterior paint-work. The Lord shines the sun on him. He should be getting on; the customer has started asking questions. Bartholomew can't blame the dormer roof for much longer.

As he replaces his brush in the paint can, some of the white undercoat slops onto the patio. He scoops it back in with his palette knife and removes the rest of the stain with white spirit. He sprinkles more spirit on his hands and wipes them down with the rag from the pocket of his shorts.

His fingers aren't clean, but pale like a white man's. He needs a wash down with soap and water. But he doesn't want to go into the house as the customer's wife is at home. She might ask him why he's stopped again.

He sits on the edge of the patio. The step down to the lawn is low and his paint-flecked knees come up high in front of him. The grass is yellow, even though he's seen the owners using a sprinkler every evening. He's heard them talking of having it re-turfed – as soon as the decorating's finished. He sighs. Perhaps he should tell them that God will replenish their lawn long before Hedges House Painting Services retouches their eaves.

He's surprised they gave him the contract at all. He knows the man didn't want to and he can't blame him. As far as he was concerned Bartholomew had already proved himself unreliable. In February he'd been due to start on their dining room – a big job to take off the Anaglypta wall covering, cross line it and paint over in mushroom gold. Bartholomew had to cancel at two weeks' notice when he couldn't find his steam stripper. It would have taken a month of God's sacred Sundays to scrape off Anaglypta without a steamer.

The machine disappeared from the back of his van one night, but there'd been no sign of a break-in. Had he forgotten to lock the van? Convincing himself that it was his own foolish mistake, he hadn't gone to the police or contacted his insurance company. Back then, the possibility that someone else could get hold of the van key hadn't crossed his mind. Bartholomew wipes his chin with his forearm and wonders whether that suspicion had been in his head all along but he'd chosen to ignore it. February? Were the signs already there?

He shuffles along the patio edge to his toolbox. Underneath his Thermos flask of Cherry Tango is his Bible, wrapped in a plastic bag. He longs to take it out, ask it the questions, and seek solace. But he can't touch it until he's washed his hands.

The same passage comes into his mind. It's been there almost constantly for three weeks now. Proverbs 10: 1: "A wise son makes his father proud of him; a foolish one brings his mother grief." The words have been pressing against his brain ever since he saw his own son, Saul, being … doing …

He shivers. The fear comes back and he thinks of Job 20: 16: "What the evil man swallows is like poison." Is Saul evil? Every day he prays for a sign, for the Lord to reassure him. Bartholomew needs to know that the evil lies elsewhere, not in a boy like Saul. Again and again he's asked Saul why he did it. Saul says it's like falling into cotton wool. It lets him find a warm and happy place that he wants to keep going back to. Where did Bartholomew go wrong? He's found comfort from a life of faith. Why hasn't Saul found it there, too?

A scenes of crime officer dusts a bedside locker while another hunts through drawers. I look at the unmade double bed that the Brocks must have been dragged from in the night. The room's simply furnished – a large pine wardrobe and matching dressing table – again tidy, no lipsticks or perfume bottles in sight.

The second bedroom looks like an advert for an office suppliers. A black swivel chair slots underneath a desk as if it's never been used. Even the few sheets of printed papers on top lie in a perfect pile. A plastic dust sheet covers the computer. The blotting pad looks fresh and a single ballpoint pokes out of a pen-tidy. The only incongruous item is a birdcage, complete with a bell and a seed hopper, under the desk. Two forensic officers come in behind me, so I leave them to begin a detailed search.

Whereas the rest of the upstairs appears sterile, the third bedroom is a surprise. Three walls are bright yellow and the fourth displays a magnificent hand-painted circus scene. Trapeze artists fly across the red and white striped backdrop of the big top. Clowns juggle silver hoops and two white horses rear up at each other. It must have taken someone days to complete. In the middle of the room is a large cot with a clown motif mattress, but no bedding. The drawers of the nappy changing unit next to it are empty.

I go downstairs, psyching myself up for the next round with Matthews.

He's on his mobile, rubbing the back of his neck with his free hand. "No, ma'am, nothing of interest so far. They've bagged up a few bits and pieces."

I wander into the kitchen. Dave, the forensic scientist, kneels at the opened back door, scraping at a broken pane of glass. I look beyond him into the garden. Typical new-estate small, the paved patio is surrounded on three sides by conifers.

Two familiar figures come round the side of the house and I smile in relief. "Anything interesting?" I call.

"Hi, Pippa, good to see you. Nothing out here," PC John Whitton says, coming towards the doorstep. "But Forensics pulled some clothes out of the washing machine. They want to check whether anyone's tried to wash away evidence."

"Unlikely though," PC Kieran Clarke says. "It's a towel and a few men's shirts and trousers, probably the husband's. We won't find any bloodstains. All his blood is spread across Martle Top." He gives a half-hearted chuckle.

"The relief's missing you already," John says. "So how are you getting on in CID?"

The thought of my day so far makes my insides clench but I manage a breezy "Fine". Trying not to sound desperate, I say how glad I am to see them again and go back through the kitchen.

The lounge curtains, closed when the police broke in, are now pushed back to let maximum daylight onto the crime scene. With the light comes the fire of a midsummer day. My hand goes to undo my jacket but the protective suit is in the way. Apart from the pungent smell of forensic chemicals sprinkled into the carpet, the room is orderly. Matching cushions on the sofa and paperbacks on the small bookcase. Red roses on the coffee table and a cheap carriage clock on the mantelpiece, but otherwise no ornaments or photos.

My own small lounge has every available space crammed with photos: old ones of Mum and Dad in the same frame; one of Dad's wedding to Joanne and several of their son, Jamie, from newborn to the current cheeky eight-year-old. But no photos in this house, no clues to the occupants.

I kneel over the kitchen chair in the middle of the room and get a whiff of the oily scent left by the fingerprint experts. Hard to know what colour the chair is under its dosing of white powder.

A pale wood, perhaps, and there are several paint spots, evidence that the chair has been a makeshift decorating ladder before its latest incarnation as a prison for Gaby Brock. Some of the spots are summer yellow and partly obscured by splodges of blue. The circus room with its yellow walls probably wasn't the most recent project.

On the bookcase, two shelves of light romances mingle with classic horror, and another shelf of paperback textbooks. *Understanding Shakespeare; Yoga Postures; Towards the National Curriculum; Modern Grammar; Advanced Yoga.* Which books belonged to the husband and what will the wife do with them now?

Dave, the forensics officer, puts his head around the door. "Tell Mike Matthews I'm off. I'll have my initial report ready this afternoon."

"Ok, I'll tell him. It was nice meeting you," I say.

Dave grins. "You too, Agatha". Then he's gone.

My cheeks burn. Matthews must have told him about my failed Agatha Christie joke. It wasn't that funny, was it?

PC Kieran Clarke appears at the door. "Mike Matthews wants us to make a start on the house-to-house enquiries. Find out if anyone saw Brock's Mondeo leaving in the middle of the night." He pauses to give his face time to break into a smirk. "So you'd better hurry up, Agatha."

There's more danger that her Jimmy Choo heels will pierce the forensic overshoes and sink into the melting tarmac of the Martle Top road than they will bury themselves in the dried-out grass verge, but force of habit makes DI Liz Bagley tiptoe to the edge of the ditch. She shouts across to the kneeling figure of SOCO Steve Chisholm.

"Anything?"

He stands up. "Not much. There are some tyre tracks on the grass over there." He looks towards a patch of ground a few feet ahead. "From a bicycle, I think. The grass is flattened as if someone's laid a bike down."

"That fits. The man who found the body was on a bike. Where's Dr Spicer?"

Chisholm points to the white incident tent a few metres behind him. "In there with the victim." He folds his arms, a half-smile hovering over his mouth.

In that moment Liz hates him. Clockwise Chisholm might be the station's resident anorak, with his hand semipermanently stuck up the back of a computer, but he's astute enough to realize that, to get to the tent, she'll have to cross the ditch. Its banks could harbour a few wet spots despite the heatwave. She isn't going arse over tits for anyone.

"Get me a plank," she says.

"I'll call DC Holtom."

"Not that sort of plank."

Chisholm grins. "I meant he's got the bridge."

"Tell him to be quick," she says, cursing herself for not bringing her wellies. She took them out of the car caked in mud weeks before, but forgot to put them back.

DC Holtom comes over with a duckboard. She steps across the ditch, placing one foot deliberately in front of the other. Her expression hardens against the curious gazes of Chisholm and Holtom. No way is she giving them the satisfaction of seeing her slip.

At least DS Mike Matthews isn't here. He'd enjoy watching her walk the plank. The man is dire. So polite and correct, apart from his outsize broomstick hair. "Yes, ma'am, certainly ma'am. If you want me to, ma'am." But behind the plodding reliability, Liz has the feeling he's waiting for her to fall flat on her face. It's a good thing he'll be preoccupied from now on with supervising DC Adams. He'll be too busy keeping that towering toddler on her feet to trip up his detective inspector.

Matthews and DCI Hendersen did the interviews for the

vacancy, so it's their fault they've ended up with a girl trainee. Lads are much easier to knock the corners off. They're a bit wet behind the iPhone, but they know who's boss. Women, on the other hand, make loose cannons.

Liz complained to John Wise about it, of course. That's lover's perks. But Assistant Chief Constable Wise was non-committal. There was no suggestion, on his part anyway, of wading into Hendersen's office and pulling rank.

And the upshot is DC Pippa Adams. An overgrown cheerleader, all pink cheeks and ponytail. Detective material? Unlikely. Time will tell.

As Liz steps off the duckboard, she goes down on her ankle but rights herself despite the pain. With all the dignity she can muster, she heads into the incident tent.

Chapter Four

"I didn't think you'd catch up with me this quickly," a woman's voice says through the polished brass letterbox. The door opens a fraction and the voice continues, "Can I ring Stuart – that's Mr Perkins, my husband – before you take me in? I'm allowed one phone call, aren't I?"

A pair of hunted green eyes appear and I wonder what crime I've stumbled into. Isn't that how we caught the Briggham killer – routine enquiries into another case? I glance up the road, but my colleagues are nowhere in sight, each having allocated themselves a different avenue on the Southside estate for the house-to-house. I knocked at the first house in a cul-de-sac that runs off the road behind the Brocks' house.

"I suppose you'll want to come in while I'm on the phone so I don't abscond," the woman says. She opens the door wide.

I step over the threshold. Should I call for backup? After a shaky start on my first day are things about to get even rockier?

"I must be in a lot of trouble if they've sent a CID officer," the woman says. She leads me into the lounge. What villainy could have taken place in a room where paisley pink curtains match the sofa cushions?

"What do you think will happen to me? I know it's not much

of an excuse, but I would like to say in my defence that I only saw it was back this morning."

"Back this morning?" I ask, trying to disguise my bewilderment. The woman is chatty. I'll feed her enough rope, get her to confess to whatever it is she's done and make an arrest. Maybe even redeem myself in DS Matthews's eyes.

"It was propped against the front wall. I swear it wasn't there yesterday. And Stuart walked up and down the avenue before we spoke to your officers on Wednesday. There was no sign of it. I know we shouldn't have kept it in the front garden. The way other people let their children stay out till all hours. It's asking for trouble in this day and age."

"Is it?" I ask.

"They'll take anything if it's not nailed down, even a tatty old thing like that. Except they didn't take it because it's back now. But I swear it wasn't there yesterday, not since Wednesday."

"A tatty old thing?"

"I'd had it since college." She waves a hand at the mantelpiece, which displays two graduation photographs. One is of a youth with wispy hair reaching to his oversized collar and big tie. Stuart? The other is of a young woman with sparkling green eyes and a magnificent smile, lavishly framed by lipstick. I study Mrs Perkins's tired, pale features. She must be in her late thirties but carries herself as if in middle age. She resembles an Afghan hound with messy, permed hair over her ears. Loose grey cords and a baggy cardigan conceal long limbs. Has a guilty conscience tarnished her former radiance?

"And you spoke to us on Wednesday?" I ask, trying to make a jigsaw out of the pieces the woman is giving me.

"We both came down to the station to make a statement, give a description. We didn't mean to waste anybody's time."

"You wasted our time?" I begin to think she's wasting mine.

"Are you going to charge me? We thought it had gone. It never occurred to us it would come back."

I give up. "What came back?"

"My bicycle, of course." Mrs Perkins raises her voice an octave but returns to deferential tones to explain that she and her husband had reported her bicycle stolen from their front garden on Wednesday but that it reappeared this morning. "I was going to phone you. I didn't want the police force out looking for it any longer than necessary. I know wasting police time is a serious offence. I'll just phone Stuart, or should I phone a solicitor?"

My eyes move back and forth between the woman and her graduation photograph. Intelligence manifests itself in so many ways. I reassure Mrs Perkins that the Brigghamshire Constabulary won't be taking any further action on this occasion. Doubtless my fellow officers will be delighted that Mrs Perkins's property has been returned safe and sound. Mrs Perkins launches into a torrent of thanks. When she pauses for air, I explain the real reason for my visit and find myself accepting an offer of a cup of tea.

"Not to worry. Thanks for your help anyway," DS Mike Matthews says outside number 23. He puts away his notebook. All of them wise monkeys. No one saw or heard anything, and they aren't saying much either. Not even: would you like to come in out of the heat and have a drink, officer.

Chance would be a fine thing.

"Have another piece of chocolate cake," Mrs Perkins offers. "It's lovely to see a young woman enjoying her food. I'm afraid with this talk of murder, I've rather lost my appetite."

I hastily swallow. "Quite. Did you see anyone in the avenue during last night?"

Mrs Perkins shakes her head. "We're heavy sleepers. Perhaps if we weren't, we'd have seen what happened to my bicycle."

"Maybe you saw something before you went to bed. A car, perhaps, a Ford Mondeo?" I'm anxious to steer the conversation away from the bicycle.

"I've got an awful feeling we've met the victim. I don't think I've seen him round here, but there's a chap we see up at the allotments now and again that matches the man you've described. Big, scruffy. Stuart says he'd lose a bit of weight if he put his back into it. His plot's a mess. Not like Stuart's. He's up there every evening. We grow all our own veg."

She smiles at his graduation photo, no doubt proud that a man in a psychedelic tie could evolve into one with green fingers. "Things taste much better when you grow them yourself. All those additives these days send children into orbit. Give them a home-grown diet and they're good as gold," Mrs Perkins continues. "We're doing runner beans this time. It makes a change from courgettes. I've still got tubs of puree in the freezer from last year. I'll give you some to take home. Let me put the kettle on again."

Matthews puts a tick against number 27. It always amazes him how many people are at home during the day. Only three doors didn't answer. He hasn't found out anything from the others, but at least he can cross them off. Someone must have seen something. Two men forcing another man into his own car and then driving off intent on murder. It's hardly a routine occurrence, not on Southside. On the Danescott estate, maybe, but not round here.

He goes back to the car. Perhaps the uniforms or Agatha will have had more luck. Agatha. He screws up his face and clenches his fists. *Agatha*. He's only just met her, and yet … He's worked with junior DCs before, so why does this one wind him up so much?

"Is that the time," I say, standing up.

"I'll get your courgette puree," Mrs Perkins says. "Time does fly. The children will be coming out of school soon."

Despite the risk of venturing into what must be another pet subject for Mrs Perkins, I can't resist asking another question. "How old are your children?"

The hunted look returns to the woman's eyes. "I don't have any of my own. I meant the children in general would be coming out of school. Stuart and I haven't been blessed." She stops speaking, her eyes watering. I feel bad and sit down again to coax Mrs Perkins back to the happier topic of her vegetables.

"One, Agatha! Just one!" The blood pulses visibly through the veins in Matthews's neck, and he grips the steering wheel. "We covered half the estate, while you interviewed one householder. So what did you get, a full confession? A request for several previous capital offences to be taken into consideration?"

I stare blindly out of the window. All I see is misery. "It's people like that who spot things," I offer without conviction. "And the lady seemed unhappy. She needed someone to talk to."

"Tell her to phone the Samaritans. If I spend much more time with you, I'll be needing them myself."

Chapter Five

I follow Matthews into the main entrance of Penbury General Hospital. Glad of the wide corridors, I keep my distance. He isn't about to play the caring supervisor and whisper words of reassurance en route to the mortuary. He wants me to squirm and his wish might well be granted. Thinking about the post-mortem I attended three years ago during police training still brings me out in a sweat. I'll have to draw on the skills I learnt in my performing arts degree to appear in control.

When we reach the mortuary anteroom, I drop my bag alongside DS Matthews's brown briefcase. I put on a gown, fumble with the plastic overshoes and take a deep breath as Matthews pushes open the wide swing doors into the main lab.

The smell triggers a kaleidoscope of memories. I'm back in Matron's room at school. I only went there twice, both times to escort a sick friend, but there's no forgetting the stench of disinfectant designed to terrify any virus into submission. The mortuary shares not only the same fragrance but also, bizarrely, the same cosy warmth. At the training post-mortem, all the police cadets on my intake remarked on the unexpected heat of a morgue.

I rub my dripping forehead and decide that Penbury's mortuary needs better air conditioning. The stuffy room isn't much bigger than Matron's office, but there's an ominously empty space in the centre.

A masked and gowned man sits at a computer screen, making notes on a clipboard. He stands up to greet us. "Ah, Mike Matthews and …?" He looks from Matthews to me.

"I'm DC Adams," I explain.

"Charles Spicer, pathologist. What's your first name, DC Adams?"

"She's called Agatha," Matthews says.

"Actually, Pippa," I say coolly, not about to show him how rattled I am by the nickname. I'm grateful for the distraction of Bagley's arrival.

"Good. Everyone's here," Bagley says, shuffling through the door in the plastic overshoes. "Can we make a start." It's a command, not a request.

Dr Spicer rolls his eyes but says nothing. He presses the button on the intercom next to his computer. Before I have time to rehearse my reaction, the wide double doors at the far end of the room fly open and two young men dressed in white tunics push in a trolley bed containing the lifeless body of a man. They line the trolley up parallel with the doctor's desk and leave through the doors.

My stomach lurches and I'm glad I declined a second slice of Mrs Perkins's cake. I study the coveralls on my shoes, but like a bystander at a traffic accident, can't resist a morbid peek at the horror. A crisp green cloth covers most of the corpse, but has been turned down to show his waxen head. A large head, made even larger by the crop of tangled hair and the dense stubble that frames it. He looks like Moses.

"Have you already stripped him?" Bagley asks and there's no mistaking the accusation in her voice.

Dr Spicer peers at her above the silver frames of his spectacles, much as a kindly uncle might view a cheeky child. "If you recall, he was only wearing boxer shorts when we found him. You saw the body for yourself. If a body is clothed when found, we remove the clothes after it has been photographed. After twenty years in the profession, I have not chosen today to deviate from this practice."

He makes his point in amiable tones but Bagley's face takes on a darker tan below her face mask.

"Glad to hear it," she says quietly.

I take little interest in this battle of wills; I've got my own struggle. I try to imagine I'm standing outside the scene. If I can escape, I might be able to keep my emotions at bay. I force myself to look at the large feet resting in a wide V at the other end of the sheet. They're broad and strong, load-bearing. Tufts of dark hair protrude from short, thick toes. The toenails, crusty and yellowing, are long and misshapen. I think of the living man getting by in ill-fitting shoes. At least he's now free of that irritation. I stifle a sigh.

"According to the photo driving licence found in the car in the lay-by, this is Carl Edward Brock," Dr Spicer says, checking his clipboard. "I still require a formal ID."

He directs this comment at DS Matthews who jots something down in the notebook that's poised in his steady hands. I envy his professional neutrality.

"It is the body of a white male, aged between thirty and forty. The driving licence says thirty-six. He's six feet tall, of large build, a bit overweight."

"Can you give me a time of death?" Bagley asks.

"It was a warm night. He'd been dead at least two hours when I examined him on Martle Top. I'd say it was between midnight and seven this morning. A detailed PM should give a more precise time. Cause of death would appear to be a single stab wound to the heart."

"Is there any sign of a struggle?" It's Matthews who speaks.

"None whatsoever. No defensive injuries and no apparent scratches or bruising. Death seems to have occurred swiftly but I'll need to do the PM to be sure."

"Any sign of sexual activity?" Inspector Bagley hammers out her question.

Dr Spicer gives the inspector another avuncular gaze. "We've already established he's 'boxer short *intactus*' so you'll have to wait a little longer for that one. There is an older injury to the right knuckles. I'd say it occurred several hours before death. He banged his fist against something sharp. However, cause of death seems to be one thrusting action up through the ribcage."

I keep looking at the doctor's face, not at the descriptive movements he makes with his hands. My nails dig into my sticky palms. And this isn't even the full PM. I force my eyes onto the ivory face and try to think of him as the corpse, the victim, the case, but he's still Carl Brock, a human being. The darkly shadowed eyelids will never again open to scan the books on his bookcase. The unshaven jaw won't need the razor from the tidy bathroom cabinet. The stiffening shoulders, fleshy and wide, will never again share the warmth of the double bed.

"It's a boat-shaped wound, suggesting a knife with one sharp edge. And long," Dr Spicer says.

"We found a blood-covered kitchen knife close by the body," Bagley replies. "Could it have been suicide?"

"Not with that angle of penetration."

"Can you tell us anything about the killer?"

"You won't find the assailant soaked in the victim's blood, a few spatters at most. There was little external bleeding. He haemorrhaged internally."

I swallow hard and concentrate on the doctor's face.

"Man or woman?" Matthews asks.

"Hard to tell. The blow was strong and quick. It's a clean incision and it seems to have taken the victim by surprise."

"So we are looking for someone big and powerfully built," Bagley concludes.

"The height of the killer is difficult to gauge. The attack apparently took place on the side of a ditch. The victim may have been standing on lower ground. With a sharp knife, the attacker would have needed little force. Even a woman could have managed it if that was how they were standing. Once the knife had penetrated the skin, it would've been like stabbing a water melon."

"When will you do the full PM?"

"Tomorrow at eleven but we need a formal ID before that. Even when we've stitched them up, the deceased never look the same after we've had the hacksaw to them. The bereaved don't like to see that."

Queasiness wraps itself around me like a tight woollen blanket.

"We'll get the wife to do it when we know what state she's in," Bagley says.

"The police surgeon examined her about an hour ago," Dr Spicer says.

"Do you mean Dr Tarnovski?"

"Of course."

There's a pause as Dr Spicer and DI Bagley exchange a glance.

Dr Spicer resumes his briefing. "Apparently she's being treated for shock. Mild concussion, badly beaten up. Black eyes, cracked cheekbone. Fresh bruising to the arms and legs consistent with being chained and handcuffed." He looks at Bagley again and adds, "No sign of sexual assault."

"Is she fit to interview?"

"You'll have to check with Dr Tarnovski. She's suffered a major trauma. Her own ordeal was bad enough and now she has to cope with her husband's murder."

"Of course, doctor. I realize that. DC Adams and I will be back for the full PM tomorrow."

My heart drops like a stone.

Dr Tarnovski sits at his desk and scrutinizes the lines of text. His eyes linger over every weight and schedule as he crosschecks them against the recesses of his encyclopaedic memory. He'll find a match, an absolute, however long it takes. He just needs to locate The Evidence. He takes a sip from the plastic cup by his hand, smacking his lips together and rubbing away the taste. With The Evidence, he could make his predictions and test his hypothesis. His elbow nudges a half-eaten curry tray, relic of another late night at the office. His methodology deserves perseverance. It will reap its own rewards – soon.

What time is it now? He lifts his sleeve in an automatic gesture, forgetting that his wrist is bare. A temporary setback. He reaches across the paper-strewn desk to the old transistor radio. It crackles weakly as he turns the dial. If only he hadn't been called out to that assault victim, Gaby somebody. At least the examination was straightforward. She'd had a good beating but not life-threatening. It's up to her if she chooses not to take the sedatives and sleeping tablets he suggested. Another ill-informed hippy isn't his problem. She can always try her own GP for some alternative therapy.

He ponders for the nth time why he remains a police surgeon, calculating an exponential rise in his job dissatisfaction. Of course the profession has its value. Its contribution is not without merit. Someone has to treat traumatized victims and assess prisoners keen to feign illness.

He's a strategist, a mathematician, a man of reason – and speculation. It's a case of horses for courses. The creases in his face deepen into a grin. He marvels at his gift for irony. Police duties take him away from his real work, although he has to admit that the income is useful. The allowance and expenses – thank the Lord for travel claims and a DCI who doesn't probe them.

Only Mary probes. In the early years of their marriage, he tried to explain the nature of his empirical investigations. But she isn't a scientist. He has no time to listen to her weakminded debates and to counter her abstract reasoning. He's taken the pragmatic line and concealed his research, continuing in secret to build the necessary experience to achieve results.

He scans the page again. He must have missed it. He drains his cup. His head begins to ache but he forces the print back into focus. Suddenly, there's The Evidence. Yes, The Evidence, but are the conditions viable? He snatches up a page of formulae and scribbles in the numerical values. The first equation balances. Now to manipulate the figures on the second one. Adrenaline starts its familiar stampede around his body. One more test needed, then it will be irrefutable. He roots through a pile of charts and diagrams and retrieves some graph paper. Hand shaking, he plots the data and joins the crosses. There it is, a straight line. Better than he'd dared hope. Perfect positive correlation. It's incontrovertible. After so many challenges – not sacrifices, as Mary called them – here is the eureka moment.

With his eyes fixed on the newsprint, his right hand opens his top drawer and his left dials the sacred number.

It takes an age to be answered. Such impudence. He has an urgent theory to verify.

At last. "The name is Tarnovski. I have an account." He takes the whisky bottle out of the drawer and refills the cup.

"What limit? … I can't hold. There isn't time."

During the silence on the phone line, he strains to make sense of the buzzing sounds from his radio.

"I see. And you can't override it? I'm a long-standing account holder … Well, of all the nerve. Wait a minute …" Another confounded woman who doesn't understand the science. He slides open the top drawer again and removes a debit card from underneath a second, empty, bottle. It slips in his clammy fingers.

"It's the eleven thirty at Lingfield. I want to place …" He hesitates as another, weaker, force tugs against his resolve: Sara's gap-year fund. But he'll be more than able to replenish it. And retrieve his wristwatch from the pawnbrokers. A statistician of his standing doesn't miscalculate.

"I want to place £800 on number five, The Evidence." He drains his cup again. It's an absolute constant, a dead cert.

Chapter Six

Still feeling flushed after the meeting in the mortuary, I take off my jacket and clutch it to my stomach as I follow DI Bagley into the interview room. Gaby Brock sits at the table holding a plastic beaker. She looks like a battered baby. The forensic suit she's been dressed in is way too big and she stares out of her swollen face with wide eyes. She seems unaware of our arrival and equally oblivious to the arm around her shoulder. It belongs to the large, sobbing woman beside her. The woman looks up as we sit down opposite. I drop my jacket over the chair.

"Thank you for coming in at this difficult time, Mrs Brock. We're sorry for your loss. I'm DI Bagley. This is DC Adams."

"I'm Linda Parry," the large woman says, "Gaby's sister-in-law, Carl's sister." She swallows hard.

Bagley ignores her. "I need to ask some questions about this morning. Are you up to it, Mrs Brock?"

Gaby Brock blinks her doe eyes.

Bagley seems to take this as a yes and presses on. "Can you tell us what happened?"

Gaby's pale mouth remains closed for a moment, apparently still frozen by her ordeal. When she finally speaks, her voice is soft and pretty – like honey. It doesn't seem right for a voice like that to come out of such a damaged face.

"We were asleep in bed," she says. "Two men burst in and dragged us downstairs. One of them punched me in the face and I fell. The other grabbed my arms and pulled me up again."

"Can you describe these men?"

She blinks again as if searching the images in her head for the faces of her attackers. "They were black," she whispers eventually, "and big."

"How old were they?"

This time her pause is so long that Linda Parry squeezes her shoulder and prompts, "Come on, Gaby, love. You can do it."

I see Gaby wince. The shoulder squeeze must have hurt. It's a stark reminder that, although the face pummelling is there for all to see, there are other injuries hidden under the forensic suit.

"Well, Mrs Brock? How old were your attackers? Teenagers? Twenties? Thirties? Older?" Impatience steals into Bagley's voice.

Gaby's hand tightens on the empty plastic cup. Somehow she's managed to consume an entire outpouring from the interview suite coffee machine. The trauma must have affected her taste buds.

Gaby's answer rolls out at the same hesitant pace as her previous ones. "They weren't kids, but I don't know how old."

Bagley studies the woman's face, weighing up her reliability as a witness. "What were they wearing?"

"I couldn't see. It was dark."

"You mean they didn't turn the lights on?" she asks, more irritation creeping in.

How long ago did the DI attend the Dealing with the Traumatized Victim course, I wonder. Do they offer refreshers?

Gaby shakes her head slowly. "They shone torches in our faces. And I was too scared to look at them."

"Did you see their hair? Was it long or short?"

"They wore hats. Woollen ones."

"Balaclavas?"

"No, I don't think so, but I couldn't see. I'm not sure."

"Did they say anything?"

Gaby Brock blinks again and her sweet voice cracks. "They told Carl to get a chair and chain me to it. One punched me on the shoulder and I fell back into the chair."

Linda lets out a sigh and tightens her arm around Gaby. I turn away, not wanting to see Gaby Brock flinch again.

DI Bagley ignores Linda once more. "Did you notice any kind of an accent?"

There's another pause as Gaby considers her answer. "I think one was local and one was sort of West Indian."

"And they brought the chains with them?"

Gaby's body tenses as if reliving the memory. "They brought metal chains and handcuffs. They made Carl tighten the chains around me and handcuff my arms to the chair. They gave him the keys and told him to put them in my pocket." She taps her chest to indicate the spot where her pyjama pocket had been. "Then they took Carl away." Her words are faint and slow.

Her eyes are watery, empty. Victim's eyes. Victim ... Still living, still breathing but a victim nonetheless ... No one could know how that felt except another victim ... The hairs on my arms bristle but I won't go *there*. I concentrate on the interview.

A thought comes to me but I'm not sure of my role. Does Bagley want me to remain the silent trainee or should I take part in the interview?

"Did they say anything else?" Bagley asks.

Gaby Brock takes a deep breath. "They said to Carl, 'You need a lesson of your own, teacher.'"

"He was an English teacher at Swan Academy and a damned good one," Linda explains. She pats Gaby's hand. "Everyone liked him, even the kids."

I think of the literature textbooks on the Brocks' bookcase.

"And the kidnappers definitely called him 'teacher'?" Bagley asks.

Gaby lowers her head, too weary even to nod. My heart races. Dare I ask my question?

"Would you recognize the men again?" Bagley continues.

"Maybe but – I don't know – it was dark. The torchlight in my face … I couldn't see …"

As the woman's voice tails off, I expect Bagley to fill the silence. When she doesn't, my question pops out.

"How did your husband cut his hand and get the bruising? Was it during the assault?"

Bagley's jaw tightens at my interruption but she looks at Gaby Brock, waiting for the answer.

"His hand?" Gaby's eyes glaze over and she seems to retreat into her private thoughts. "I don't know. I don't think he tried to fight them off. How could he? He might have done something to his hand at school, but it hardly matters now that he's …" Gaby shakes her head. Her right cheek is black, and a purple blotch, visible through her thin fringe, spreads from her left temple across her forehead into her hairline.

Bagley lets out a small, defeated sigh. "That's all we're going to ask you at the moment. I want you to look through some images later to see if we can identify your attackers but for now you can leave the station. Where can we find you?"

"She's staying with me," Linda says. "I'm not having her go back to *that* house."

"Good. I can't let you go home anyway, Mrs Brock. It's a crime scene. We'll be doing an appeal to the public, so it would help if we had a recent photo of your husband. If you tell me where to look, I'll send an officer into your house to get one."

"Photo," Gaby echoes as if she's never heard the word before. I cast my mind over the barren walls and tables of the Brocks' lounge. Photography does seem to have been an alien concept to the couple.

Linda Parry comes to her sister-in-law's rescue, offering to provide something from one of her own family photo albums. DI Bagley closes the interview with a cursory "thank you" and stands up.

I follow her to the door and look back at the two women. "Goodbye," I say. "It was nice to meet … I'm sorry for … Goodbye."

DI Bagley speeds along the corridor. "I want you to join DS Matthews in Forensics. See what they've got so far. Good question, by the way, well done, but no need to be overfamiliar with the witnesses. This is a murder inquiry."

"Yes, ma'am, thank you," I say to the back of the gingham skirt as it disappears through the door at the end of the corridor. I can't help grinning to myself. I've asked my first question in CID and, despite it coming out in a gabble, the inspector was impressed. Not that the answer told us anything. The cut hand is still a mystery. Dr Spicer has already said there's no other sign of a struggle, so Gaby's vague suggestion of an injury at school simply confirms that it didn't happen during the attack at the house. At least both sources are consistent, making it likely that Gaby Brock is telling the truth. I all but tap dance along the corridor. Things are looking up.

"DC Adams," a voice booms behind me. "Hoped I'd catch up with you. Everything going well, is it?"

I spin round to see the advancing hulk of Detective Chief Inspector Hendersen, the chairman of my interview panel. So huge in his tweed jacket that I think he must have at least two more on under it. He moves at quite a speed for a man of bulk, jowls flapping. A rhino charge? Or a Saint Bernard dog?

"Very well, sir, thank you," I manage.

The DCI catches up but doesn't speak again. The silence unnerves me and I fill it with basic facts about the case. The longer he remains mute, the more disjointed my explanation becomes. While my mouth moves, my brain wills him to talk. His eyes are boring a hole in my middle. The dreadful realization dawns that I've left my jacket on the chair in the interview room. I'm standing in front of a senior officer exposed in my royal blue T-shirt.

DCI Hendersen's gaze takes in every letter of the sparkling silver *Boogie Babe* motif before moving on to the Barbie girl below it. After what seems like an age, he resumes his military bellow. "Jolly good work so far, DC Adams, but remember this is a police station not a night club. CID is the *plain*-clothes branch. How would it be if I pitched up in my pyjamas?"

My eyes hit the ground in search of a gaping hole to swallow me up, royal blue T-shirt and all.

"Carry on, detective constable, carry on." He strides past me, muttering to himself, "And they expect us to take them seriously."

Chapter Seven

After retrieving my jacket, I join Matthews in Forensics. Blood pounds in my cheeks. How could I have undermined my credibility with the DCI on my first morning in the job?

Matthews is sitting with a man who has the same air of scientific inquisitiveness as Dave, the forensics officer I met at the Brocks' house.

The man grins. "I'm Steve Chisholm. You must be Agatha. I've been hearing all about you."

Same appearance and same sense of humour. Thanks again, DS Matthews.

The room is a jumble of desks, each with its own spaghetti tangle of telephone and computer cables. Two or three small, heavy-duty suitcases of forensic equipment lie on the floor. I wheel a swivel chair over and sit on the edge, trying to slide my back down to their level. I daren't touch the handle to alter its height. Landing spread-eagled on the floor is the only indignity the day has so far spared me, but I still have the afternoon to endure.

Evidence bags litter Chisholm's desk. Matthews has his notebook open.

"Steve's going through the forensics for both crime scenes," he explains. "Dave's team has scarpered back to Briggham."

"Did you know that it's the fifth fatal stabbing in Brigghamshire this year, but only the second kidnap?" Steve says. "Quite a puzzle for you. Good job you can call on forensic science." He points at two large see-through bags. One contains a heavy metal chain and the other holds a set of handcuffs. "We got these from the lads at the Southside crime scene. We've only found one set of fingerprints."

"Anyone we know?" Matthews asks.

"Definitely not the wife's. So, if she did handle the chains, she would've been wearing gloves." Steve grimaces. "But there were no gloves anywhere near the lounge where she was found."

"She says the assailants got her husband to chain her up."

"We'll get the prints off your corpse. If they match the prints on the cuffs and chains that would fit with her account."

Matthews holds up a bag containing two small keys.

"We got a partial on one of those," Steve says, taking the bag. "The prints were smudged." He shrugs. "Not unusual on something like this."

"I take it they do fit the cuffs?"

"One key for the cuffs, one for the padlock on the chains. It was a pretty sick joke, putting the keys to unlock them in the pocket of her pyjamas – these pyjamas." He lifts another bag. "Mrs Brock was wearing them when we found her."

DS Matthews takes the bag, looks at it and passes it to me. The pyjamas, folded with the top pocket visible, are like something I'd buy in Marks & Spencer. Paisley pattern, lemon and white winceyette. I have a pair like them for winter.

"And that's about it," Steve says, retrieving the pyjamas. "We couldn't find anything in the bedroom. There were a couple of bits of rubbish on the lounge carpet. This piece of cotton thread and a fragment of toilet tissue." He points at the relevant bags on the desk. "The other thing of significance might be this." He passes round a small bag containing a single black hair. "It's hair uprooted from a human head, probably IC3. We're working on the DNA, so if you find your suspects we may have evidence which places one of them at the house."

"Let's have the DNA as soon as you've got it," DS Matthews says. "The chances are they've both got previous."

Steve nods, closes the file on the desk, and slides it to one side. He pulls another manila folder towards him. "Moving on to the murder scene at Martle Top. The boys are taking the car apart as we speak. Lots of prints everywhere, especially on the steering wheel, which match the prints on the handcuffs. So probably the husband's." He flips the new file open. "Also a few of the wife's prints, as you'd expect in the family car. But there's at least one other set. The boys are looking for DNA."

"What about this?" DS Matthews points at the bag containing a large knife, the blade partially obscured by dried crusts of blood.

"No prints on the handle. That would be too easy. We've taken a blood sample to match to the victim. A foregone conclusion, I'd say." He lifts a bag containing a large pair of black and white trainers. "We also found these shoes in the footwell of the driver's seat. We think they belonged to the victim. I'll confirm this as soon as I can."

"Brock was barefoot when we found him," Matthews says. "If they're his, he was probably wearing them on the way to Martle Top and took them off before he got out of the car or was dragged out. But why would two brutal killers get into his house, pull him out of bed and then let him stop to collect his trainers?" He rubs his chin and pauses. "Or did he always keep them in the car?"

"You tell me, Mike. You're the detective. But if they wanted him to drive the car, they might have let him put something on his feet."

Despite the run-in with Hendersen, I have a residue of confidence left over from the interview with DI Bagley. I interrupt. "Was anything else found in the ditch near the body?"

"Yes, *Agatha*." Steve points to three bulging plastic sacks at the back of the desk. "All the usual crap you find in an English country hedgerow these days. It's all bagged and labelled. I've got to go through it, but I doubt that any of the fag ends, condoms and cola cans will lead to a major breakthrough."

Squashed down to foolish, I remain quiet for the rest of the meeting.

"You can go home now, Agatha. Catch up on your bedtime reading," Matthews says as we make our way downstairs.

"I don't mind staying on."

"You go home and psyche yourself up for what you've got to do tomorrow."

I dread he'll mention the post-mortem, but he has another task in store.

"First thing you're taking the grieving widow to identify her husband and then bringing her back here to view some mugshots. The inspector thinks it requires the softly, softly approach of a woman constable. Best not stay up all night with Hercule Poirot. We want you looking fresher than the corpse."

Chapter Eight

Zelda's eye goes straight to the towering figure exercising at the *barre*. Her heart skips. The prodigal has returned – for the second time. She takes in the shiny blonde hair scooped into a ponytail and the baggy blue T-shirt that matches the friendly eyes. And the woollen legwarmers, of course – so old-fashioned and yet so becoming on Pippa Adams.

"Just join the end of the line, Pippa. We're starting with 'Happy Feet'," she says, offhand, doing her utmost to her hide her delight at seeing Pippa back in class. She hasn't been in a lesson for over three months – ever since Zelda mentioned doing a veterans' number at the summer show. She'd misread the look of horror on Pippa's face, putting her reluctance down to false modesty. "You've still got it, you know. Three years pounding the beat hasn't made you completely flat-footed."

"I've retired from performing," Pippa had replied, and now Zelda hates herself for frightening her away. She had thought that time had put a safe distance between Pippa and her unknown demon. But how wrong she'd been. Pippa stopped attending the class after Zelda mentioned the summer show. She still comes to the studio sometimes but after-hours and she dances alone. Zelda has never talked about the show again or Pippa's absence from class, too nervous of opening the old wound. But tonight, for whatever reason, she's back in a dance class.

Zelda sets the iPhone in the speaker and looks along the line of dancers, all poised with their backs to her. Her gaze lingers on Pippa. She knows her statuesque presence will dominate this line-up as it has every other one for almost twenty years. Tears prick her eyes as her thoughts turn for the thousandth time to what might have been. What should have been. Until three years ago.

Zelda has been Pippa's dance teacher since she was five. She seemed an unlikely ballet dancer at first – big for her age even then, thighs chubby in white nylon tights, her round face as pink as her ill-fitting leotard. But Zelda spotted the child's innate sense of rhythm and ability to interpret the music. She looked beyond Pippa's sturdy build and saw that special sparkle. She coached Pippa to the position of lead junior, tutored her in the holidays during her boarding school years, encouraged her dance degree and finally recommended her for her first professional role on a national tour with Marcos Productions.

Never before or since has she used a friendship to further a student's career. But she went all out for Pippa, calling in a favour from her old flame, Barry Marcos. He wasn't at all keen to see Pippa because of her height, but Zelda badgered him until he finally agreed to go through the motions of an audition. Zelda knew he still didn't intend to take her on, so she set to work on Pippa. Her coaching, always thorough, became intensive. Hour upon hour of time steps, line after line of Suzy Qs, shuffle to shuffle of Buffalos, Zelda hammered out her demands like an overzealous drill sergeant. Pippa, the eager recruit, responded with pinpoint precision.

They both made sacrifices. She knew Pippa missed her brother's fifth birthday party and incurred the not inconsiderable wrath of her young stepmother. For her part, Zelda cancelled two summer workshops to concentrate on Pippa. The loss of earnings and dent in her reputation seemed worth it. There was no doubt of their ultimate synergy: the expert coach teasing out the best performance and the talented pupil always willing to give it.

And Barry Marcos was so impressed that he not only accepted Pippa but also rearranged his chorus line to give her a solo spot. All of Zelda's efforts seemed to have paid off until Pippa walked out on the opening night of her first professional show and rushed headlong into the police force. After all Zelda had done to get her the job, the betrayal ripped at her insides and she didn't even know the reason. She still can't believe it was down to acute stage fright, as Pippa's mother suggested whenever the two met to mourn the loss of their golden girl.

"I'm so sorry I've let you down," is all Pippa ever says if Zelda broaches the subject. Zelda has stopped asking. It's like the most terrible bereavement. For Zelda, knowing that Pippa would never again perform on stage was like being left with only the photographs of a departed loved one. They drifted into a distant teacher/pupil relationship and things settled down until Zelda was stupid enough to mention the summer show. Now with her mouth firmly shut, she watches Pippa heel-toe smoothly over the dance floor, grateful for the third chance her reappearance offers.

I kick high. After the day I've had, staying in with a book, as Sergeant Sarcasm suggested, is the last thing I want. I needed to get out and do something I'm good at, but I didn't want to practise alone tonight. I wanted to belong again, to be part of a dance troupe to get the companionship I used to love.

It's great to be back, even in this improvers' tap class. I owe it to Zelda to keep a low profile. By joining the advanced group I might force her to mention the summer show and neither of us wants that conversation again. I've caused Zelda enough hurt over the years. Besides, in this class, I don't have to concentrate too hard on arms and legs. I can let my ears take the rhythm and my mind is free to wander.

As I grapevine my way across the studio, my thoughts turn to Gaby Brock. How must she be feeling – wrenched from her bed in the dead of night, beaten up and chained to a chair in her own home while her husband suffered an even worse fate? I miss a step as my insides drop. Gaby Brock has been through an ordeal. Ordeal, agony, trauma, nightmare – whatever they want to call it, I know how every single one of those words feels. Gaby Brock's pain lasted several hours, which seemed like they'd never end, like time had stopped and there was no way out, no one else there except you and … My heart rate rockets and I miss another step.

I pull back from the precipice of my past and keep my thoughts on the case. What went through Gaby Brock's mind as she sat bound and gagged in the darkness? She must have waited in complete dread of the brutal kidnappers returning. What kind of monsters abducted Carl Brock but let him bring his shoes with him? Matthews thinks it's drugs. Was Carl Brock, schoolteacher, leading a double life: public servant by day, drug dealer by night? First rule of detection: know your victim. DI Bagley will get us digging into his past. Maybe we'll find out he led a blameless existence. Then what will be the motive? A bungled kidnap, perhaps; the killers hoping to extort money from the Brocks. But what kind of money would a schoolteacher have?

DI Bagley seems battle hardened enough to find the men who did it, and so does DS Matthews – ready for a long fight, knowing the rules of engagement, but with a complete disregard for those on his own side. Is he as brusque with the other detective constables, or has he singled me out for special attention? I seem destined to be his whipping boy just as he appeared to be Bagley's. Maybe, he doesn't like women. I can see how spending time with DI Bagley might colour his view of the opposite sex.

The dance routine switches to a series of single time steps. With every *shuffle, hop, step*, I hear Matthews: *Ag A Tha*. A nickname on day one. It took three weeks for one to ferment at police college but that was worse: Lady Double-Barrel.

It was my fault then, too. I joined the police force as Philippa Woodford Adams. That was the name on my birth certificate and it had been unremarkable at boarding school. But the name and my private school accent nearly led to an early exit from the police course. The jokes and pranks from the other recruits became less funny and more merciless, but I dug in. No way would I give up. Never again would I cower or sob or beg. Police officers took control. They stood firm and stopped bad things, bad people. I needed that.

So I stuck it out and found a new use for my drama skills. By the end of the course I'd flattened my vowels and beaten my diphthongs into neutrality. I didn't try for a regional accent. It wasn't like the theatre where an actor learnt and repeated the same lines every night for the duration of the play. This had to be for my entire police career. Sounding more BBC than Berkeley Ball was enough to get me off the hit list by the time I joined my first police station. I also took the precaution of consigning "Woodford" to the "Middle Name(s)" box on my staff form. Thus I became Pippa Adams and fitted in.

Now I'm depressingly visible again. The only way to re-establish my anonymity will be to prove myself a good detective. That'll mean sticking close to the disagreeable DS Matthews. He already seems to have worked out a motive. His suggestion of a drugs connection is no doubt based on experience. He's probably met one or both of the murderers on a previous case.

"Line up everyone." Zelda breaks into my thoughts. "Take your positions for the show number." I sit down at the side and see the expectation in Zelda's face change to resignation.

Chapter Nine

It's like walking through treacle, trying to shorten my stride to match Gaby's. I tell myself to feel more compassion; the woman has been beaten to a pulp, walking must be painful. Linda Parry, who flanks Gaby's other side, is struggling with her heels on the vinyl floor of the hospital. No doubt she's grateful for the plodding pace.

Maybe there's a chance that the formal identification process, the follow-up paperwork and then the trip to the station to view mugshots will make me miss the 11 a.m. post-mortem. I'm clutching at straws.

The atmosphere in the glazed corridor is stifling. Glad I ignored Mum's advice and opted for bare legs. If it's good enough for DI Bagley, I can get away with it too.

"Sorry it's such a long walk," I say. "This place is worse than the police station. Corridors everywhere and they all look alike. I forget where I am sometimes."

Linda smiles, but Gaby seems not to hear.

When we reach the door to the viewing area, Linda cuts through my chatter. "You don't have to do this, Gaby. I can go on my own."

Gaby glances wearily at her sister-in-law. "I'm fine," she says and pushes open the door.

A blue curtain is drawn across a large window. When I press a button on the wall, a hand appears around the curtain and pulls it back to expose another room. In the centre is a table draped by a cream sheet, with the contours of a body visible. The scene reminds me of the chapel of rest where I last saw my grandfather, except that this room lacks the yellow lilies and burning candles. Instead, several harsh fluorescent ceiling tubes light the space.

The attendant turns down the sheet to reveal Carl Brock's head and shoulders. The morticians have taken great care to comb his hair and tidy his chin.

"Oh, my God." Linda presses her hands against the window, sobbing.

Gaby Brock also steps nearer. Her eyes burn through the glass into the closed lids of the corpse. "Yes, this was my husband, Carl Brock."

The vivid black and purple bruises around her eyes and across her forehead make it hard to gauge her reaction. Her eyes linger over his face, studying all his features. Despite the circumstances, she carries her battered body with poise, arms by her sides. Is she indifferent to her husband's death? Or enveloped in a grim and silent grief?

Linda's sobs become louder.

"Would you like to go to the hospital chapel for a few minutes, before we do the paperwork?" I ask, glancing at my watch, still lots of time until my date with post-mortem destiny.

Gaby shakes her head. "Better get it all over with."

When we arrive at the police station, the sergeant handling the ID photos says that he can manage without me and I'm free to report to DI Bagley for the post-mortem. He suggests Linda get a coffee while Gaby goes through the photographs.

"I'll show you where the canteen is, Mrs Parry," I say, grasping the opportunity to delay my return to Bagley.

"I'm sorry about your brother," I say, handing Linda a steaming polystyrene cup and sitting down opposite.

Linda peers into the coffee. "We weren't that close, but it's still a shock to see him lying there."

She rests her open fingers against her throat. I note the gesture. If only I could remember what I've been taught about body language.

"It's awful to think that Gaby was inside, all tied up when we called round," Linda says, close to tears.

"You called round? What time was that?" I try to keep the eagerness out of my voice. And the smugness. This is news. DI Bagley was so intent on grilling Gaby Brock yesterday that she ignored Linda Parry.

"We dropped the kids at school and called on Gaby at about nine. We were supposed to be taking her to the Monday market. I thought she'd forgotten and gone out, although she doesn't go out much."

My excitement fades; the kidnappers would have been long gone by 9 a.m. Whether Bagley knows about it or not, it's highly unlikely that Linda's visit to the Brocks' house will have a bearing on the case.

"Did you hear or see anything near the house?" I ask, but it's hardly worth asking.

Linda shakes her head. "Only their milk on the doorstep. I moved it into the shade."

"Will your sister-in-law be all right? I'm not sure it's sunk in yet. She's very quiet."

"Gaby always is. That's her way. She was the same when Pipkin died."

"Who's Pipkin?" I ask. Maybe getting some background information on the family will give a lead.

"Her pet cockatiel. He died a couple of months ago. Mangy

old thing. First his tail feathers went black and then he started pulling them out of his chest. He was practically bald before he finally fell off his perch. Gaby adored that stupid bird. It became her world after she lost the baby." She fishes a soggy tissue out of her handbag and blows her nose. I wait for her to continue and hope she will without prompting. I need to know, but am reluctant to probe into the obvious tragedy.

"She had a miscarriage last year. Didn't say much then either. Didn't even cry. Carl took a week off school to look after her. He wouldn't even let me visit so she had complete rest. When I did see her, she was quiet. Didn't want to talk about it." She cups her drink and blows on the surface. "After another week she picked herself up and carried on as if nothing had happened. Threw herself into her yoga. Not classes though; she said it was more restful to use tapes at home. I expect she'll return to it now."

My eyes moisten. At least the books on yoga on the Brocks' bookcase will be read again. I'm about to give Linda's hand a sympathetic squeeze but pull back when I remember Bagley's earlier rebuke about being overfamiliar.

"How long were Gaby and Carl married?"

"Two years. A whirlwind romance. She was a classroom assistant at the school where he works. They got married soon after they met."

"Does she still work there?"

"She gave up work after they married." She takes a sip of coffee and wraps her arms around herself. "They hoped to start a family."

"Did Carl like being a teacher?"

"He loved it. He thought he could make a difference. Especially to the ones everyone else had written off as the no-hopers." Her fingers touch her throat again, and she breaks into loud sobs.

Grief. I remember: an open hand to the chest means the woman is grieving despite saying she wasn't close to her brother. Ditching

Bagley's instructions, I pull my chair around, lean a consoling arm around Linda's shoulder and let her cry. I catch sight of my watch and sigh; acres of time to spare.

Chapter Ten

"You can skip the post-mortem," DS Matthews says when I return to the general office.

"Has it been postponed?" It's bound to be his idea of a joke and next he'll tell me I have to go to it after all.

"The DI is doing it on her own. She wants you to see some real CID work." He slips his jacket over his shoulders. "The desk sergeant says Gaby Brock picked out one of the mugshots. It's Samuel McKenzie."

I recognize the name. "Isn't he a suspected drug dealer?"

"He's a known dealer, Agatha. Dealing, running a brothel, illegal gambling, blackmail. A regular pillar of the community. We're off to the Dynamite Club to rattle his cage."

"The night club?" I've made a fair few drunk and disorderly arrests outside. "Will it be open at this time of day?"

"Calling it a night club is like saying the Danescott Kebab House is a gourmet restaurant. The Dynamite is little more than a strip joint. The sort of facilities McKenzie offers have a steady supply of punters twenty-four seven. It's supposed to be members only before six, but McKenzie wouldn't let a little thing like the licensing laws get in his way."

As expected, Matthews drives in silence along the endless rows of industrial units and warehouses. This time I make no attempt at conversation. Don't want to give him more ammunition. I intend to limit his weaponry to the Agatha tag.

The silence gives me a chance to mull over the events of the morning. The chat with Linda Parry answered a few questions. Poor Gaby, how could so much tragedy attach itself to one person? The Brocks' circus-themed room was intended for the baby they lost, and the cage in the study was for the recently departed pet cockatiel. Pipkin is the kind of daft name I might have given one of my teddy bears, if they weren't named after Christie characters.

And Linda Parry displays her sorrow whereas Gaby Brock conceals hers. I remember how Mum and I clung to each other, wailing long and loud, when my grandfather died. I can't imagine keeping grief to myself. Other emotions – terror, rage, despair – I can hold those, but not grief.

We turn right into Minster Meadow, the dual carriageway that forms the eastern approach to Penbury town centre. It's bordered by elegant town houses, many displaying discreet Bed and Breakfast notices. Two pubs stand on either side of the road like a pair of bookends. Hanging baskets with patriotic displays of salvia, alyssum and lobelia front them both, while banners proclaim their respective commitments to family menus and Sky Sports.

Matthews slows down as Minster Meadow narrows to two lanes and becomes dwarfed by the minster itself. The 800-year-old walls stand solid and clean on velvety green lawns. No errant daisies or incipient clover here, thanks to the Briggham diocese grounds maintenance team. Although I see the minster as an ancient monument rather than a place of worship, I rarely visit. Crossing its slavishly swept threshold is like trying to penetrate a precious jewel. I've no business defiling its stone-carved floor with my size eight deck shoes. I content myself with frequent trips to the adjoining refectory for spaghetti bolognaise followed by apple crumble and custard.

Beyond the minster is a parade of shops. I make out a hardware store, a bank and a sandwich bar. Across a side road is a high-wire fence around a school playground. *Swan Academy. No unauthorized entry.*

We drive over the East Bridge, built fifty years earlier to span the River Penn. At this time of year its vast stone arches seem ostentatious for the grubby stream of water trickling below. However, by October, heavy rains in the Welsh mountains will swell the river and hide its banks. They currently stand naked and filthy. Another week of drought and they'll reveal the river's insides: rusted pushchairs, buckled bicycle frames, fleshless mattresses.

The town centre proper begins after the bridge. There's a multi-storey car park, an antique shop, two estate agents, a health food shop, three pubs – without hanging baskets – and any number of shoe shops. And then, on the right-hand side, is the Dynamite Club.

Matthews pulls into the deliveries bay in front of the club. "We ought to be able to arrest him just for that." He shakes his head at a neon sign that promises *Live Music.*

The building is by all other appearances a genteel Georgian-style mansion with greystone walls and bull's-eye windows. In a previous life it was Penbury's town hall. The council relocated to bigger premises west of the river and cashed in some of the town's architecture to pay for the move. The town hall was sacrificed when Samuel McKenzie waved a big enough chequebook. And the result was Dynamite.

Even before my eyes grow accustomed to the dimness after the brilliant sunshine outside, there's distaste in my mouth. Not so much for the shabby scene inside the club, unworthy of the building's heritage, as for the fact that it's taking place before noon. The sun not over the yardarm, my grandfather's expression passes through my mind.

There are women cocooned in cigarette smoke and laughter. Office workers taking an early lunch break or on an all-day bender. They don't notice me, but take in an eyeful of DS Matthews, nudging each other and laughing even louder.

A table of young men study the women and sip their beer. Elsewhere, at least three overweight, elderly men sit alone, clenching their pint glasses. When one of them lifts his rheumy eyes towards me, I hurry on, trying hard to shake off a feeling of revulsion.

Two skinny girls sit near the bar. One twists the rings on her fingers and the other picks at her nail lacquer. They wear cropped tops and leggings, but look as if they'd be more comfortable in the green school sweatshirts that peep out of the bulky holdalls stuffed under their stools.

A heavy woman in tight pink jeans passes us carrying a tray of empty glasses and makes the air heady with hairspray and cheap perfume. Matthews indicates we should follow her to the bar. As we weave between the tables in the dark room, a strobe light swoops across us and onto a small, low stage. Once there it changes to a series of whirling spotlights. An ageing speaker system starts with a muffled saxophone track. Its deep base makes my throat throb.

The circling spotlights settle on one side of the stage as three figures in white glide forward to the sound of a drum roll. My ears ring when the women erupt into wolf whistles and shouts of applause. I squint across the room. The young men have switched their gaze to the stage but still drink their beer. The fat old men are no longer holding their pints, their hands have disappeared below the tables. I'm ice-cold as a buried memory threatens to resurface. Crepey skin, florid neck, bulging eyes, acid breath. I turn to the stage, forcing my mind away from the past.

As we reach the two schoolgirls, they bow their heads guiltily.

I sense them relax as we move on. They must think they've dodged the truant officers for another day.

The woman in pink jeans is already behind the bar when we get there, slamming half lagers onto the tray. Matthews speaks and I strain to hear the barmaid's reply above the noise. She points to a large man sitting at the far end of the bar. Matthews moves towards him, holding out his ID card.

I try to stay tuned in but miss bits of what Matthews says as the tortured saxophone music works itself into a frenzy. The man stares at Matthews. Dreadlocked hair scooped into a ponytail. Expensive-looking purple suit with matching shirt and tie. Unlit cigar in one fist and a tumbler in the other. He sees me looking and I flinch. I flick my head back to the stage, cross with myself for feeling intimidated.

The dancers' manoeuvres are sluggish, not in time to the marching drawl of the music. What would Zelda say? With each step their ankles turn out sloppily. They push their hands above their heads, stroking the air with red fingernails. Their hips thrust to the left, flashing shiny brown thighs through the criss-cross of white fishnets. The music cuts out and the dancers amble off to raucous applause from the female parties.

"I know who you are. We already met." With the death of the soundtrack, the man's voice is loud and clear.

Matthews ignores the man's tone. "That's correct, Mr McKenzie. I interviewed you about a cocaine consignment which hit the Penbury club scene."

"It's summer," he drawls. "Ain't no snow here."

He looks me full in the face with his hard eyes.

"I'm DC Pippa Adams," I hear myself say in an over-friendly way.

"What you people doing in the Dynamite?" The menace in his eyes chills me.

"We want to ask you about a kidnap and murder which took place yesterday." I try to sound businesslike despite the intimidation. Blood whirs in my ears. I've seen eyes like this before. One time they'd bored me in half and I couldn't get away. I gasp for breath.

McKenzie lights his cigar and takes a deep draw on it. He leans towards me then breathes out with his mouth open wide. I manage not to cough despite the sweet smoke and sour breath that violate my nostrils.

"Errol, show these people the door. They not members." McKenzie calls out to a large, shaven-headed man who's appeared at the other end of the bar.

"We don't want to take up more of your time than necessary," DS Matthews says, apparently undaunted and opting not to remind him his smoking is breaking the law. "We need you to tell us where you were yesterday between two a.m. and seven a.m."

"With my woman, of course. Now leave my place."

"We'll have to speak to her to confirm it. And we would like to ask you for a sample of your DNA to eliminate you from our enquiries."

"Ask my woman. She gets my DNA." He discharges a belching belly laugh and leers at me. I want to bolt, need to even, but I hold as firm as I can on jelly legs.

"All we need are a few cheek cells, Mr McKenzie," I say quickly, eager to reach the end of my sentence before an old fear freezes my voice. "We can compare your sample with the one we found at the Brocks' house."

I see the brief but unmistakable flicker of recognition on his face. The name Brock means something.

"Errol. They going now," he says.

Errol moves in front of DS Matthews.

Again, Matthews ignores the threat. "We'd like you to come with us to the station. A witness has placed you at the kidnap scene."

McKenzie stands up slowly, extinguishing his cigar in his glass.

He leans towards Matthews. "You get some evidence first." He turns to leave.

Errol blocks the way. Without challenging him physically there's nothing Matthews can do to reach McKenzie.

McKenzie saunters off. Without thinking, I make a grab for his back and catch his ponytail. After what must feel like a gnat bite to a rhino, he brushes me off with a flick of his wrist and keeps on walking. I take a few strands of his hair with me as I fall and bang my face on the grubby carpet, with its stench of beer and undigested food. Stomach heaving, I pick myself up.

"We'll be back, Mr McKenzie," Matthews shouts as Errol moves aside.

McKenzie ambles through a door by the bar.

"Shall I call for backup?" I whisper, rubbing my cheek.

Matthews shakes his head. "He'll keep."

Chapter Eleven

One wall of the general office displays a board of photographs and diagrams. DI Liz Bagley has her back to the assembled officers and writes on a white board, her silver bracelets jangling against her tanned arm. A desk is piled high with her papers, briefcase and handbag.

Chairs have been dragged into a line in front of her. I slip in beside an older detective. He nods, his eyes lingering on my injured cheek. Two young officers at the end of the row appraise me, smiling. I manage a smile despite the tension in my jaw. When they finally return to their own chat, I relax.

DS Matthews stands next to a small, attractive man close to the display board. The man catches my eye and grins. I look away, blushing.

"The victim," DI Bagley says, turning round and pointing to the stark crime scene photograph of Carl Brock, "was found in a ditch on the Martle Top road, by a pensioner, at just after eight yesterday morning."

The room falls silent.

The DI looks at her notes on the desk. "The pensioner was a Reginald Arthur Kenny – out for an early morning bicycle ride." She paces in front of her audience. Her toenails, polished in the same red as her fingernails, peep out of her high sandals. "A blue Ford Mondeo was parked nearby with the passenger door open and the car radio on. Uniformed officers found what looked like the victim's photo driving licence in the glove compartment – in the name of Carl Edward Brock. A PNC check confirmed that the Mondeo was registered in the same name."

She sits on the edge of a desk, her thighs pressing against her leather skirt. "Uniform called at Brock's house in Southside at nine twenty." She points at a street plan on the board behind her. "On hearing banging noises inside, they broke in and found Gabrielle Brock, the victim's wife, semiconscious on the floor, gagged, chained and handcuffed to an overturned chair." She taps a photograph of the Brocks' lounge. "And the keys for the handcuffs and padlocks were found in the breast pocket of her pyjamas.

"Mrs Brock has been able to tell us that two men burst into their bedroom in the early hours. They made her husband, Carl, tie her up and then took him away. She remembers them saying ..." She checks her notes. "'You need a lesson of your own, teacher'.

"I attended the post-mortem this morning. Carl Brock died from a single stab wound into the heart." She scans her notes again. "Dr Spicer says the actual cause of death was cardiac tamponade – that's heart failure to you lot. The stabbing caused blood to accumulate in the space between the heart muscle and the outer covering of the heart. Death occurred within a few minutes. Brock also had a gash on his right hand from a day or so before his death, consistent with smashing his fist against a sharp surface. It might be something. It might be nothing."

She surveys the assembled officers and, when she's sure they've noted down the information, she continues. "Dr Spicer is running further tests as there is some evidence of long-term nerve damage. Although, in my opinion, any underlying chronic disease pales into insignificance compared with the terminal condition of a stab wound." She waits, giving us time to acknowledge her brand of humour, and turns to DS Matthews. "Did you learn anything from the house-to-house enquiries?"

"Nothing useful," Matthews says and pauses.

I examine the weave in my skirt, waiting for him to tell the room about my encounter with Mrs Perkins and how I managed the "house" but failed the "to house" bit of the operation.

He resists the temptation. "I tracked down the Brocks' milkman. He called at around six thirty but saw and heard nothing. He couldn't tell me anything about the Brocks except that they kept themselves to themselves. They always paid for the milk by cheque, direct to the dairy."

"So we can rule out the wife having an affair with the milkman and the husband catching them in the throes of a bondage game," Bagley says.

"You'd be the expert on that, ma'am," Matthews says. The older officer next to me blows his nose and hides a smirk under a greying handkerchief. The others, less discreet, laugh out loud.

"Expert on motives, I mean," Matthews says calmly.

"And I learnt everything I know from your mother." Bagley grins, but the smile doesn't reach her eyes.

Matthews resumes his briefing. "The only prints found on the chains, handcuffs and keys used on Mrs Brock were Mr Brock's, which supports the wife's version of events. A bit of tissue and cotton thread were found by her chair, but there's no evidence that they are linked to the crime."

"That's probably the separate crime of being a bad housewife. She hadn't vacuumed the carpet for a week." The handsome man next to Matthews speaks, a mischievous twinkle in his eyes. My face heats again.

A hearty chuckle ripples around the room and even Liz Bagley laughs. I find myself smiling at the joke, too, but a thought stirs in my mind. I try to make sense of it, but Matthews continues the briefing and I have to let it go.

"Forensics say that the strand of hair found in the hall is

definitely IC3." He pauses to look at the other detectives. "Odd they found hair when the attackers were wearing woollen hats."

"Maybe they didn't have hats on at first, but put them on before attacking the Brocks upstairs. Anything in the bedroom?" Bagley demands, her laugh a distant memory.

"Forensics have found nothing, and they're starting to rule out an inside job. They are still checking Mrs Brock's pyjamas, but there are no obvious blood spatters. She was barefoot when uniform found her. Forensics have tested for pollen or soil on her feet and shoes to place her on Martle Top with Brock, but it's looking unlikely."

The grey-haired detective near me raises his hand.

"Yes, Bradshaw," Bagley says.

"How did the kidnappers gain entry to the Brocks' house?"

Matthews turns to his colleague to answer. "SOCO found a broken panel of glass in the back door with a key in the lock on the inside. It looks as if they just put a fist through the glass and turned the key."

There's a general tutting and shaking of heads. We never cease to be amazed by people's disregard for crime prevention: leaving the key in the door is asking for trouble.

"Any prints?" DC Bradshaw asks.

"None, but SOCO did find blood on a shard of glass. They're checking it out."

DI Bagley addresses the room again. "Mrs Brock has formally identified the victim as her husband and picked out our old friend Samuel McKenzie from the family mugshot album."

A brief chorus of "I might have guessed"; "typical"; "sounds about right", interrupts her.

"Are there any similarities with Briggham's Easter Day kidnapping?" Bradshaw asks suddenly.

Bagley pauses before answering. "Doubtful. Briggham CID is pretty sure it's the Smith End Gang behind that."

"Does McKenzie have links?"

"Not that I know of. He's a pain in our arse, but he's small fry. Smith End would have his bollocks for breakfast," Bagley says. "So, Matthews, what's the latest on the McKenzie line of enquiry?"

Matthews clears his throat. "DC Adams and I visited McKenzie at the Dynamite Club this morning. He refused to give a DNA sample and had a flimsy alibi for the time of the murder."

Before they can register the hesitancy in Matthews's voice, an electronically whined version of "Mission Impossible" rings out and distracts everyone. His good-looking neighbour reaches into his jacket for the offending noise. Liz Bagley beams again. I beam too. It's hard not to. The man's dazzling. As he moves to the back of the room and speaks into his mobile phone, a grin plays on his agile mouth and he rubs his fingers through his smooth blond hair. He's in blue jeans, and his New Balance trainers pick out the matching red and white in his T-shirt. He must be the other sergeant, DS Danny Johnson. I let out a sound as I imagine myself assigned to work with him instead of Matthews.

I turn hastily to the meeting, relieved that no one has heard my sigh.

Bagley's in mid-rant and exacting her revenge on Matthews for his bondage joke. "I'll give you resisting arrest. How could you let McKenzie get away? How many other scumbags in Penbury do we know who fit the description and are capable of this? I'll lay odds on the hair at Brock's house being his."

Matthews stares into her face impassively. The only sign of his discomfort is the pulsating skin above his collar.

"Is that how you got that shiner, Adams? It took two of you to fail to do the job. Put some make-up on for goodness' sake," Bagley snaps. I rub my cheek as she continues. "Get him, Matthews. And be quick about it. I want that low-life in here before he can firm up his alibi and brief his fancy lawyer."

I'm not sure what makes me do it. I haven't planned it. A discreet word with DS Matthews was my intention. But in a reflex action against Bagley's comment about my face, I stand up and, after a moment's scrabbling through my bag, fetch out a tube of Smarties. "Will this speed things up?"

The two young officers smirk. Bradshaw chuckles.

"What's that, DC Adams?" Bagley says, irritated.

"During the scuffle …" I hesitate as I see the anger in Matthews's eyes. "I mean when McKenzie resisted arrest, I managed to grab some of his hair. It's in here." I shake the sweetie tube.

Another, louder chuckle goes round the room. But Bagley's in no mood to join in. "Do you mean to tell me you obtained a sample of a suspect's hair without his knowledge?"

"I just thought …"

"Against every police protocol ever written?"

"I, well …" I hear my voice squeak and die.

"You took it upon yourself to get an unlawful DNA sample from Samuel McKenzie. Is that what you're telling me?"

I nod.

"Well, don't just sit there glowing brighter than your sweeties. Get it down to the lab. It's strictly illegal but if it gives us a positive match on the hair in the hall, we'll find something official to nail him with later. Good effort, DS Adams." A brief smile appears at Bagley's mouth but vanishes quickly. "Now, jobs for you lot …"

"Ma'am, that was Forensics on the phone," DS Johnson cuts in, replacing the mobile in his jacket. "They say the death definitely occurred in the ditch. They can tell from the small amount of blood pooling at the site. They also confirm that the knife found in the ditch was the murder weapon. They've finished going over the Ford Mondeo. Most of the prints belong to Mr and Mrs Brock, but they've got a match for a third set, too." He looked gleefully at Matthews. "It's Samuel McKenzie."

"Right, Danny," Bagley says, "let's not wait for the DNA. Get uniform to arrest him. They know what they are doing." She shoots an icy look to Matthews.

"But we don't have enough evidence to make it stick. What's the motive, ma'am?" he says.

"That's for you to find out, detective sergeant. The wife says the attackers knew Brock was a teacher. They told him he needed a lesson of his own. You and Adams get down to Brock's school. Find out all about him."

"Ma'am." I stand up again, on wobbly legs but emboldened now that I've impressed Bagley with the hair sample. "His sister, Linda Parry, said he cared for his pupils. Maybe he discovered that McKenzie had dealers at the school."

"Promising theory. But she would say that, wouldn't she? The bereaved always turn their loved ones into heroes. It's up to us to cut through that." Bagley looks at the officer beside me. "Bradshaw, do the rounds of the hardware stores. See if they've sold any chains to anyone fitting our kidnappers' description. You'd better do the kinky shops for the handcuffs, although they were probably mail order.

"Holtom, Connors, I want you to run a check on Reg Kenny. Let's make sure he was just a passer-by on a bike ride who stumbled on the body."

The two young detectives write furiously in their notebooks.

"And do PNC checks on Carl and Gabrielle Brock, and Linda Parry, formerly Brock. I'm puzzled why the murderers needed to tie up Mrs Brock. Why not meet Brock at the school gates and take him for a ride into the country? Why involve his wife? Was she an intended victim, too?"

"Maybe, they wanted to extort money from Brock by threatening to hurt his wife," Matthews says.

Bagley nods. "We can't rule it out. When you've finished at the school, check out Brock's bank statements. Blackmail was one of McKenzie's early career moves."

"Do we know anything about the wife?" DS Johnson asks.

I look around, but no one responds. After a deep breath, I have another go – I'm on a roll now after all. "She is a full-time housewife. She gave up her job as a teaching assistant two years ago when she married Carl. They planned to start a family, but she suffered a miscarriage last year."

Danny Johnson's pale eyes twinkle in my direction. "Good girl, DC Adams. Anything else?"

My heart dances. Buoyed by yet another, albeit patronizing, compliment – and this one heading my way courtesy of the sparkling sergeant – I let my tongue dance too. "Her cockatiel died recently. I saw his old cage in the Brocks' study. He was called Pipkin and his feathers fell out."

My heart quits dancing. Several loud guffaws echo in my ears. I fix my eyes on a cracked carpet tile by Bagley's desk, willing the words back into my mouth.

"Thanks for sharing that with us, Agatha." I hear Matthews's voice full of scorn.

"Let's get on with it, shall we?" Bagley barks and sweeps out of the room.

Chapter Twelve

"The location is right for drugs," DS Matthews says as he swings into the last remaining space in Swan Academy's car park. "A short stroll over the bridge to the town centre, only ten minutes' walk from the Dynamite Club. Perfect for McKenzie's brand of tuck shop."

The school looks utterly respectable to me. I've been to a couple of other secondary schools to give talks on the dangers of drugs. *You did Drama at college, Adams. You can get up on your hind legs and spout*, Sergeant Conway said when the schools liaison officer phoned in sick one day. The schools I inflicted my unprepared presentation on looked scruffy – litter in the playground, broken fences, patches of graffiti. Whereas this one, with its stone-carved nameplate *Brigghamshire Education Committee Swan School 1936* above the main entrance, has a solid, traditional air. Like my own school, Tadcote.

Matthew helps when I struggle to open the heavy oak door. We go up six marble steps to the vestibule. On the left-hand side of the high-ceilinged entrance hall is a lift, looking like an upstart, squeezed in beside a wide staircase. The wall next to it displays a row of paintings and collages: *An Owl* by Daniel Tanner; *Firework Fantasia* by Ned Downey; a vivid and chaotic watercolour by Saul Hedges; and a pencil-sketched self-portrait by Sarah Link. What impressive young talent.

Ahead is a corridor that probably leads to classrooms. Off to the right, the entrance hall becomes an open-plan office. A middle-aged woman types into a computer, cradling a phone against her shoulder. Two boys in their early teens hover in front of her. They wear trainers and dark grey trousers a faction too short. Their open-necked shirts must have been plain white once upon a time but have taken on the hue of an aged treasure map. A far cry from my uniform – white knee socks, polished shoes, blue tartan skirt and a crisp white blouse with a firmly fixed tie.

When the woman finishes on the phone, the boys move forward, but she looks past them to us. "Do you have an appointment?" she asks, peering through her bifocals.

"Police. Is the head teacher about?" Matthews takes out his ID. The boys exchange an excited glance.

"One moment, please." The woman presses three buttons on her phone with pronounced finger movements. People often exaggerate their gestures to hide their fluster when dealing with the police for the first time. But this woman keeps her voice steady. "Mr Cunningham, I've got two police officers here who'd like a word." There's a short pause, but only a short one, before she replaces the handset. "Mr Cunningham can see you now. If you'd like to come this way."

She leads us down the central corridor. When we reach a door marked *Head Teacher*, she knocks, shows us in and leaves immediately. A tall man of about forty-five with laughing brown eyes comes round the front of his desk to shake our hands before motioning to two easy chairs.

He returns to his leather chair. "How can I help you, officers?"

"Thank you for seeing us without an appointment, sir," Matthews says. Is the "sir" out of cordiality or because of some vague memory of his school days?

"No problem at all. Don't mind Trish. It's only irate parents who need an appointment. Trish protects me from the worst of them."

"We are here to talk to you about one of your staff, a teacher called Carl Brock."

Cunningham adjusts some papers on his desk before answering, "He teaches English here, but he's off sick today. At least we think he is. He's not answering his phone. Didn't come in yesterday either or email cover work. Most unlike him."

"We have bad news, I'm afraid. Mr Brock is dead."

"Oh my god. That's terrible." Mr Cunningham raises his hands to his mouth in a show of horror. "I wondered why he didn't ring in." He must have seen my frown and adds, "What happened?"

"He was murdered yesterday morning."

Mr Cunningham grows pale and moves the papers again. "Not the stabbing on Martle Top? I heard about it on the local news. The victim hadn't been named. I never thought it could be … This is dreadful." He flicks his fingers through the papers. "Nothing like this has ever happened to one of my staff before." He sounds apologetic. "Do you know who did it?"

"Our investigations are at an early stage."

"Of course. Well if there's anything I can do to help." He adjusts his position in his chair. "He was a good teacher. He got reasonable results given the material he had to work with." He grins at me. On the desk is a framed newspaper clipping with a head and shoulders photograph of himself. The headline: "A Head of his Class". The words "flash" and "salesmen" cross my mind.

"Is the school poorly funded?" I ask.

He presses his hands together and leans his chin on them, adopting an academic pose. "Not really. Not that I would say so to Brigghamshire Children and Young People's Services Department. What I meant was his results were satisfactory for our students. Our catchment covers one of Penbury's largest council estates, the Danescott. I'm sure you must be familiar with it in your line of work. Need I say more?"

"Does the school have a drugs problem?" Matthews asks. Clever; he's used the headmaster's disparaging comments to lead into his main line of questioning.

"Certainly not." Cunningham lays his hands flat on the desk and looks steadily at Matthews. It seems to be a well-practised response to a question he's faced before. "Our students may not be the brightest stars in the galaxy but they understand the penalties for breaking school rules. I can't control what they do in their own time, but I can assure you there are no drugs in this school."

"Glad to hear it," Matthews says, holding the man's gaze. Cunningham's the first to look away. Matthews chooses not to press his advantage and changes the subject. "To build up a picture of Carl Brock, we would like to interview staff and pupils."

The headmaster's hands are back on the papers, gathering them up and tapping them into one neat pile. "There are nearly a thousand students and they'll all be going home in half an hour so I don't see how—"

"I don't mean today. We have to inform the parents first of our intention to interview their children. We can come back tomorrow. We just need a list of names and an interview room. Your office, perhaps?"

Cunningham coughs. "I need access in here at all times. I receive a number of important telephone calls throughout the day." He smooths his sleeve like a cockbird tidying his feathers. He must be used to his "I'm a very busy man" routine being accepted without question. But DS Matthews isn't his receptionist.

When the sergeant doesn't respond, Cunningham's plumage shrinks. He picks up the phone on his desk. "Trish, lock the Year Eleven common room for the rest of the week. The police need it. Any Year Elevens in for exams can go in the playground or, if they're desperate, the library."

"Thank you, sir," Matthews says, jotting in his notebook. "We'd like to start at nine tomorrow, but we can only interview children if the parents have been invited to attend. Perhaps your secretary would be kind enough to type out a letter for the pupils to take home tonight? Or send an email?"

"If it's really necessary, but don't expect a response. Most of these parents don't turn up to the annual consultation meetings. Unless, of course, you're planning to arrest any of their offspring? They'll demand their rights soon enough in that case."

"We just want to ask them a few questions, but we need an appropriate adult present. Perhaps one of the teachers could stand in if the parents can't attend?"

"I'm afraid that's out of the question. They all have classes of their own to supervise."

"What about you then, sir?"

He pauses. "I'll allocate a teacher," he says eventually.

"We'd like to kick off with the children who were taught by Mr Brock. Did he have any particular class that he spent time with?"

"His registration group. He didn't teach many of them English – luckily for him." He rolls his eyes. "But he had half an hour with them first thing every morning and fifteen minutes after lunch to take the register."

"We'll start the interviews with the form class and then work through his English classes. When can we interview the teachers?"

"I'm afraid that will be difficult to arrange. It's the end of GCSEs this week. Free periods are few and far between and taken up with lesson-planning and marking." He moves the pile of papers to his empty in-tray as if he's somehow closing the matter.

But DS Matthews isn't finished. "What about after school?"

Cunningham gives a sharp intake of breath. "Curriculum development meetings most nights. We have one tonight in fact."

"Will all the staff be there?"

"The English, History and Drama departments."

"I wonder if we might take up a short part of your meeting to interview the English teachers? It shouldn't take long."

Cunningham shakes his head. "We've got an Ofsted inspection coming up."

DS Matthews stares back at him. "We've got a murder inquiry."

The headmaster swivels his chair. "I can let you talk to them for the first half hour. We start at three fifteen prompt. You may use the reception area."

"Isn't that a bit public?" I ask.

"You won't be disturbed. We let the students out at three o'clock and you can see the skid marks on the carpet tiles. The place is deserted by five past."

"Thank you, sir. You've been most helpful." DS Matthews manages to sound sincere.

Bartholomew Hedges is outside his son's closed bedroom door. Should he knock, does the boy still deserve that courtesy? He and Sonia have always respected Saul's privacy, but have they been wrong? Privacy leads to secrets, and secrets lead to misery. Should he have been a stricter father, demanding to know Saul's every move and breathing brimstone for every minor misdemeanour? His heart drops in his chest, weighed down by another rush of the guilt that has swept over him in the last few weeks. Since that day when he *had* breathed brimstone – breathed, slapped, struck, shook and punched. Why is he so concerned about Saul's privacy, when he's violated a more precious right?

Or was his action justified? Did he act as any caring father would? Didn't God Himself, the most caring father of all, punish his children? Bartholomew has read it often enough: Numbers 16: 46–50; Romans 1: 18–20; Romans 2: 6–10. If the Holy Book tells of chastisement, then how can Bartholomew have been wrong? He ought to talk it over with Pastor Michael. Several times he's waited behind after the early service, but lost his nerve, too ashamed to talk about it outside the family even to a man of God.

Is the boy in his room? A flicker of hope. Perhaps Saul's in there drawing again. But the hope dies because the room is silent. Saul hasn't picked up his pencils for weeks and, anyway, he always draws with a racket in the background. Saul's favourite noise-music can no longer blare out, since he took his phone apart at two o'clock one morning when he couldn't sleep. Bartholomew isn't sure Saul still has the components to put it back together; he's probably sold them off.

Not since he was a toddler has he slept so erratically. In those days he ran his mother ragged, rushing around, into every piece of mischief, not wanting to miss out on any fun by succumbing to sleep. On the day they moved into Hare Close, Bartholomew took him outside to the grass in front of the flats to keep him out of Sonia's way while she unpacked. It was one of those gloriously bright, chilly mornings that the Lord God provided every once in a while during a dull, damp autumn. Saul rolled in the leaves, then found a stick and tried scooping them into a pile.

"Big 'tick bru'… Daddy," he exclaimed over and again as he continued with his game. Bartholomew's heart swelled to hear his baby telling him the stick was a brush. Such a bright child and what a talker! He toyed with looking for a proper broom for the boy to use but he didn't want to break the magic by taking Saul back inside. He carried on watching Saul coax his leaves into a scrappy heap and then scamper after them as the breeze blew them away.

Despite Sonia telling Saul to keep his bobble hat on properly in the cold weather, he pulled it back so that his ears stuck out, making him look like the cheeky imp he so often was. In the muddle of the unpacking, Sonia could only find the navy duffle coat that had belonged to his big cousin. Saul tripped over many times because it came down below the tops of his wellington boots. But none of those tumbles made him cry, so intense was his concentration on catching and herding the leaves. His magnificent son: active, enquiring, focused. Bartholomew sighs. When did these admirable qualities free-fall into something else?

He knocks gently on the bedroom door, and then harder. Soft tapping will show weakness. He has to stay strong in front of

Saul at all times. They'll get through this ordeal with strength. He puts his ear to the door. Saul could be sleeping. He doesn't sleep often, but when he does, he's out for hours. Bartholomew sighs again.

He feels the familiar tears prick his eyes. There's no more little boy who peeped transfixed through the stairwell railings at the first snowfall of winter, who sang in the choir in his Sunday shirt, Weetabix stains hidden under his tie, who won a children's painting competition and had his photograph in the *Penbury Evening News*, who swept the autumn leaves with a big 'tick.

Bartholomew has never forgotten that autumn morning, not least because he managed to capture it on camera. Pastor Matthew, the old pastor, used to lend him his video camera once in a while, saying, "It will be joyous for you and Sonia to share with Saul's own children one day."

He turns away from Saul's room without waiting for an answer. No one can watch the DVD of the little boy in the leaves; their DVD player is missing.

Chapter Thirteen

Judging by the pained expressions on the faces of the five people sitting at the back of the deserted reception area at 3.15 p.m., Mr Cunningham has passed on the news of their colleague's death.

A distinguished-looking man in a navy pinstriped suit offers his hand to Matthews and, as an afterthought, to me. "I'm Donald England, head of English." He catches my grin and adds, "A good name for the job, I know. The source of much mirth and merriment among the troops." He pauses to allow his colleagues time to chuckle. "And this is Mrs Howden, my second in command." He points to a plump, middle-aged woman with dyed black hair. He waves generally in the direction of the others. "These are Ms Yardley, Mrs Ferris (who's leaving us at the end of term) and our newest recruit, Miss Wickham."

"Thank you for seeing us," DS Matthews says. "As I think you know by now, your colleague, Carl Brock, was murdered yesterday."

Sombre nodding of heads.

"We need to find out as much as we can about Mr Brock. Build up a picture of what sort of person he was. Who were his friends, and his enemies if he had any? Who did he mix with, where did he go? That sort of thing."

"Seemed a decent chap to me. He came here about three years

ago. I was on the appointment panel," Donald England says, taking his seat.

"Did you ever see him socially, Mr England?"

"Not I." England turns to his colleagues. "But I don't know about any of the ladies."

"I'm not sure Carl had much of a social life," a thirty-something woman says. Tie-dyed skirt and heavy boots. Ms Yardley? "He seemed to spend most of his time here. He ran an after-school homework club twice a week."

"That's right. A noble gesture to give some of the weaker pupils a helping hand with spelling and grammar and the like," England explains. He straightens the crease in his trousers.

"Did many kids go along?" Matthews sounds sceptical.

"Most just tried it out a couple of times, but he had a core of regulars."

"Who were they?" I get out my notebook. It would be good to speak to pupils who knew Carl Brock well.

"Mostly boys in his form class," Ms Yardley says. She looks to Mrs Howden, the older woman, to help her out with the names.

But Mrs Howden doesn't respond until she realizes that we're also looking at her. "Joe Walker, Sam Turner, Will Gleeson." She glances at Donald England. "And a couple of others, probably."

"It would help if you could remember all the names," Matthews says. He must have seen her hesitation.

Donald England gives a small nod.

Mrs Howden says, "The only other one I know was Saul Hedges."

"We're interviewing the pupils tomorrow," Matthews says. "I'd like it if you could arrange for us to see these boys first."

Mr England exchanges another glance with Mrs Howden, then nods to Matthews.

"Did any of you know Gabrielle Brock, Carl's wife?" I ask, trying to concentrate on their answers but I'm distracted by a half-thought I can't grasp. Something Mrs Howden said is grating but I can't work out what.

"Didn't even know the chap was married," Mr England says.

"He mentioned her to me once. He told me she had a miscarriage last year." One of the other teachers speaks for the first time. When she lays a protective hand over her enlarged tummy, I make a guess that she's Mrs Ferris, the teacher leaving at the end of term.

"Didn't any of you know her?" I ask, letting go of the missing thought. "I thought she used to work here as a classroom assistant."

"I worked with an assistant called Gaby, but she left ages ago," Ms Yardley says. "Was she married to Carl?"

"Oh, I remember little Gaby," England says. "Quiet as a mouse. Didn't stay long. Shame she left."

"She wasn't that quiet. Not at first anyway. She was great at engaging the children, but said she wanted to spend more time at home with her new husband, so she left," Ms Yardley says.

"That sounds like Gaby Brock," I say. "Isn't it a bit odd she didn't tell you she had married one of your colleagues?"

"Many teachers choose to keep their personal relationships under wraps." England casts a sideways glance at Mrs Howden. "It seems to get the children overexcited otherwise."

Mrs Howden looks away. Are they withholding something?

"I think we should organize a collection. I can take some flowers round to Gaby. Carl's address will be on file here somewhere," Ms Yardley says.

"Excellent idea," Mr England declares. "I'll get the Head to issue an email."

"Mrs Brock is staying with a relative at the moment," I say. "If you'd like to leave the flowers with me, I'll make sure she gets them." I colour under Matthews's stare. He clearly doesn't appreciate the domestic interruption.

"If I could just ask you a few more questions," he says. "Does the name Samuel McKenzie mean anything to any of you?"

Miss Wickham, who's been gazing at DS Matthews and hanging on his every word, speaks for the first time. "He runs the Dynamite Club. I go there every Friday and Sat … I mean I go there occasionally with mates. But I've never met him." She stops speaking and looks at the floor. I sympathize with the gesture, which matches many of mine over the past two days.

"Do you know how Carl Brock hurt his hand?" I ask, trying to rescue the young teacher from embarrassment. "His wife said it might have happened at school. It would have been last Friday."

The teachers shrug and shake their heads. So much for my line of enquiry. I wait for Matthews to take over.

"Did Mr Brock have any visitors in school in recent weeks?" he asks but his question meets with more shaking of heads. "Perhaps parents of his pupils?"

"I saw him talking to a woman a few weeks ago. Shoulder-length bleached hair and big looped earrings. She looked quite agitated," Ms Yardley says. "I think she's the mother of one of the pupils in his form class. But I don't know who. I don't teach that class."

At this point Trish interrupts us to say that the Head needs his English staff for a critical "ideas-slamming" exercise. As none of the teachers can shed any light on the mystery blonde, Matthews closes his questioning and we leave them to slam away.

"His form class might know who the woman was," I suggest as we cross the school car park. "It's odd that the homework club regulars are all boys."

"I thought that, too, Agatha. Teenage boys aren't noted for their conscientious attitude to homework."

"What did you think of Brock's colleagues?" I ask. "Do you think they know more than they are letting on?"

"I don't think the women are mixed up in this. Howden is too ancient, Ferris too pregnant and Wickham too much of a raver."

"What about Ms Yardley?"

"I wouldn't like to get on the receiving end of those Doc

Martens, but she's harmless enough. The one I don't trust is England."

"I thought he was charming."

"Exactly, Agatha. How many teachers do you know who wear pinstriped suits and talk with a plumy accent?"

I think of my own teachers; it's best not to give a truthful answer. "I did wonder whether he and Mrs Howden were hiding something."

"They're probably at it. Even the over-fifties have been known to partake now and again."

"What about the headmaster?" I ask quickly. Why the hell am I blushing?

"Seemed all right to me. A bit of a poser, maybe, calling his school kids 'students'."

"He didn't strike me as very caring."

"He's a typical headmaster, a paper shuffler." He stops walking as we reach the car. "Press the flesh with the governors, look paternal in assembly and Bob's your uncle."

I wonder how he'd be sum up the professor of a music academy and make a mental note never to tell him what my father does for a living.

"Do you think Mr Cunningham is right about there being no drugs in the school?" I ask.

"Every school has a drug problem and he knows it. But he also knows that it's career suicide to admit it." He unlocks the car. "We can't do more till we speak to the kids. Do you want a lift home?"

"It's only four o'clock."

"You'll put in your hours soon enough. I see an all-weekender coming up. So where do you live?"

"I'm sorry?" My voice quivers. Why is his question so distracting?

"So I can drop you off."

"Thank you, but there's no need. It's out of your way." It must be a joke. Any minute now he'll mention St Mary Mead.

"Don't you live in Penbury?" he says.

"Yes, but—"

"It can't be far out of my way, then."

"That's very kind." What else can I say without sounding rude? "It's Riverside," I mutter, pulling on my seat belt.

"Nice." Matthews switches on the ignition.

I chew my lip as he drives us over the Ramparts, past the Boys' Grammar School and the West Bridge, and on to Riverside. Several of my fellow PCs and Sergeant Conway have been round to the flat at one time or another, but I'm dreading Matthews seeing the warehouse conversion that featured in the *Daily Telegraph* property section as well as *Brigghamshire Life*.

Will I have to invite him in for a drink and let him cast his sarcastic eyes over my living room? Storing up snide remarks about the women's magazines on the coffee table and the rows of crime novels on the bookcase, with one Agatha Christie well-represented? I take a deep breath as we turn into the leafy courtyard and park in front of my block.

"How do you afford this on a constable's salary?" he asks, looking up at the building.

I wasn't expecting such a direct question and blurt out the truth. "My grandfather bought it as an investment when they were built and left it to me in his will."

"He must have loved you very much."

"Would you like a cup of tea?" I offer. So disconcerted by the first civil words he's spoken since I started the job, the invitation comes easily.

I feel an odd mix of relief and disappointment when he declines, pleading paperwork. I fumble in my bag for the door key as he effects a three-point turn behind me. I make a point of not turning around to avoid the decision of whether to wave.

Once inside, I head along the ground-floor corridor. The door to my flat opens before I reach it.

"Darling, you're home early."

Chapter Fourteen

"What a lovely surprise." I put my arms round Mum, breathing in the exquisite perfume and touching the soft fabric of her smart navy T-shirt.

"What happened to your face?" She lifts wisps of hair that have come loose from my ponytail, her eyes full of concern.

I rub my cheek where it connected with the carpet at the Dynamite Club. "It's nothing. I slipped over, chasing a suspect." Almost true.

"How frightful. I'll make some tea." She moves easily to the kitchen, slim and elegant in her polka dot trousers.

I follow. "What brings you this way today?"

"I met the girls for a spot of lunch at Bundies, and I decided to pop over to see how you were getting on in the new job. I thought you might have phoned last night."

"I stayed on at the studio. It was too late to ring when I got back." I curse myself for bringing up the dance studio and quickly change the subject. "I didn't see your car outside."

"It was Diana's birthday, so we had champagne. I thought I'd better pick up the car this evening." She stands on tiptoes to reach the teapot from the cupboard where it resides between her visits. As she cranes her neck in search of the matching teacups, her thick hair shimmers in the light from the window. The greying gives it a stunning silver quality.

"The mugs are on the bottom shelf," I say, wandering into the bedroom.

"Let's have cups," she calls after me.

I toss my jacket on the immaculately made bed. Half a dozen cuddly toys are propped up on the pillow beside a folded nightshirt.

I emerge a few minutes later, barefoot and in loose-fitting shorts. "Thanks for making the bed. You didn't have to."

Mum reaches into the fridge. "My goodness, darling. What on earth is that mould?" She retrieves a milk carton and hastily closes the door.

"It's courgette puree. Would you like some? I've got plenty. The proceeds of a housetohouse enquiry." Mrs Perkins was true to her word and pressed two margarine tubs of green liquid into my hands as I made my escape.

Mum gives a declining smile and hands me a cup and saucer. "So how is Brigghamshire's newest detective?"

"My feet haven't touched the ground, and I'm investigating a murder and an assault."

"I read about it in the *Evening News*. How's it going?"

Despite my mother's deep fondness for gossip, I know she'll never breathe a word to anyone about my work. I tell her what little I know. "The murder victim and the assault victim were a married couple. The wife was left bound and gagged at home while the husband was taken away and killed. We are trying to find a motive at the moment."

"The poor woman, subjected to that terror and then being told her husband had been murdered," she says. "I can't imagine having to face anything so dreadful."

She holds the hot cup to her mouth, taking careful sips. She's been through traumas of her own: her husband's adultery; her beloved father's death; my desertion to the police from my dance career. Although she hasn't faced a crazed kidnapper, she's fought off her own demons.

"Are you going to see Jamie on Saturday?" she asks with the false brightness that's in her voice whenever she mentions my half-brother, the product of Dad's remarriage.

"My sergeant says we'll probably have to work all weekend."

"How awful for you." She tries to sound sympathetic, but I see the relief in her face. She's glad her daughter won't be playing happy families with the enemy.

"We need to make some headway with this case."

"Who's in charge of it?" she asks.

"Detective Inspector Liz Bagley."

"I thought it would be James Hendersen."

"I haven't seen the DCI yet." I decide not to mention the *Boogie Babe* T-shirt debacle.

"He's a good man, you know," she says. "Your grandfather knew him in his regiment."

"I think you may have mentioned it already." Ever since I became a police constable, Mum has clung to the knowledge that her father, Brigadier Nairn Woodford, commanded Major James Hendersen. On retirement from the army, Hendersen joined the Brigghamshire police force. In Mum's eyes this gives my new career far greater respectability.

"You must invite him round to supper."

"I'm not even sure it's the same James Hendersen." I've lost count of the number of times I've regretted telling her the name of the officers on the CID interview panel. "Even if it's the same one, he's a chief inspector and I'm a detective constable."

"Darling, you make it sound worse than the army. No fraternization between the ranks. He's a family friend."

"Well as I said, I haven't seen him. I expect he's busy investigating other aspects of this murder."

"Who do you think killed the man?"

"It could be someone he met through his work as a teacher."

"Surely not even a pupil at the grottiest of comprehensives could hate a teacher enough to do that."

"We think it might be drug-related."

"Of course. The scourge of the twenty-first century. I don't envy young people today. The worst temptation I ever faced was when Lydia De Cornez smuggled a bottle of sherry into the dorm. We didn't have any glasses, so we used our toothbrush mugs."

"That explains why you never drink sherry now," I laugh.

"The next morning matron had us cleaning the lavatories as punishment. It was colourful to say the least." She takes a long drink from her tea, leaving the imprint of her pink lips on the cup. "What are you doing tonight?"

"I'll probably go to the studio unless you'd like to stay for a meal?" I kick myself for mentioning the studio again.

"No, thanks, darling. I want to get the car back." Then she looks into her teacup and says, "Is Zelda doing a show this summer?"

"It's in a couple of weeks." It's my turn to take a long drink.

"Did you audition ...?"

I shake my head with the cup still obscuring my face.

"Shall I make more tea?" She goes into the kitchen, extracting us both from the hazardous conversation.

"Yes, please," I say, relaxing back into the sofa, the danger over.

"Thank you for ringing," Sonia says.

Bartholomew watches her replace the handset. She's almost smiling. Almost. But not the old smile, broad across her bright face, from one hoop earring to the other. That grin has died. The new half-smile is grey. Just grey.

"That was Kyle Stewart, the senior manager. They've had a cancellation," she says. Her voice is trembling. With excitement? Or more tears? "Saul can go in tomorrow."

Her eyes find his, but he looks away. They used to be close. A marriage blessed in church before the eyes of the Lord, even if

Sonia didn't worship and not everyone accepted their union. They were strong through the hard times. A match for the wolf at the door. But for the one in the home, not a hope. He can't look into his wife's eyes anymore.

Sonia turns away too. "I'll go pack Saul a few things." She hurries to the door.

Don't rush, he thinks, it's too late to rush.

Chapter Fifteen

I drag two bulky chairs across the Year Eleven common room to a coffee table. Matthews takes them from me and brings two more for the other side of the table. I clear its debris of tatty magazines and sit down, landing heavily when the chair's lower than I expect. I don't catch Matthews's smirk, but assume it's there.

Peeling posters cling to the walls with yellowing Sellotape. "Are your trainers fairly traded?" asks one, while another gives details of "SnoopeeeZ MegaParty", partially obscuring one for the Penbury Careers Advisory Service. A far cry from the Senior Girls' Lounge at Tadcote, with its solid oak panelling and reading tables, displaying undisturbed copies of the *Daily Telegraph* and *The Economist*.

Matthews also takes in his surroundings. "This dump makes the station restroom look regal. Did you ask Trish to start sending them in?"

"She said Ms Yardley would be coming down with the first one after they've called the register."

Right on cue, the common room door bangs open and the first awkward adolescent interviewee ambles in. Matthews points to one of the chairs opposite us. As the boy flops into it, the twin scents of body odour and stale cigarettes waft across the table.

"Hi," I say, putting on a warm smile.

"What's your name?" Matthews asks without any introductory pleasantries.

"Joe Walker," he mumbles in a buzzing, newly broken voice.

The door opens again and Ms Yardley creeps in and takes her place next to Joe. Matthews acknowledges her and continues questioning the boy. "We want to talk to you about Mr Brock. See what you can tell us about him, okay?"

Joe shrugs his shoulders and keeps his eyes focused on a spot between my head and Matthews's. His jaws move constantly, working a piece of chewing gum behind his closed mouth.

"You went to Mr Brock's after-school homework club, didn't you?"

"Not me," he mutters.

"Are you sure? You're on the list of pupils who did. That must be a mistake." Matthews glances at Ms Yardley.

She nods. Does that mean it was a mistake or not? I can't read the gesture.

Matthews doesn't seem to know either. "So are you good at spelling then, Joe?" he asks.

The boy shrugs.

"What are you good at?"

Joe says nothing and puts a hand through his greasy, unkempt hair. Matthews could do more to put him at ease. How does probing his scholarly inadequacies help the case?

"Do you like school, Joe?" I ask.

"Nope."

I glance at Ms Yardley. Her face is impassive.

I try again. "What do you like?"

He shrugs again.

"What do you want to do when you leave school?"

Another shrug.

"Did you like Mr Brock?" Matthews asks. No doubt he'll blast my failed line of questioning later.

Joe opens his mouth but only manages a "'S'pose." He chews the gum with renewed vigour.

"Has Mr Cunningham told you what happened to Mr Brock?"

"He's snuffed it."

Ms Yardley shifts in her chair and casts me an apologetic smile.

Matthews begins tidying his papers on the coffee table, rather in the manner of Head Teacher Cunningham. I see the veins pulsating in his neck. "Okay, Joe, send in the next one," he says without looking up.

The boy saunters out without a backwards glance.

"Are they all like that?" Matthews says, giving an exasperated breath.

"Not all," Ms Yardley says, her earrings jangling furiously.

The next boy enters. Carrying a leather jacket over his shoulder, he walks confidently to us and sits down. He rests the jacket loosely between his knees. His green polo shirt shows off an athletic frame.

"Hi, what's your name, please," I ask.

"Will Gleeson." His voice is deep.

"We need to ask you some questions about Mr Brock. He was your form teacher, is that right?"

Will confirms that he's in 10B. Although only fifteen, he looks older. His skin, free of pimples, has a warm glow.

"Did you go to his homework club?" I ask.

"Sometimes. Not often."

"We were told that you were a regular."

"I've been a few times but not for ages."

"Do you have any idea who might have wanted to harm Mr Brock?"

"No idea." He pulls the leather jacket further onto his knee.

"There could be a drugs connection," Matthews says, taking over the questioning. "Is there any of that in school?"

Will draws the jacket up to his stomach. "Not that I know of."

"Anything you tell us is in complete confidence." Matthews lowers his voice, flicking his eyes at the teacher.

"I don't know anything about drugs or Mr Brock. He was just my form teacher." He speaks calmly and maintains eye contact with Matthews.

"Thanks for your time," Matthews says, leaning back in his seat.

"I can go?" Will looks at Ms Yardley.

"Yes, Will, you can," Matthews says, breathing out. "Thanks for your time."

"You're welcome." The boy smiles broadly. I detect relief behind the gesture. Have we let him off the hook too easily?

"He seemed polite but—" I begin.

"Don't be taken in," Matthews says, not letting me finish. "He didn't give us any more than Joe Walker did."

"Of course not, sarge," I say, suppressing my indignation and not looking at Ms Yardley. What must she think of us? Of me?

"A cool lad like that always knows things, but he's not as laid-back as he thinks he is," Matthews says. "Anyone lugging a leather jacket around in the middle of June is insecure on some level. Didn't you see the way he held on to it like a security blanket when I mentioned drugs?"

"Do you think he's hiding something?" I say, addressing the question to both Matthews and Ms Yardley.

"I haven't made up my mind yet. Let's see what the next one doesn't know," he says.

Ms Yardley says nothing.

Matthews tosses down his notes as another pupil, Sam Turner, leaves the room. "He was nearly as mute as Joe Walker. We've only got Saul Hedges left from the homework club and he's bound to be like the others. This is useless."

Mr Cunningham appears in the doorway and makes a point of addressing himself to Ms Yardley. "Eve, I'll start sending the rest of 10B now. Duncan Josephs is off with severe hay fever today. He should be back tomorrow or Friday."

"What about Saul Hedges from the homework club?" I ask, looking down at Matthews's list of names.

"I'm afraid Saul is off sick, too," Cunningham replies, still looking at Ms Yardley. "Has been for some time. I'm not sure when he'll be back."

"What's wrong with him?" Matthews asks.

"I'm not exactly sure. I'd have to check his file," Cunningham says vaguely.

"It doesn't matter. Send in the others."

I prepare to meet the next pupil but can't shake off the feeling that I need to make a connection somewhere. It's the same feeling I had when Mrs Howden spoke to us yesterday. A girl with thin black hair and painted-on eyebrows comes in. As the boys did, she launches herself backwards into the empty chair. She brings her skinny knees together and pulls her short skirt down as far as it will go. She seems familiar and this half-thought joins the other one in my mind.

"What's your name?" I ask.

"Kirsty Ewell," she says, and sighs as if talking to the police is the most boring thing she's ever had to do.

"We'd like to ask you a few things about your form tutor."

"He's dead, right?"

"Yes, I'm afraid so. He was murdered."

"Well it weren't me." She folds her arms and rolls her eyes, still faking boredom.

"Of course not, Kirsty. Did you like Mr Brock?"

"He was all right. At least he didn't treat us like little kids like most of them do."

"Did he take you for English?" Matthews asks.

"I have Howden for English." She remembers the teacher sitting next to her and modifies her tone. "Sorry, Miss. I mean *Mrs* Howden. Mr Brock was just my form teacher."

"Did you ever go to his homework club?"

"No way. I'm not staying in this dump after three o'clock if I don't have to." She doesn't catch Ms Yardley's eye. "Actually, Mr Brock mentioned the club to me a few times. He was on at me to go. My mate reckoned he fancied me." She gives her hair a gentle preen with her index finger. She sees Ms Yardley's icy face and adds, "But I never thought that." She starts picking the red varnish off her badly bitten nails.

The gesture's enough for me to place her. She was one of the under-age girls at the Dynamite Club.

I shoot a look at Matthews, but he's already asking his next question. "Do you have any idea why someone would want to kill Mr Brock?"

"No one here would. Everyone thought he was pretty sound – for a teacher." She glances at Ms Yardley. "No offence."

Matthews forces a smile and speaks softly. "We need to ask you some delicate questions. You can talk in confidence. No one will know that we got the information from you. What can you tell us about the drug scene round here?"

"Nothing." She folds her arms again. "And if I did know anything, I wouldn't tell you lot. I'm no grass." A grin comes over her face. "Was Mr Brock a junky?" She bounces in her chair, her interest well and truly roused.

"Mr Brock was not a junky," Ms Yardley says flatly and glares at me and Matthews; she isn't only saying it for Kirsty's benefit.

"We think Mr Brock's killer might have been dealing," I say hastily, trying to limit the damage, but knowing full well that Kirsty will dispatch the rumour of Mr Brock's drugtaking around the whole of Year Ten by morning break.

"Have you heard any rumours about dealers in school?"

She shakes her head.

I play my trump card. “Have you ever been to the Dynamite Club?”

“No-o”, she says slowly, peering through her straggly fringe. “It’s for over eighteens only.”

“Of course, forget I asked that,” I say, feigning an apology. I go for a different approach. “Tell me about school, do you like it?”

“I already said it’s a dump.”

“So you bunk off sometimes?”

“No-o,” she says again, turning away from Ms Yardley. “What’s that got to do with Mr Brock?”

“Just interested,” I reply, unsure what to ask next. This girl’s our best link between Carl Brock and McKenzie and I have to exploit it. If Brock found out that some of his pupils were going to the Dynamite Club, he could have decided to confront McKenzie, with fatal consequences. Does Kirsty realize I know she’s lying? The girl’s remarkably composed if she does. She doesn’t seem to recognize us from our visit to the Dynamite.

I’m still planning my next question when Matthews says, “If you think of anything which might help, let us know.”

“Is that it then? Can I go now?” Kirsty sounds even more surprised than I feel.

“I’d just like to ask—” I begin.

“We’ve no more questions,” Matthews says, turning a firm shoulder towards me.

Speak for yourself, but I’m powerless to overrule the sergeant.

During the rest of the morning, we toil through interviews with most of form 10B. Some chatter, a few charm, most grunt but none say anything useful. Eventually Ms Yardley asks for a break, pleading dinner duty.

“If we want to get in that sandwich bar next door before the school bell rings, we need to go now,” Matthews says after she’s gone. “I know most of them will head for the chippy across the road but there's bound to be a hard core of pre-anorexics ordering wholemeal lettuce sandwiches without butter."

"Maybe we should eat in the school canteen. We might pick up some gossip," I say. I'm wrestling with a question that keeps hovering out of reach.

"The only thing we'll pick up in there is salmonella. Kids who have school dinners these days are the sad ones with no mates. They'll be the last to know what's going on." He answers his mobile phone.

I collect our notes and pens, boiling at Matthews's blunt labelling. Does he put everyone in boxes? Lonely pupils in the canteen. Anorexics in the sandwich bar. Where does he see me? At least I recognized Kirsty Ewell from the Dynamite Club. He sent the girl on her way oblivious to any connection with the case. I'll enjoy telling him that later, even though he's bound to turn the information round and blame me for something.

"That was DI Bagley," he says, coming off his phone. "The strand of hair found in the Brocks' house isn't McKenzie's. It must belong to one of his cronies."

I picture Errol, the shaven-headed minder. A match seems unlikely.

"But we still have McKenzie's prints in Brock's car at the murder scene," Matthews continues. "Uniform have brought him in for questioning. The DI wants us back at the station to interview him. We better grab a sandwich on the way. I can't face that monster on an empty stomach."

I wonder whether he means McKenzie or Bagley.

Chapter Sixteen

On the journey back to the police station, I feel a surge of excitement. Not the simmering anxiety of crowd control duties or foot patrols at closing time, it's more like the buzzing nervousness before a stage performance. I thought I'd forgotten what that felt like. But there was no mistaking that stomach-churning eagerness – in the dressing room, backstage, in the wings. *Backstage.* My spine turns to ice; I've pushed the memory too far and the excitement is gone.

I force my mind back to the case. McKenzie made us look like fools at his club. I touch the bruise on my arm where his huge hand made contact, sending me to the floor. I don't need to check my darkened cheek, now concealed behind make-up as per Bagley's orders; it aches whenever I speak. This time I'm ready for McKenzie.

Matthews peers intently through the windscreen, driving fast because a long queue of office workers at the sandwich bar has made us late. What's he thinking? He has every reason to want to corner McKenzie after our previous encounter. He must be planning his own strategy for obtaining McKenzie's confession.

"Do you know what you're going to ask him?"

His response is fast. I was right: he is thinking about the interview. "We need to concentrate on linking him to Carl Brock."

He said "we". Is that a figure of speech or am I part of it? "What do you want me to do?" I ask.

"Have you ever played 'good cop bad cop'?"

"Sergeant Conway used to do it with shoplifters but he said I was too nice sometimes."

"That doesn't matter. I want you to be as friendly and as vague as you can."

"Vague?"

"Think bimbo." He pauses when my mouth drops open, then he explains. "If he thinks you're there for decoration, he'll only concentrate on what he says to me. He'll think my questions are out to trick him. While he's fencing with me he'll hardly notice what you're asking and what he's saying in response."

Decoration! My hands start to shake; I sit on them. "What do you want me to ask him then?"

"Drop in some aimless questions in-between my incisive stuff. Pick up on his answers and ask him something trivial. Then, when you've softened him up, enquire whether Carl Brock ever gave him a lift."

"What possible good will that do?" I'm truculent and hope he notices.

He doesn't. "Depending on his answer, you may need to back off. Play bimbo for a while and then ask him again. We want to lure him into giving a reason for his prints being in Brock's car."

"But he could be making up a reason."

"Doesn't matter. As soon as he admits a connection with Brock, we've got him. We can work on the details later."

He's used that word bimbo again, and he said friendly and vague. Does he mean flirtatious and stupid? I'm never a flirt, not any more. I'm chatty, but I'm like that with everyone. Girl next door, everyone's friend, no one's fantasy. I can't play the interview Matthews's way; I might be too convincing. He'll see me as even more of a lightweight. I'd rather talk tough with McKenzie. But two heavy-handed interviewers will get nowhere with a brute like him and Matthews's opinion of me will sink even lower. Better do as he says. If we crack McKenzie, Matthews might begin to see me as a useful teammate.

I mentally rehearse bimboesque questions. *Have you lived in Penbury long? I do like your shirt, where did you get it? Which gym do you use?* It comes terrifyingly easily and I'm primed for action by the time we get to the station car park.

DI Bagley's waiting outside the interview room. "He's in there with his lawyer," she tells us. "It's a shame we didn't get a chance to speak to him on his own first, but he was forewarned."

Matthews looks away. She must still see mileage in keeping alive the memory of the failed interview at the Dynamite Club.

"Right. Let's do it. Here are your questions." She hands Matthews a sheet of paper.

I hold out my hand for mine, but Bagley says, "You aren't needed here. Go back to the office and read through some past case notes."

I feel like I've been kicked in the stomach. I wasn't relishing Matthews's approach, but I still wanted in on the action. Crestfallen, I turn to leave, keeping my eyes away from Matthews for fear of seeing one of his smirks. But I have to check my hearing for what happens next.

"Ma'am," he says, "DC Adams and I have worked out an interview dialogue."

"She's too inexperienced and I've given you all you need," Bagley says, pointing at the paper.

"Can she at least go into the obs. room to watch?" he asks. "I'm sure she'd benefit from seeing how an inspector conducts an interview."

Her ego apparently massaged, Bagley agrees. "Fine, but let's get on with it. We've left him to invent an alibi for long enough."

Matthews points me to the next door along the corridor and

gives a reassuring smile, before following Bagley into the interview room.

The observation room is dimly lit. Noiselessly, I lift out a plastic chair from under the desk and sit to watch the screen in front.

"… present are Samuel Royston McKenzie, Edwin Saunders, DI Liz Bagley and DS Mike Matthews." The DI's voice comes through the speaker on my left. I see the backs of my two senior colleagues and beyond them the bulky frame of Samuel McKenzie. He grins at the police officers. Next to him sits a thin man in a grey suit. He seems to be dozing.

"Do you know why you've been brought here?" Bagley begins.

"Police harassment." McKenzie's grin gets wider.

"You resisted arrest."

"Your officers said nothing about arrest. They asked for my DNA. I'm not obliged to give it."

Bagley ignores the technicality. "Your fingerprints were found in a blue Ford Mondeo belonging to Carl Edward Brock. What have you to say to that?"

"A Mondeo? My associates drive Saabs."

Bagley nods at Matthews. He reads through the cue sheet before asking, "Did you know Carl Brock?"

"No, sir."

"You have never met Carl Brock?"

"I'm in business. I meet many people. One of my interests is the Dynamite Club. This is a very popular entertainment centre as I'm sure you know."

"So are you saying that you might have known Brock?"

"I might have known the Prince of Wales if he ever came to the Dynamite."

"Did you know him or didn't you?" Bagley cuts in.

Saunders, the grey suit beside McKenzie, is suddenly awake. "I think what my client is saying is that he meets a variety of people in the course of his work and, like any night club owner, he cannot possibly recall everyone who has been to his club. Because my client aims to be truthful, he cannot say categorically whether he has or hasn't met a man by the name of Carl Brock."

"But you've certainly been in his car. We have your prints," Bagley says, a note of triumph in her voice.

McKenzie beams again. "So it's prints in a car now. Last time it was DNA in a house. What's coming next: needles in a haystack?"

"As your solicitor will tell you, we no longer believe that the trace we found at the Brock's house is yours," Bagley says. "We know the fingerprints found in the Ford Mondeo belong to you. We've had yours on file for some time."

McKenzie and the solicitor signal to one another as if they've been waiting for this.

"My client informs me that his fingerprints were taken as a juvenile. His last conviction dates back to that time."

"Last conviction, yes, but we've had a few get-togethers since then."

"The police are stalking me, if that's what you mean."

"We have investigated you for burglary, common assault, living off immoral earnings, extortion, illegal gambling." Bagley reads from her notes.

"And there's never been a shred of evidence. I'm a businessman and I'm black. That automatically makes me a thug, a pimp and a drug dealer."

Bagley adjusts her chair. It seems to be her turn to react to something she's been expecting. Her response to McKenzie playing the race card is simply to ignore it. "I was coming to the drug dealing. We've reason to believe Carl Brock was murdered by a drug dealer." She speaks with a conviction that surprises me. I thought the case was still wide open but Bagley makes it sound certain. Is she just saying it for McKenzie's benefit?

"So not only must I be a dealer, why not fit me up for murder too."

Bagley still doesn't bite. She passes the baton to Matthews.

He reads out his next question. "Have you ever seen drugs at the Dynamite Club?"

McKenzie rests his hands behind his head. "Sure, I've seen drugs there."

The solicitor loosens his tie, looking suddenly thinner and greyer. Bagley and Matthews exchange a glance. This admission is better than they expected.

McKenzie waits until their attention is back at him. "There's a drawer in my desk, full of drugs: paracetamol, ibuprofen, vitamin tablets." He lets out a series of short, hollow laughs as his solicitor sighs and the two police officers shuffle in their seats. "I've no time to stop for illness. I dose myself up and keep going. Don't you ever need a little help like that?"

"Stop playing games and answer the question: have you seen illegal drug-taking at the Dynamite Club?" Bagley says, leaning forward.

McKenzie stares at her, tossing his head slowly from side to side.

"For the benefit of the tape, Mr McKenzie is shaking his head," Matthews says. He puts down Bagley's script and asks a question of his own. "What do you do about under-age drinkers at the Dynamite?"

"My staff ask them to leave."

"So why were there two pupils from Swan Academy in your club yesterday morning?"

I catch my breath. Matthews recognized Kirsty Ewell from the 10B interviews all along. I feel grudging admiration.

"They must have looked older. I will remind my staff to check for proof of age. I run a respectable business."

"If we discover school children on your premises again, we'll have your licence …"

Before Matthews can finish, Bagley butts in, "We're prepared to overlook this lapse, if you cooperate about Carl Brock." She stares across at Matthews, prompting him to resume his scripted questions.

"Mr McKenzie, please explain how your prints came to be in Carl Brock's car."

McKenzie shrugs his shoulders and spreads his huge hands, palms upwards, on the table.

"For the benefit of the tape, Mr McKenzie is indicating that he doesn't know. Come on, McKenzie." Bagley's almost spitting. "Your prints have been found all over the inside of Brock's car. It was found right next to Brock's dead body. Carl Brock was abducted by two men fitting your description. You're in the frame."

McKenzie turns his palms downwards and leans forward. Even through the speaker I pick up the menace in his voice. "Detective Inspector Bagley, do you know how many black men live in Penbury?"

Bagley doesn't answer.

"I'll make it easier for you. What about the whole of Brigghamshire?"

Bagley looks hastily at DS Matthews who says: "About five thousand."

"Not bad, sergeant, you're still in touch with your roots. Now Mr Saunders, tell the officers how many are subjected to their bully-boy stop and search tactics."

The solicitor speaks as if reading from an encyclopedia entry. "Ethnic minorities in the county of Brigghamshire are exposed to police stop and searches at a rate of twenty per thousand population, compared with seven per thousand for white people."

"So aren't I just another black statistic for you?" McKenzie asks, triumphantly.

Bagley busies herself with her notes.

Matthews covers her indecision. "We have your prints. I think that you met Carl Brock in his car. He wanted to confront you about selling drugs to some of his pupils and you didn't like it, so later you went to his home in the middle of the night with one of your henchmen."

McKenzie laughs. "The big black demon kills the great white

knight. Things are not always black and white, brother." The full force of his menacing glare turns on Matthews.

"Tell us again where you were on Monday morning," Bagley says, regaining her composure.

The solicitor jumps in. "As the murder occurred in the small hours, it is not surprising that Mr McKenzie was at home in bed at the time. His partner, Estelle Gittens, and her tenyearold son have confirmed this. The boy felt unwell in the night and went into their room, where Mr McKenzie helped to comfort him. As you know, Inspector, it is difficult to prove an alibi when someone is at home sleeping, but I think in this case it's pretty watertight."

"And our fingerprint evidence connecting your client to Carl Brock is water-tight. We can keep him here on those grounds alone." Bagley leans back in her chair, folding her arms. The gesture seems smug even though I only have a back view.

"They link my client to the car, not to its owner," Saunders says, with smugness of his own. "Fingerprints don't have a date on them. Are you sure that Mr McKenzie wasn't a guest of the previous owner? How long had Mr Brock owned the car?"

"Well, I …" Bagley turns to her sergeant. "DS Matthews?"

"I'll make enquiries," Matthews mumbles.

Bagley thumps her pen onto the table, clearly nothing in her notes to help her and at a loss to ad-lib. She addresses the solicitor as if he's the only other person in the room. "Your client is free to leave for the moment, but rest assured our investigations into his activities will continue."

"Of course," McKenzie says. "I didn't expect this latest incident of police incompetence to bring your harassment to an end."

Chapter Seventeen

Bartholomew Hedges applies the last strokes of undercoat to the final window frame, savouring the sun's warmth on his bare forearm. He climbs down the ladder, whistling along to an old Supremes' song on the radio. The house owner offered him her portable before she went out. He knows it wasn't an act of kindness. She was less than impressed when he turned up late again, but she must have thought there was more chance of his making up for lost time with music in the background. And, indeed, he is making swift progress. But is it because of the sound of the radio or the beat in his heart?

He woke early this morning, as he does every morning when the spiteful dawn streams into the bedroom. It began as a day like all the others, under the familiar, looming cloud that doesn't so much hang over him as invade him. Sonia was lying wide awake, too, so he got straight out of bed to avoid having to speak to her.

Less than an hour later they were in the van with Saul, still not speaking, without an inkling of the mood change to come. When they got to Alderley Lodge, he silently handed Saul's suitcase to the Scottish man in charge. He knew he was being weak and cowardly to let his poor wife comfort Saul and answer the man's questions, but he didn't have the courage to even look the man in the eye, let alone his son. He stared at the floor of the entrance hall, counting the lines of symmetry in the parquet as the Scottish man's words washed over him: *Long haul … steady progress … eventual positive outcome.*

They returned home later than he expected, because it took the man some time to persuade Sonia to leave Saul. Back outside the flats, Sonia got out of the van but Bartholomew didn't move. He felt odd – like an obese man who'd rapidly slimmed, or an invalid suddenly recovered – as if his body didn't know how to lift itself now it had been stripped of its daily burden. As he watched Sonia walk away from the van, he noticed a change in her, too. Her gait was faster than of late, more confident, lighter. Then he realized. Hope. The minute speck, the seed, the grain of hope that Saul's admittance brought them.

A voice on the radio cuts into his thoughts, "*Time for one more golden oldie before the news. Anyone remember this one by The Drifters?*"

Bartholomew resumes his whistling as he climbs the ladder to check the paintwork on the eaves. He taps it in a few places – touch-dry and ready for the topcoat. Parsonage Cream – the owners have excellent taste. A fine colour: elegant, traditional, Christian. Bartholomew's enjoying his work.

It will be the first of many joyous working days. The spring in Sonia's step will be the first of many happy strides. And Saul's first day in Alderley Lodge will be the first on the road to his salvation.

Yes, all will be well. Bartholomew beseeched God and He listened. Bartholomew will throw himself wholeheartedly into his business; Hedges House Painting Services can claim back its reputation for excellence; with the profits he'll replace the television for Sonia. Never again will she wear a face of greyness. And Saul – the old Saul, his real son – will come home.

"*Good to hear that one again. Now here's a reminder that after the news, John Castle, our gardening expert, will be here with tips on container gardening. So if you want wonderful window boxes or tantalizing tubs, give John a call on ..."*

Window boxes. Sonia hasn't done anything with theirs this year. Her mind on other things, but perhaps now ... He starts down the ladder. If he makes a few notes from the radio programme, he could help her. They'll work on the flowers together.

"Now the news at noon on Radio Brigghamshire. Good afternoon. Police have issued more details of Sunday night's Martle Top stabbing ..."

Bartholomew picks his receipt book out of his toolbox to write on the back and roots through his brushes to find a pen. A small flurry of cloud drifts through his mind as he climbs back up to the roof. A murder in Penbury – such wickedness. It's one of the mercies of no longer having a television; he and Sonia rarely hear such news.

"Police have named the victim as Carl Edward Brock, a teacher at Swan Academy ..."

The receipt book slips from his hand. It flutters slowly through the air. He watches it spin to the ground as the leaden cloud wraps around him.

Chapter Eighteen

DS Mike Matthews retreats to the general office. He groans inwardly when he sees DS Danny Johnson there too, pulling up a blind in front of an open window.

Johnson calls out of the window, waving an arm. "Come this way a bit, mate." Tucked under the other arm is a pair of New Balance trainers. "You're still too far over."

Mike curbs his curiosity. He never speaks to Johnson unless he has to and now isn't the time. The conversation would get round to the McKenzie interview. He'd rather leave it to Bagley to fill him in on that later, in the back of his sports car – as she surely will; everyone knows about the special favours DI Bagley gives DS Johnson.

Mike sits with his back to Johnson and busies himself with his briefcase. The sun floods in through the opened blind and hits his desk with its full intensity.

"Right, that will do. Now lie down," Johnson shouts. He waves the trainers in his hand in a downward direction.

"On my back or my front?" The disembodied voice of DC Martin Connors wafts up to the window.

"On your side. Not like that; you've got to be able to keep still when she looks out."

She? Mike takes his briefcase over to Darren Holtom's empty chair. He brushes aside the empty plastic cups that litter the desk. He's out of the sun here and facing Johnson. If he's pulling a prank on Bagley, Mike wants a good view. She'll eat Johnson alive afterwards, special favours suspended. Mike might even buy him a pint. Might.

"I've got them." Darren Holtom bursts into the office and stops dead when he sees Mike in his chair. "Hi, sarge," he mutters, his face approaching the same shade as his hair.

"Darren," Mike says. The junior officer has nothing to fear on his account. It can be open season on DI Bagley for all he cares. Besides they'll all be for a roasting when she finds out that Sergeant Johnson and two of her constables are still hanging around the station during a murder inquiry.

Holtom holds out a handful of plastic sachets to Johnson. "The canteen would only let me have four."

"Some bloodbath then." Johnson takes the sachets and chucks them out of the window. "Catch these, mate. She'll be here in a minute."

An uneasy thought creeps into Mike's mind. Bagley won't be there in a minute. She's more than likely holed up in her office, sticking pins in his effigy. She won't venture down the CID corridor again today.

Johnson throws more orders out of the window. "Smear two on your head and squirt the other two on the ground."

"I don't want ketchup in my hair, sarge." Connors shouts back.

"Stop being a poof and get on with it," Johnson yells. "Even she won't fall for it otherwise." He brings his head back into the room and instructs Holtom to stand guard by the office door.

Realization dawns. Bagley isn't the target. Mike clenches his fists as he tries to crush his fury. Danny Johnson and his crass cruelty.

Holtom closes the office door and gives Johnson a thumbs-up sign.

Johnson takes the New Balances, soles upward, in each hand and bends over the windowsill. "Help! Somebody, help! I can't hold him!"

His timing's perfect. He looks back into the room just as his victim enters. "DC Adams, thank God you're here. Quick, girl, I can't hold him any longer. Help me pull him in … Oh, no. Oh, no!" He holds up the empty shoes and then crouches over in staged agony. "Oh, God. Don't look!"

Mike's timing's also perfect. In an instant, he places himself between the writhing Johnson and the pink-faced Agatha. "You're late," he snarls at her. "We've got witness statements to go through."

"But what about …?" she begins.

"Don't bother with that. It's DS Johnson's idea of a joke. Come and sit down," he says, iron in his voice.

He feels a glow of satisfaction as Johnson tosses out a two-fingered salute and quits the room.

We sit at our desks opposite each other in total silence. The general office lacks its usual background noises of phones ringing and computers printing. Darren Holtom has followed Danny Johnson out of the room.

Once or twice I resolve to speak to Matthews, but whenever I glance across, he bends lower over his files.

"Thanks," I say eventually.

His jaw tightens and he says nothing.

"I thought it might be a prank."

"Yeah, right," he mutters.

"Really I did. I noticed he'd used his own trainers. He was standing there in stocking feet."

Matthews stares into my face. I wait for the customary rebuke but, instead, the corners of his mouth lift into a magnificent smile and he begins to laugh. It's a rich, infectious sound that takes me with it. It's several minutes before we get back to the paperwork.

Chapter Nineteen

Dark for the time of year when I walk to the studio. The sky's heavy with rain clouds and the atmosphere sticky. I stayed late to type up the school interviews, such as they were, and missed the group lesson with Zelda, much to my disappointment. I already feel part of that family, even though I've only just rejoined. Zelda and I have reached an unspoken understanding that I won't perform in public again and everything's easy once more.

After I've laced my tap shoes, I select a high-speed rock and roll number and leap into a routine, the twenty-minute walk from my flat having warmed my muscles. I grapevine across the floor, throw my arms forward and cause my bruise to ache.

I think about the way DI Bagley dismissed me from the McKenzie interview in front of Matthews. As if he hasn't witnessed enough of my embarrassments in the three days we've worked together. In a way I'm glad she removed me from the interview. I couldn't have fielded McKenzie's questions any better than she did. I'd no idea about the ethnic make-up of Brigghamshire. One of the tutors at police college used to throw statistics at us, but I never really tried to catch them.

Shuffle, hop, tap step. After a series of split double-time steps, I find myself thinking how well DS Matthews handled himself.

He kept his cool despite Bagley's attempts to choreograph his questioning. His smile as he showed me to the observation room before the interview wasn't mocking but conciliatory, almost kind. And it was his idea to let me observe the interview.

Suddenly DS Matthews seems less oafish. I might have misjudged him. He indicated to the DI that he wanted to do the interview with me. *Shuffle step, shuffle ball change.* But that was probably because he disliked DI Bagley more. If he had to be with one of us, better the bimbo than the battle-axe. My step slackens and I miss a beat.

I cue "Happy Feet", the routine I practised with the troupe. I take up a star-shaped stance as if I'm performing to an audience. *Stamp, stamp, toe, heel, toe, heel.* I can't gloat that Bagley's interview with McKenzie failed. He's guilty of something even if it isn't Carl Brock's murder. I saw the evil in his eyes. If I'd made more of an effort to restrain him when he walked away in the Dynamite Club, he'd have probably hit me, even put in a kick for good measure. My gut says he's no respect for women. Not much for men either.

Side step right, left, right. The humiliation of the interview will no doubt make Bagley more determined to nail him for something – and that something will be whatever sticks.

Toe, heel, toe, heel, toe, heel, turn. And despite my dislike of Bagley, I want to help her. Better the control freak than the cold-blooded killer. *Shuffle ball change, stamp.* But if McKenzie can outwit a DI in a controlled interview, I don't see how being vague or decorative, or any of the adjectives Matthews might attribute to me, would work on McKenzie.

Crossing my arms, I stamp forward. I still don't get why Matthews wanted me to go softly, softly with McKenzie when he looked daggers at my attempts at familiarity in the pupil interviews. Perhaps he realized afterwards that the formal approach at school hadn't got us very far. We learnt nothing in a half a day of enquiries.

Most of the Swan pupils displayed the requisite stroppiness with folded arms and crossed legs when talking to old people like me and Matthews. *Stamp, ball change, hop, hop.* How can an age gap of less than ten years make such a difference? I'm only twenty-four, but 10B must see me as ancient.

I toe-heel my way to the close of the music. I've got to win their trust. No good sitting on the opposite side of the Year Eleven common room, with my notebook poised, crisp in my pale grey suit. I have to soften the setting. Putting the copies of *Glamour* and *PlayStation* back on the table where we found them would be a start. Matthews won't be keen but I'll have to convince him. Let him see me in action.

I barely notice the first spots of rain as I sprint home, preoccupied with mentally creating a teenager-friendly wardrobe. My pedal pushers will be perfect for the warm weather. And I've a particular top in mind. The slogan might appeal to some of the pupils. Doubtless Matthews will make some fatuous comment, but I'll just have to explain my strategy. Because I'll be at the school all day, I won't bump into DCI Hendersen and risk repeating the *Boogie Babe* T-shirt dressing-down. It's one time when a plain-clothes officer can go a little fancy.

The next morning the rain buckets down. I throw a raincoat over my carefully chosen outfit and head outside. Discovering I haven't got my car keys, I'm about to cross the road to catch the bus towards Swan Academy when I receive a text, asking me to call at the police station for a briefing. I dash to the other bus stop and jump straight on the bus towards police HQ. I congratulate myself on not having to wait in the rain for the next one.

Chapter Twenty

I get off opposite the station, wait a few moments for a gap in the traffic and dash across the road. Bright patches in the sky hint at the sun to come, but the shoulders of my raincoat are soaked by the time I reach the main entrance.

Shaking off the excess drips I lay the coat on the back of my chair. Matthews is at his desk, hunting through the top drawer.

"What have you come as?" he asks when he sees me.

"It's for the school. To gain the pupils' trust," I sniff. The move from the cool rain to the warm office has made my nose run.

His eyes scan my T-shirt. "'Born to be Wild,'" he says. I can taste the derision.

"Well it's worth a try. We haven't got anywhere so far," I say.

"True, but I'm not sure today's the day to try it." He loosens his red tie.

"I don't see why not. After the briefing we're going to the school again, aren't we?"

"We're going to the school all right, but the headmaster is holding a memorial service for Carl Brock this morning." He takes a black tie out of the drawer and lays it round his shoulders.

I'm glad of the tissue already en route to my nose to hide my mortified face. There's no way my crimson and purple ensemble will pass for mourning clothes. "How long have you known?" I ask through gritted teeth.

"Keep your hair on, Agatha. I only found out this morning. Headmaster Cunningham called Bagley yesterday evening. He told her that the press had been phoning the school and a photographer even turned up. Now that the victim's been named, they want more than Hendersen's initial briefing. Cunningham and Bagley decided on a memorial service for the whole school followed by a press conference with the two of them on the charm offensive. She's called us here to give us our roles in the pantomime."

Danny Johnson, Kevin Bradshaw and Martin Connors have arrived by the time DI Bagley enters. They eye my outfit, desperate to put voice to their ridicule.

Bagley does it for them. "Are we keeping you from other things, DC Adams?" The sniggers behind me are out before she adds: "A day at the seaside perhaps?"

After a swift admonishment to Matthews to advise his constables of the dress code, she begins the briefing. "At nine thirty, David Cunningham, the head teacher at Swan Academy, is giving a short assembly in memory of Carl Brock. If the weather fairs up, it will be held outside in the playground so that all the pupils can attend. The school hall's not big enough apparently. The local media have been invited. Afterwards Mr Cunningham and I will hold a press conference. Our press office is taking a couple of uniforms with them to marshal the hacks. We're expecting people from Mids FM, Radio Brigghamshire, and maybe Mid TV too, and a photographer from the *Penbury Evening News*.

"I want you lot there as our eyes and ears. Don't watch the memorial service, watch the audience, or should I say the 'mourners'. I want you to mingle, keeping a low profile." She turns to me. "Which might be quite a challenge in some cases."

My nose needs blowing again.

"Look at the teachers," she continues. "Who's weeping into

their hankies? Who's turning cartwheels? Watch the kids, too." An icy glance to Matthews. "The interviews with students may have failed so far, but you can still crack them through observation."

A vast assortment of children in white or green polo shirts mill about the playground. Some of the smaller ones head for the puddles left by the earlier downpour. There's a hum of excited chatter that I associate with a school fire drill. A level of noise never tolerated inside school but somehow acceptable in the fresh air.

On the far side of the playground a tarpaulin covers half a dozen stage blocks. Two police officers raise a line of police tape, its job to corral the media that comprise: a longhaired man with a large movie-type camera; a stocky man snapping photos of the crowd and two young women with shiny hair. One holds a tape recorder, the other a notebook.

I stand among the children, uncomfortable in my raincoat now that the sun's out again.

Mr Cunningham mounts the stage. His movements are slow and considered, with a welldefined pretence at gravitas. He surveys his empire, lapping up the ripple of attention that moves through the assembled children, aided by taps on shoulders and shushes on lips from their teachers. After several moments, too many in my opinion, he sits in one of the two chairs that have been placed on the stage.

Then I spot the occupant of the other chair. How on earth was I so wrapped up in the buffoon Cunningham that I missed her arrival? Although she's seated, I can tell that she's tall and lean, definitely lean. A panther of a woman in a black, short-sleeved trousers suit. I'm no fashion guru but I can tell it's expensive. Her legs are lightly crossed, revealing a dark brown ankle and a slim foot in a flat leather sandal. She's at her most striking from the shoulders up – long neck, small head framed by cropped black hair, high cheekbones and huge brown eyes.

Matthews, who's been moving through the pupils, comes into earshot.

"Is that …?" I whisper.

"Superintendent Naomi Chattan, our glorious leader," Matthews answers.

"Where's DI Bagley?"

"Gesumpt. The Super pulled rank."

A warm glow comes over me. Bagley bounced me off the McKenzie interview yesterday and now she's been bounced off the press conference. Poetic justice.

When Cunningham's sure that the audience has reached an approximation of silence, he signals to Trish, the school secretary, below him on the tarpaulin. She slips on her spectacles and gingerly examines an old-fashioned tape player. Eventually she finds the appropriate knob. Strained organ music bleats out of a speaker at the far side of the stage. The music has the same effect on the children as headlights on deer. They stand transfixed for almost half a minute before the usual shuffling and whispering begins. Cunningham holds his nerve for another thirty seconds before motioning Trish to kill the music. The fidgeting dies down as he stands up. He switches on the induction loop around his neck sending a loud clang through the PA system. One of the uniformed constables sticks a finger in his ear, and the cameraman moves his equipment back a few feet.

"Colleagues, students and welcome visitors," Cunningham begins. He pauses for effect as I silently fill the gap with *lend me your ears*.

"We are gathered here today." Another pause. *In the sight of Mid TV*. "To pay tribute to one of our own who was cruelly and savagely taken from us earlier this week. We, at Swan Academy, are a family, always there for one another."

"Agatha, forget the soap opera," Matthews whispers. "Watch the kids."

I snap back to my duties and look about me. Keenly aware of the renewed warmth in the now cloudless sky, I put my hand up to undo my raincoat.

"And keep that mac on," he growls. "We aren't here to provide the cabaret."

Stuffing my hands into my pockets, I scan the crowd. The teachers have edged their way to the sides of the playground and formed two lines against the wire mesh fences. Mrs Howden and Mr England take up sentry posts on either side of the open gates to the car park.

"Carl Brock was a charming colleague and true friend," Cunningham continues.

A few teachers raise eyebrows, reacting to the "true friend" description from a head teacher who doesn't seem to know any of his staff, including Carl Brock. Most of the male teachers balance with feet apart and heads bowed, concentrating on the patches of drying tarmac. The women's eyes dart across the sea of pupils. Mrs Ferris, who's been provided with a chair, engages in this activity too. Her hands rest on her enlarged belly but her gaze is animated.

"I greatly respected his abilities as a teacher and as a man." Cunningham's eulogy continues.

There's a new ripple through one group of girls, the word "man" having set off a mild hormonal frenzy, which is quelled by a sharp glare from Ms Yardley.

"He was a fine teacher. He imparted a great love of his subject, English, to all of you." Cunningham stretches out his upturned hand towards the children. Complete bafflement seems to be their only discernible response. "And he achieved excellent results for our already high-achieving school." This rocks even the dozing male teachers into shifting their weight. "And he was a caring teacher. Always eager to go that extra mile to support all of you in whatever way you needed."

Out of the corner of my eye, I see Ms Yardley push through

the crowd, holding a box of tissues. She hands one to a small boy who wipes his face and blows his nose. *Bless.* At least one pupil feels the need to mourn his teacher.

Ms Yardley is about to place a maternal hand on his back when the scruffy teenager next to him takes her attention. Her expression hardening, she holds a tissue up to his face, then waves it towards the ground and hands it to him. The scruffy boy hesitates as if about to defy her but drops to his knees and wipes the tissue across the floor. He stuffs it in his pocket as the teacher moves away. He's Joe Walker, our first interviewee, his chewing gum presumably now residing in Ms Yardley's tissue in his trouser pocket. Why did he choose that precise moment to spit it out?

"I would now like to hand over to Superintendent Naomi Chattan to say a few words." Cunningham turns to his neighbour. The panther uncurls her legs and reaches her full height.

"Thank you, Mr Cunningham. I am most grateful for this opportunity to add my words of comfort to you all at this sad time." Her lilting accent works like a charm on the children and she has their rapt attention. "I did not meet Carl Brock but from what I've heard here today I do know he was a first-rate teacher. I'm sure he has instilled in all of you your own sense of worth and dignity. I am grateful to those of you who have already spoken to my officers. I thank in anticipation those of you who are still to be interviewed. I am confident that with your help we will get justice for Mr Brock." She sits down gracefully.

Cunningham's on his feet again. "Whatever your tradition, please join me in a minute's silent contemplation for our dear colleague and teacher, Mr Brock." Eyes down, he assumes the same stance as his male staff.

The women teachers reluctantly leave their lookout positions and bow their heads. The younger pupils follow their lead. Some of the older ones hunch shoulders in semicompliance, others look about them for guidance from their peers. Two youths with cigarette papers, use the cover of prayer to roll their own. The scowling face of Joe Walker stares towards the car park. Kirsty Ewell, standing close to me, plays on an app. But no one speaks.

The sound of a throaty car engine breaks the silence. I can't see which car's moving but Mr England and Mrs Howden edge towards the noise in the car park. When a car door opens, the two English teachers lean into a dark coloured car, holding onto the driver's door so it can't open further. Mr England shakes his head and Mrs Howden appears to pat the driver's arm.

Back in the playground, the PA system springs into life with a reprise of the organ music. Cunningham dismisses the assembly with an expansive wave of his arms. The female teachers siphon off some of the children to a side entrance and lead another posse round to the front of school. I look back at the car park in time to see the dark car reverse out of its space and speed to the exit. The driver comes into view for a split second. Blonde and glaring.

Chapter Twenty-One

As the last crocodile of children leaves, Trish pushes the tape recorder away on its trolley. A man in a brown jacket, the police press officer, steps forward to escort the press visitors onto the stage. The long-haired cameraman lifts his equipment onto the blocks and clambers up behind it. The press officer puts out more chairs as Trish passes them up the steps. I stay in the playground with my colleagues.

The press officer sits beside Superintendent Chattan and whispers something to her. Then he looks across her to Cunningham and nods. All set, the superintendent faces the press pack.

"Thank you for coming," she purrs. "I'd like to thank Mr Cunningham for letting us use his school for the press conference."

Glancing only occasionally at the note cards in her long fingers, she launches into her formal press statement. "Carl Brock's body was found just after eight o'clock on Monday morning on a stretch of the B456, known locally as Martle Top. We now know that he was stabbed and killed there during the previous night. His blue Ford Mondeo was parked close by and we are anxious to hear from anyone who saw it during that night or early on Monday morning." She pauses to find the car registration number.

"We would also like everyone to come forward who drove along Martle Top between midnight and eight a.m. on Monday." She talks directly into the TV camera held by the longhaired man. "Even if you don't think you saw anything, you can still help with our enquiries.

"At approximately nine twenty on Monday morning, my officers visited Mr Brock's house and found his wife bound and gagged. Mrs Brock has been able to tell us that two men entered their bedroom in the middle of the night, tied her up and took Mr Brock away with them."

"Was she able to describe them?" the stocky, middle-aged journalist asks, his digital camera now slung over his shoulder.

"We have an initial description," the superintendent continues, unfazed by the interruption. "The men were both black, approximately six feet tall and of heavy build. One spoke with an Afro-Caribbean accent, the other sounded local." She stresses the "rib" in "Caribbean", causing the man to give her a good-natured smile.

She looks into the TV camera again. "Both of them appeared to be wearing woollen hats. We are anxious to hear from anyone who thinks they may know who these men are. All information will be treated in the strictest confidence.

"They may have arrived at the Brocks' house on foot, so they could have been seen walking in the Southside area before the crime. Or someone may have seen them later in the night with Carl Brock in his Ford Mondeo. There is a recent photograph of Carl Brock in your press pack. Do you have any questions?"

"Will we get a Photofit of the suspects?" One of the young women, with shiny hair, holds out a microphone.

"We hope to issue a more accurate description later today."

"Has a murder weapon been found?" The other shiny girl joins the questioning.

"A long, kitchen-type knife found at the scene has been

confirmed as the murder weapon. It was produced by a leading manufacturer and is widely available at department stores nationwide."

"Was Mrs Brock injured?" the stocky man asks.

"She was badly beaten and has been treated for shock."

"Have you any idea of the motive for the attack on the Brocks?"

"We are pursuing several lines of enquiry."

"Was it a burglary gone wrong?"

"We are still working with Mrs Brock to establish whether anything was taken from the house."

My mind skims over the well-ordered bookcase and bathroom cabinet. The Brocks' house wasn't ransacked. Theft seems an unlikely motive but I admire the reporter's logic. Sensible questions. However, his next one surprises me.

"Is the fact that the two kidnappers are black likely to cause a rise in racial tension in the town?"

The superintendent doesn't flinch, her voice still smooth, "We have no reason at this stage to believe the crime was racially motivated."

"The last kidnapping we covered had a drug connection. Is it the same thing here?" The man warms to his theme.

"I think you're referring to the Easter Day kidnapping and gang shooting in Brigham. We cannot rule out any possibilities. However, that scenario looks improbable."

How would DI Bagley have handled that question? With the same grace and polish? Unlikely.

The reporter fires his last salvo. "But you're not sure of the motive. Is the lack of progress on this case yet another example of police under-resourcing?"

Superintendent Chattan replies in the same calm, tuneful voice. "Brighamshire Constabulary has pledged to recruit an extra 300 officers this year. We are already on target to exceed this total. One in three of the new recruits is an experienced officer from other forces."

"Spoken like a future chief constable," Matthew whispers behind me.

The reporter's less impressed. "So why are your detection rates so lousy? Aren't you disappointed with your new job?"

"Far from it, I'm pleased to have joined the Brigghamshire Constabulary at such a positive time in its history. My officers have a lot to offer. I'm seeking to build on our reputation as one of the safest and most crime-free regions in the UK."

"Tell that to Carl Brock's widow," is the reporter's ready retort.

Instead of unsettling the superintendent, it enables her to effect a slick closure to the questioning. "Indeed so. It is important that we use this press conference to help catch Carl Brock's killer. The contribution of the media to law and order in Penbury is crucial. We need you to enable us to appeal to the public for vital information. I'm going to hand over to Mr Cunningham who will make his own short appeal."

"Thank you, Naomi." Mr Cunningham stands to address the press line.

Matthews and I exchange a glance, registering his informality. *Naomi?* She called him Mr Cunningham.

"Carl Brock worked here at Swan Academy for three years. He was a talented English teacher, well-liked by colleagues and students. He was an honest, hard-working guy who didn't deserve this." Cunningham stares into the television camera, adopting a theatrically emphatic tone. "I urge anyone who knows anything about his murder to get in touch with the police immediately. As Naomi said, all calls are treated in the strictest confidence. Please help us to catch the people who committed this terrible crime."

I smile at Matthews to share the second "Naomi" and the "us". He rolls his eyes, then moves forward to usher out the press as the conference breaks up.

Chapter Twenty-Two

A small boy is hovering outside the common room when we head back to resume the interviews. His white socks peep out below his half-mast trousers and he hops about restlessly. His school polo shirt, emblazoned with the Swan logo, hangs off his narrow shoulders. I recognize him as the child who cried at the memorial service.

"You're the detectives, aren't you?" he says in a high, choirboy voice. "I'm your next witness."

We haven't finished interviewing 10B pupils and aren't expecting to move on to the younger ones. Matthews asks him what year he's in.

"Year Ten. I'm in Mr Brock's form class," the boy says, rubbing his nose. "I'm Duncan Josephs."

Matthews eyes the small child sceptically, but invites him to go in.

The boy rushes into the common room and goes straight to the seats. He might actually have something to tell us; he seems eager to help.

Ms Yardley arrives and Matthews commences the interview, having located the boy's name on the 10B register.

"What can you tell us about Mr Brock?"

"He was my form teacher and he taught English." The boy adopts an earnest tone that makes him sound even more child-like.

"And?" Matthews says.

"And?" Duncan Josephs looks bewildered. His hand attacks his nose again.

"What kind of a person was he?" I prompt.

"He was a very nice teacher." Another solemnly delivered response.

"Did you go to his homework club?"

"Mr Brock invited me." He bounces proudly in the chair.

"So you went to the club?" Matthews's tone softens.

"Twice a week." Duncan pulls his mouth into an odd position as if trying to clear an irritation in his nose without picking it.

Matthews seems thrown off course, having long since abandoned the hope of finding a pupil prepared to admit to attending the homework club. He asks a filler question while he refers to his notes. "What kind of work have you been doing there recently?"

"Recently? I haven't been recently. I haven't been since before Christmas."

Matthews puts down his notes and folds his arms. Another brick wall.

"Mr Brock asked me to stop going," Duncan says apologetically. "He said he was pleased with my work and I didn't need the extra lessons."

"Well done, Duncan," I say. "So are you getting good grades now?"

"Mrs Howden, my English teacher, doesn't think so. She doesn't like me." He twitches his nose again.

"What work did you do at the homework club?" Matthews asks, sounding disinterested.

"We did a bit of spelling but mostly we talked about stuff."

"What stuff?" I ask. "Grammar? Punctuation?"

"No, real stuff." The boy laughs nervously. "About life and what we think, you know."

"Did you have to write essays about it?"

"We just talked."

"So was the homework club different from your other lessons?"

The boy bounces again. "It was, you know, really grown-up. You could put your feet on the table, walk around, even swear. People could smoke and everything." The words tumble out before he remembers who he's talking to. He addresses Ms Yardley, attempting damage limitation. "I promise I didn't smoke myself, Miss. I get asthma and my mum doesn't like me swearing."

"That's OK, Duncan. We won't tell anyone. We just need to know as much as we can about Mr Brock," Matthews says, using a kindly voice I haven't heard before. "We appreciate your help. Did the others smoke?"

Duncan glances from Ms Yardley to Matthews. "They all did. Joe, Sam, Saul and the others who came sometimes. And Mr Brock, too. It was very grown-up."

Too grown-up for little Duncan, I wonder. "But you started to get better grades than the others, so Mr Brock said you didn't need the club anymore?"

"I was surprised because I thought Saul Hedges was better than me. But Mr Brock said I was the best and the others still needed the club."

"Do you know what the others have been doing at the club since you left?" Matthews asks.

Duncan shakes his head. "I don't hang around with any of them. They don't talk to me much." I picture Will Gleeson and Joe Turner and couldn't imagine Duncan in the same frame.

"Do you know anyone who would want to hurt Mr Brock?" Matthews says.

I'd have used the word "hurt" too. "Kill" seems too strong for this fragile child.

"I don't know anyone who would murder anyone – not even

a teacher." Duncan lets out a laugh. "Can I go now? I've got Health Studies. We're watching a film."

Matthews sighs and closes the interview with the same exasperation with which he's closed so many this week. Duncan scurries towards the door.

"You were the boy who was off sick yesterday, weren't you?" Matthews calls after him.

"I had bad hay fever. I get it a lot." He halts by the door and rubs his nose. He looks to Ms Yardley. "The teachers are always having to give me extra tissues, aren't you, Miss? Like you did at assembly this morning."

My image of the grieving pupil shatters. "You had hay fever at the memorial service, didn't you? That's why your eyes were streaming," I say. "Do you miss Mr Brock at all?"

"Miss him? He was just a teacher." He turns to Ms Yardley. "Do you know who our form teacher will be now?"

"Come on, love, I'm sure this Bible reading can wait until tonight." Sonia sits down at the dining table beside Bartholomew and touches his arm. "Why don't you go back to work?"

He shakes her off. How can she utter such blasphemy after what she's done to bring destruction on the family? *She* might be a nonbeliever, but *his* only hope is to study God's word. Work will have to wait. Surely she can see that. "Why do you take the Lord's name in vain at a time like this?"

"What do you mean 'at a time like this'? Things are getting better, aren't they?"

"Why didn't you tell me? Instead I have to hear it on a radio."

She lowers her head, then looks up and touches him again. "I knew it would upset you. But it doesn't matter now. You said it yourself yesterday: Saul's going to recover; the Lord has listened."

"But why didn't *you* listen? What made you go to that school? They'll make a connection now."

"I want them to know." She glares at him. "That's why I went.

I wanted to say it where no one could hush it up. Everyone should hear what happened to this family."

Rage surges through him. "We have to be silent. It's the right thing. It must be." He shuffles his chair away from her and scans the Bible in front of him. He lives the Ten Commandments and shuns those who transgress them, but sometimes people can be forgiven, can't they? There must be a sign somewhere in the texts.

"Why are you so afraid of scandal?" Sonia says. "Saul will have to face up to what's happened if he's to get well again and so should we. I want everyone to know who's responsible. It won't hurt Saul. He's safe at Alderley Lodge."

He slams shut his Bible. "Safe? What will those counsellors do against the might of the Law? Don't you see? We must do whatever it takes to protect Saul, *whatever* it takes. They must never see the link. Do you hear me? *Never*."

"Calm down. I don't understand." She stares into his face. "Is there something you're not telling me? Do you know something about the …? About—"

"Don't say it." He shouts louder than she deserves, but he has to stop her saying it.

"Oh, God. Oh, God," Sonia cries. She buries her head in her hands. Between her sobs, she tells him that he must be mistaken, that he must have misunderstood, and that she knows in her heart he's wrong.

Tears prick his eyes; he no longer knows where his heart is.

"Sorry. It's mine," I mouth.

Zelda's face is frozen in indignation but her feet continue the routine. The other dancers copy.

It must be work. I retreat to the ringing phone in the changing room. Friends and family know I have it switched off at the studio on Zelda's very strict orders. I've only left it on tonight because of the case, although I didn't seriously expect any of my colleagues to consider me important enough to call out of hours. The noise becomes louder and more urgent as I search the voluminous compartments of my bag. The press conference must have led to a tip-off. Bagley needs to brief me on a new line of enquiry. What if it's Matthews ringing? My breathing quickens. When I tip up the bag, the phone spins out of the first compartment I look in.

My heart sinks when I see the caller ID. Of course, it isn't work.

"Joanne here," the snappy voice says. "Can you collect Jamie by nine thirty on Saturday morning?"

Blast. I meant to phone her. I take a breath. "Sorry, but I don't think I can have Jamie this weekend. I have to work."

"But it's your turn to have him."

I've never quite worked out how having my half-brother to stay every other weekend has become my turn. I love spending time with Jamie, but resent my stepmother Joanne's suggestion that it's somehow my duty. I explain apologetically that I have to work overtime until the murder is solved.

"But I've got a manicure booked. What about Sunday? I've told Jamie you'll take him to Magica."

I sigh. Of course, Joanne would promise him that. Magica is the jewel in Penbury's crown. It developed from a static circus company into an interactive visitor centre offering workshops, live shows, puppets, and several fairground rides. When I was a child, I went just once as a special treat. My father declared it a child's venue at adult prices, so his family would boycott it on principle. He relented as a reward for me scraping through my first (and last) cello exam. His second wife gets round his obstinacy by promising Jamie a visit when it's my "turn" to have him.

I take another breath. "I'm working all weekend."

"Well, that's very inconvenient. What about my manicure … and Jamie? I don't know what your father will say."

I apologize again and ring off. I pack the phone into my bag along with the other belongings that spilled across the tiled floor. I'm shaking from the encounter, but can't help smiling. I know exactly what my father will say. He'll tell his young wife to cancel her manicure – a waste of money. Years ago, whenever my mum caught me in the act of some minor misdemeanour and used the same threat of involving my father, I was terrified. He would never hit me or even shout much, but he had a way of reducing me to abject wretchedness, conferring on me his complete and utter disdain with his ice-blue eyes. These days Wife Number Two is the more likely recipient of that death stare than Child Number One.

I return to the studio and slot into the back row. Zelda doesn't look my way and keeps on directing the routine.

Chapter Twenty-Three

"We'll have to work through the lunch hour," Matthews says, as we head to the common room on Friday morning. "Let's get finished here today. I want next week to be an acne-free zone."

"Are we allowed to see the pupils during their dinner break? Shall I check with Mr Cunningham?"

"Agatha, this is a murder inquiry not choir practice. I'll tell Cunningham. If we let them get hungry enough, they might cooperate. It's amazing how the lure of battered sausage and chips can loosen the tongue."

Mrs Ferris readily agrees to swap places with Eve Yardley and sit in on the interviews. The chance to take the weight off her swollen ankles must have strong appeal. We see a succession of Carl Brock's GCSE English pupils who are in school for maths revision. According to Mrs Ferris, they're a bright group expected to do well. They're polite and give full answers to every question, but none of them seem to have known Mr Brock well. Several mention his efforts to support weaker pupils. Some even suggest that he preferred the stragglers to the high-fliers. They've all heard of the homework club, but only a handful ever went to it. As top GCSE students, none felt the need for extra coaching with basic spelling and grammar.

At half past one Matthews finally declares a break for lunch. "You'd best feed that stomach of yours, Agatha. It sounds like a washing machine on fast spin. But be back in half an hour."

I dash into the school canteen, thinking, if I get something to eat immediately I'll still have time to get to the shops to buy Jaimie a present to make up for missing Magica. There's a keen smell of gravy but the hall's almost deserted, just a few children in there, mostly eleven and twelve year olds. They bolt down helpings of pink custard, ready to sprint out the moment they've finished. Duncan Josephs sits by himself, stirring thick red syrup into a bowl of rice pudding.

A woman in a dark blue overall is wiping down the food rail by the serving hatch.

"Am I too late for lunch?" I ask.

"Last entry to the hall is one o'clock," the woman says without looking round.

"But could I have some of those vegetables?" I point at two aluminium trays of dried-out potatoes and tired broccoli.

"I said we're closed." The woman goes round the other side of the hatch and releases the shutters.

I give up and march away. I've wasted several minutes and have no chance now of going shopping.

Three people are waiting ahead of me when I get to the sandwich bar. One of them, a man in a business suit, pockets his change and leaves carrying his white paper bag of food. I know the two remaining customers. Kirsty Ewell from 10B and another thin-looking girl are deep in conversation, oblivious to me behind them and to the assistant in front who's waiting to serve them.

"She thinks Jordan nicked her mobile," Kirsty is saying.

"No way," the other girl replies. "What's she gonna do?"

"She's given him till tomorrow or else she's setting her brother on him."

"Bloody hell." The girls finally look up at the shop assistant.

"A salad sandwich on brown – no butter or mayo," Kirsty says.

"Just one?" the woman asks.

"We're sharing it."

I grind my teeth. Matthews's stark assessment of the "pre-anorexics" on half a lettuce sandwich is spot on.

As the girls count out their money, I place my order.

"Is that with butter or mayonnaise?"

"Both please," I say.

Kirsty suddenly grins when she sees me, as if she's just remembered something. She whispers excitedly to the other girl.

"No way," the girl says. "You're having a laugh."

"Ssh," Kirsty says and leads her out of the shop. I'm fairly sure I've witnessed the rumour about Mr Brock being a junkie embarking on its maiden voyage.

"Do lots of the Swan pupils come in here?" I ask the shop assistant, showing my ID card.

"A fair few of them, officer," the woman says, suddenly formal.

"You must sometimes overhear what they say to each other, like we did just now."

"I don't pay much attention. It's kids' stuff."

"Have you ever heard any of them mention Carl Brock?"

"I've heard the name. Is he on the school football team? The girls are always on about those lads." She spreads a hearty helping of butter over two slices of wholemeal bread. In the heat, the bread soaks it up like water.

"Mr Brock was a teacher. He's died."

"Oh, the murder. That's why I've heard of him. Terrible business. I read it in the paper. But when the kids come in here, teachers are the last thing they want to talk about."

Given the interviews we've so far conducted, I'm not surprised at the pupils' lack of interest in their teachers, even a freshly murdered one. Unless they think he was a junkie, of course. The good ship *Gossip* and her captain Kirsty Ewell will see to that. I fish out my notebook and find the names of the pupils in the homework club. "What about Sam Turner or Will Gleeson?" I ask. "They're pupils. Do they talk about them?"

"They sometimes mention a Will. A lot of the girls have taken a shine to him."

I remember the young man's athletic frame from the first round of interviews. "I can imagine. Have they ever mentioned Joe Walker?"

"Don't think so." She adds a dollop of mayonnaise to the filling.

"Saul Hedges?"

She stops shaking her head. "Is he the one who disappeared?"

"Disappeared?"

"It was a couple of weeks or so ago but some of the kids were buzzing about a boy who suddenly stopped coming to school and no one knew why. I think his name was Saul. I heard a couple of the girls say he'd missed an art exam. Apparently he was good at art."

I run up the marble steps into the school vestibule, clutching the sandwich bag and stop at the painting gallery that I noticed when we first entered the school three days ago. It dawns what's been bothering me ever since Mrs Howden listed the boys in the homework club. I pass Daniel Turner's *Owl* and Ned Downey's *Firework Fantasia* and come to the vivid watercolour at the end of the row. The brushstrokes are certainly skilful but the whole composition seems somehow desperate, bordering on mad even. The artist is Saul Hedges.

DS Matthews is already in the common room when I burst in. "Sarge, we need to interview Duncan Josephs again."

"Welcome back, Agatha. Had a nice lunch?"

I'm getting good at ignoring his sarcasm. "Duncan might be able to tell us something about Saul Hedges."

"Saul Hedges. That's the boy that Cunningham said was on long-term sick leave."

I catch my breath for a moment, then continue quickly, throwing out words before he can interrupt. "It seems he didn't turn up to school one day and never came back. He missed an art exam. He likes art. One of his paintings is in the foyer. It's wild and scary, sinister, delusional almost. I think it might be drugs."

"Creativity under the influence, you mean. What on earth did they put in your sandwiches?"

"I haven't eaten them yet," I reply, missing his joke. "Shall I go and ask Mr Cunningham to get Duncan Josephs back?"

"Explain to me first why you think Duncan Josephs will know more."

"He's the only one who's given us anything."

"But he's told us everything he knows."

"How can you be sure?" I say, irritated by the finality in his voice.

"He's an anorak and doesn't realize he's not supposed to help the police. But, because he's Billy No Mates, he's not on the school grapevine and doesn't know anything worth telling us."

I think of Duncan eating his lunch alone and grudgingly concede to Matthews's logic. The bubble of enthusiasm in my chest deflates and I see it's pointless to press for another interview with Duncan. I try a different tack: "Perhaps we should speak to Mr Cunningham then."

"Cunningham isn't going to tell us if he's got a pupil off sick with drug addiction. Not with his precious inspection coming up. No, let's get Joe Walker in again."

"Walker? The first boy we interviewed. He was monosyllabic." Even my idea of trying Duncan is better than that.

"Let's ask him how he came to be detached from his chewing gum during Brock's memorial yesterday." Another point to Matthews. I've all but forgotten the spitting incident. "I was being too nice on Wednesday," he continues. "We need to try an alternative approach."

Chapter Twenty-Four

Joe saunters in, chewing gum again.

"Come in, Joe, have a seat," I say.

Matthews raises his eyebrows impatiently.

I carry on. "We need to talk to you again about the homework club, but we just need to wait for—"

Matthews interrupts. "We know you went to the club. Mrs Howden told us."

Just need to wait for the teacher. I close mouth again.

Joe stares ahead mutely.

"You went there with Saul Hedges," Matthews says.

Joe crosses his arms at the mention of the name but doesn't change his defiant expression.

"But Saul's not here now," Matthews continues. "Where is he?"

My eyes slip to the coffee table. Silently I will Mrs Ferris to return. In the unlikely event that the boy speaks, it'll be inadmissible without an appropriate adult present.

But Matthews doesn't seem to care. "Don't tell me you don't know what happened to your best mate?"

The boy jerks his eyes off the wall and on to Matthews. "He wasn't my best mate."

Matthews shifts in his seat, apparently pleased that he's forced a response. "But you know about his drug addiction, don't you?"

Joe crosses his legs and begins bouncing the top one up and down.

"Did Mr Brock know about it, too?"

Joe watches his moving foot and still doesn't reply. Has he realized we should wait for Mrs Ferris?

"Was Mr Brock trying to help him?"

His head shoots up. He glares at Matthews but remains silent.

"Everyone tells us what a caring teacher he was," Matthews says. "The sort of person to try to help a kid in trouble."

I look at the door, praying for the teacher to reappear. Joe Walker could cry foul at any moment.

The boy continues to stare at Matthews, his face blackening.

"I think Carl Brock found out who Saul's supplier was. Is that what happened, Joe?" He doesn't wait for an answer. "But you know too, don't you? You must do. You were a good friend of Saul's, spending lots of time with him at homework club. Mrs Howden has told us that."

"Howden knows bugger all." Joe leans forward in his chair, glowering at Matthews. "I left the homework club months ago."

"Why did you leave, Joe?" Matthews still sounds calm despite Joe's outburst.

"It was crap."

"I'd have thought you'd like a club for you and your mates with a laid-back teacher who even let you smoke in class."

Joe slowly leans back and folds his arms. He swallows.

"You don't know you're born." Matthews is almost shouting now. "There aren't many teachers like Carl Brock who care about their pupils – all of them, not just the brainy ones. I'd have thought you would want us to catch his killer. It's the least he deserved. He was a good man."

"He was pond life," Joe whispers. His shoulders sink. "He wasn't trying to help Saul Hedges get off drugs. He's the one who got him started."

There is a moment of silence. Joe's foot has stopped moving. I stay still, not daring to look at Matthews. His call. He's brought Joe to this. He'll have the skill to run with it if I keep quiet.

"Go on, Joe, I'm listening," he says eventually.

Joe uncrosses his legs. "Brock let us smoke at homework club and he even bought us the fags. Then one day he brings in some cans of lager. It's just me and Saul, Sam and Will. They got pretty raddled, but I can handle my drink." His eyes lift towards me as if he's hoping this last remark will impress me.

"What happened next?" I ask, abandoning thoughts of waiting for the teacher. I'm as desperate as Matthews to hear Joe's revelation.

"Brock gets out some weed. Saul and Will take it. Sam's too drunk. Pretty soon Saul and Will are giggling and climbing over the chairs. Brock sits there with his feet on his desk, laughing to himself." Joe tries to sound angry but I sense something else in his voice. Relief that the truth's out or pleasure at telling a convincing lie?

"Why didn't you smoke it?" I ask.

"I grew out of that stuff in Year Eight."

"So what have you grown into now?" Matthews says.

"I'm not that bloody stupid."

"Is that why you left the homework club?" I ask.

"Brock looked like such a dickhead, sitting there. He was supposed to be teaching us to spell not to score."

"Did the others leave, too?"

Joe shrugs. "Saul was my mate but he changed, got hyper. He kept asking me to stay out all night with him and did his nut when I wanted to jack it in and go home. Other times he'd crash out, fall asleep in class. Twice he started crying. I don't do mates like that."

"Cannabis did all that to him?" Matthews asks, scepticism in his voice.

"Brock got him on speed and God knows what else."

"Speed? You're telling me that your form teacher, Mr Brock, was supplying Saul Hedges with amphetamines?"

"Saul said Brock could get him wraps for cheap."

Matthews shuffles his papers. He seems to be trying to suppress the incredulity that's setting in. The battle won, he looks up impassively and asks: "Why did Saul leave school?"

"Don't know. I went round to his house when he'd missed a couple of days. No one answered the door, but I'm sure his mum was in. I guess she knew that we weren't such good mates anymore."

"What about Will Gleeson. Did Brock supply him, too?"

"How should I know?"

"Don't want to grass on a mate. Is that it?"

The boy shrugs again.

"Right, Joe. You can go back to your class," Matthews says, unexpectedly halting the interview. "We're going to check out everything you've told us, so you'd better be telling the truth. Giving false statements to the police is a serious offence."

"I'm quaking in my boots." Joe takes back the mantle of surly teenager and ambles out.

"Why did you let him go?" I say. "I thought you'd want to cross-examine him more."

"What he said would be disallowed without a teacher present, as you were itching to point out. I want to get some corroborative evidence first in case the little toerag is spinning us a yarn." He leans back in the chair, rubbing his chin. "In many ways Brock does sound too good to be true. The homework club could have been a good cover to cultivate friendships with vulnerable boys and later offer them drugs."

"Boys like Duncan Josephs?" *Itching to point out? How dare he?*

"Exactly. From what Duncan says, Brock pestered him to join

the club but then dropped him, probably when he realized that he could never keep a secret. Sooner or later, a boy like that would end up blabbing. And according to Joe, there's plenty to blab about. But Joe Walker could have made the whole thing up. He's had two days to invent this fantasy since we last questioned him. Despite his protestations, he could well have taken drugs himself. And if he's still a user, he'll want to distract attention from the real supplier – out of fear of reprisals and the need to keep getting his own fix."

"Should we see Will Gleeson again? He doesn't look vulnerable, but we should try to help him if he is on drugs."

"He looks healthy enough to me at the moment. Surely you haven't forgotten those rippling biceps of his, Agatha? I don't think he's progressed beyond the occasional spliff. He'll keep for now. First we need to find Saul Hedges. Let's go and ask Sir."

Chapter Twenty-Five

"I'll call you back. Something's come up." Cunningham drops the phone into its cradle when we walk into his office without knocking. "Good afternoon, officers. Would you like to sit—?"

"Where is Saul Hedges?" Matthews says without a greeting.

A brief look of anguish clouds Cunningham's face but it's sandwiched between two of his usual smarms. "Saul Hedges," he says. "Now let me see." He heads for the filing cabinet behind him.

"Cut to the chase, Mr Cunningham. Where is he?"

He faces us, a man unused to being challenged. "Well, I … how dare … student details are confidential. I don't know whether I should say."

"Just tell us, Mr Cunningham. Or we can apply in writing to the governors."

The threat works. He sighs. "His parents are keeping him at home until he can get a place at Alderley Lodge."

"The drugs rehabilitation centre near Briggham?" I say. I know of it from the drugs talks I gave to schools.

He nods. "Mrs Hedges phoned me about three weeks ago to say that Saul had confessed to having a problem – a minor problem – with drugs."

"Did she mention Mr Brock?"

"Actually she did. She said to thank Mr Brock for his help and that her husband would be in touch to get some extra homework for Saul." He resumes his seat behind his desk as if taking back his throne.

Matthews doesn't seem impressed. "Mr Cunningham, you do realize I could charge you with wasting police time. Why didn't you tell us about this in the first place?"

Cunningham finds his patriarchal school assembly voice. "I don't see the relevance to your enquires. Saul Hedges left three weeks ago and I've heard nothing from his parents since the phone call."

"So Mr Hedges didn't come to school to collect the extra work for Saul?"

"Not to my knowledge."

"And you didn't feel the need to check? One of your pupils is seriously ill, awaiting treatment and you don't think to ring the parents?"

"He was an addict. School rules are very strict," Cunningham speaks rather weakly for a patriarch.

"Who else knows about Saul?"

"No one. The parents didn't want it broadcast. Mr Hedges is a proud man. He's a reader at his church. He'll be devastated if you make it public now. Can I rely on your discretion for his sake?"

Matthews ignores the question. "We may need to interview you again. Don't go on holiday. Oh, I forgot you can't with your inspection coming up. I'm not sure we'll be finished here by then."

A look of horror creeps onto the headmaster's face.

"There's one more question for now. Who were Mr England and Mrs Howden talking to in the car park during the memorial service?"

"I'm afraid I've no idea. You'll have to ask them," Cunningham blusters, still reeling from Matthews's implied threat to his inspection. "I instructed them to look out for any unexpected visitors. It was paramount that the press conference ran smoothly. I have Swan Academy's reputation to uphold."

Matthews is unappeased. "I wonder whether the governors know how valiantly you guard the school's name. Perhaps someone should tell them of your dedication."

For a moment Cunningham is silent.

"Goodbye for now," Matthews says, running his hand along one of Cunningham's filing cabinets.

Cunningham leaves his chair, opens the office door for us and offers up a few closing pleasantries as he battles to regain his voice. He manages to ask me to collect from reception the flowers that the teachers have bought for Gaby Brock.

"Tight wads," Matthews says, pointing to the posy of red roses and white gypsophila as I lay it on the back seat of the car. "How many teachers work at that school? They must have only coughed up a few pence each."

"I think they're rather pretty, better than a grand bouquet." But then I don't suppose DS Mike Matthews appreciates subtlety.

"DS Matthews to Control," he says into the radiophone. "I need a check on whether a patient by the name of Saul Hedges has been admitted to Alderley Lodge. Out."

"So it looks as if Joe Walker was telling the truth," I say. "And I wasn't itching to tell him to wait for an adult before answering your questions."

"What he said about Saul Hedges being on drugs seems to be true, but I'm not sure I believe the rest. If Brock was the supplier, why didn't Mr and Mrs Hedges phone the police or at the very least tell his head teacher? And they'd hardly ask Brock for extra homework. I know you weren't itching."

I pinch myself. Has he just apologized? "Thank you." The words are awkward in my throat. "Perhaps they did tell Mr Cunningham and he decided to hush it up."

"I don't think he'd dare mess us about anymore. He knows we could make trouble for his inspection. Failing to tell us about a pupil's drug problem is one thing, turning a blind eye to a teacher being the pusher is quite another."

"Maybe Saul didn't tell his parents who the supplier was."

"Control to DS Matthews." The car phone crackles into life.

"Come in, Control."

"Alderley Lodge has confirmed that Saul Mark Hedges was admitted as an in-patient on Wednesday."

"Thanks, Control. Out." He turns to me. "We'd better get some fuel. We're driving to Briggham."

Chapter Twenty-Six

"It's a good job this is a pool car," Matthews says as the exhaust scrapes on another speed bump.

I feel queasy, although I can't blame his driving. He crawls along the private road, alternating between first and second gear, and breathes a sigh of relief when the way's finally blocked by a row of metal bollards, displaying the notice: *All visitors to Alderley Lodge park here.*

We draw up between two other cars. One's a brilliant blue Mercedes, the other a dark green, rusting Citroen. Matthews eyes me quizzically as I open my notebook and jot down their registration numbers.

"Still thinking like a plod?" He scoffs. "I suppose it is only your first week out of uniform. I'll let you off."

We exit the car, step round the bollards and set off up the shingle track beyond them. When the pathway begins to climb, I have to rub sweat from my forehead, hoping Matthews hasn't noticed. Dancing keeps me in shape, but I'm struggling with the lack of shade and bits of grit have got into my deck shoes. I'd stop and shake them out but don't want to give Matthews the satisfaction of seeing me hop about stupidly on one leg and work up an even bigger sweat.

We reach the top of the hill and catch our first glimpse of Alderley Lodge, a Georgian house with a geometrically perfect mix of beige chimneys and white window frames.

"Thank God for that. It's time we got out of this sun. I'm ready to melt," Matthews declares and, when the gravel track becomes a concrete drive, he empties stones from his shoes, balancing awkwardly on one leg as he does so.

Just when I think I've got the measure of the disagreeable sergeant, he becomes almost human again. I slip off one of my shoes and tip out the gravel. With one foot clear of the ground, I stand stock-still. Why was I worried about hopping? Have I forgotten I'm a ballet dancer? So graceful is my one-legged pose that Zelda used to say I had flamingo feet. But flamingos don't have detective sergeants watching them. My leg buckles. Matthews catches my arm. Before I can fully register the movement of his upper arm muscles through his cotton shirt, he strides off towards the building. Despite the odd constrictive feeling in my chest, I set off after him. It must be the heat, that's all.

Two young men with close-cropped hair and wearing grass-stained jeans and baggy Tshirts are kneeling over a flowerbed by the main entrance. They grunt an acknowledgement but carry on turning the soil with their trowels.

The front door, framed by a white-pillared porch, is wide open, as are most of the windows. The indistinct thud of a bass guitar comes from upstairs. We ignore the *All visitors ring bell* notice and step inside the long oak-panelled hallway. A woman with two thin teenage girls in jogging suits exits a room at the far end. The girls' skeletal frames remind me of Kirsty Ewell and her friend from the sandwich bar, but their eyes don't have Kirsty's spark. They cross into another room with a green door without looking at us.

No sooner have I obeyed a second notice to ring for attention, than a plump young woman with braided auburn hair appears at the reception desk. "Hello, how can I help you?" she asks pleasantly.

"Police. We need to speak to one of your patients, a Saul Hedges," Matthews explains.

Her smile vanishes and she disappears into an office behind her without another word.

R&B music blasts from behind the green door. I wander up the hall towards the sound and peer through a porthole window into the room. The blinds are closed, but I make out half a dozen people lying on their backs and waving their limbs in the air in time to the music.

"Can you come back here and wait for the manager," the receptionist calls out when she reappears. I duly return to the front desk.

Another door down the hallway opens and a white couple emerge with a mixed-race teenager. The man leads the woman and the emaciated boy to the room where the music's playing. He stops by the door, squeezes them both on the shoulder and then walks purposefully towards us. Early forties, dressed in faded denim. Behind him, the woman embraces the boy, who stays still, neither resisting nor reciprocating the hug. A good few inches taller than the woman, he bends forward as she holds him but when she lets go of him, his stance remains stooped. He slopes away into the music room.

"I'm Kyle Stewart, the senior care manager," the man says when he reaches the reception. "Do you have a warrant?"

The woman who said goodbye to the boy also heads down the corridor in our direction. Her dyed blonde hair is scrunched into a ponytail. Despite showing a healthy tan on her arms, her face is grey and her eyes red and swollen. She looks at the floor as she passes us.

"Take care, Sonia. I'll ring you later," Kyle Stewart calls after her, but she doesn't respond.

I think for a moment that we've met before but the woman's out of the front door before I have chance to place her.

"You need a warrant. This is a care centre not a prison," Stewart says, turning back to us.

"We are investigating a murder," Matthews says.

"Our residents are all here of their own free will. They haven't committed any crimes. They're here to get control of their lives." He's speaking quickly in anger, making it difficult for me to understand his accent.

"We're not here to arrest anyone. We believe that one of your residents, Saul Hedges, may have information which could catch a brutal killer," Matthews explains.

"Saul Hedges is a frightened young man who has to face his own monsters before he can sort out anyone else's."

"How long will he be here?" I ask.

"That's entirely up to him. Those who make good progress stay about three months and then they attend as out-patients for a year or so."

"And after that they stay off drugs?"

Stewart's mouth softens and he launches into a well-practised reply. "It works for some, but it has to be the right time. Recovery is about life change. Addicts have to be ready to change their entire belief system about themselves, their relationships and their need for drugs. Not everyone can do that straight off."

"Is there a waiting list?"

"You bet there is. We have a higher success rate than most of the nonresidential drug services available. That's why so many people want to come here. Detox only goes so far. It's what happens after that which makes the difference. Our waiting list is ten weeks and growing. Every kid who asks for help faces a wait with more time on the downward spiral of addiction." He shakes his head. "You police come here talking about crime, but it's a criminal outrage that desperately needy kids have to wait because the great and the good of Brigghamshire Health Authority have seen fit to cap our budget. If you want to arrest somebody, start with them." He waves his arms around the foyer. "We've got the space here to open up another wing. We could accommodate ten more people easy but we don't have the funding for staffing. Saul was lucky. He got in early due to a cancellation."

"A cancellation? Someone changed their mind about getting help?" I ask.

"Either that or else they died of an overdose," he says, his jaw tightening.

"How's Saul settling in?" I ask, hoping that the man will relax again.

Instead his voice hardens. "I won't discuss patient details."

"Look, Mr Stewart," Matthews seems to struggle to keep his approach polite, "our killer is probably a drug dealer who's not only got into Saul's veins but also into other kids at Saul's school. You could help us get him off the streets. One less dealer could cut your future waiting lists. We're not your enemy or Saul's."

Stewart frowns at Matthews, pondering his words. When he replies, his tone's conciliatory. "All I can offer you is a chat with Saul's key worker, Raz. He won't tell you much more than I've said already, and you'll have to apply in writing. I'll get the paperwork. Wait here." He and the auburn-haired receptionist head into the office behind reception.

When they don't return, I peer into the music room again. Six figures writhe on the floor but the boy sits with his arms wrapped round his knees, rocking backwards and forward. An Asian man kneels behind him, massaging his shoulders. The boy's so thin I'm surprised the man doesn't snap him in half. For a brief instant the boy looks up at the window before he returns his soulful gaze to the floor. Through the gloom, I get the impression of a pair of scared eyes amid the gaunt features of his face.

"I said wait here." The angry Scottish voice resonates along the corridor. I scurry back to the desk.

"We promise our patients absolute privacy." Stewart screws up the printed form he's holding. "You'll have to get a warrant if you want my cooperation. We run this place on trust. I think we're done now."

"We'll return with a warrant if necessary, sir." The vein in Matthews's neck pulses but he keeps his tone civil. "We're on the same side. Sorry to have troubled you."

He remains silent as we leave the building, but as soon as we're on the drive and out of earshot of Kyle Stewart, he starts. I dodge his insults as we trudge down the track.

"Unprofessional … no thought … Miss Marple … back in uniform."

The sun's even higher now. Is this man, his smooth hand and powerful arms a distant memory, about to combust?

He flings open wide his car door, the Citroen having gone. Careful not to catch the Mercedes, I squeeze in my side and get blasted by the baking hot air inside the car while the other blast, the one from Matthews, continues.

"Now we'll have to phone Cunningham and get the parents' address. See if they know anything, as we can't interview Saul, or his key worker without a warrant. You can ring Cunningham. I've had enough of jobsworths for one day."

I pick up the car radio set.

"You need your mobile," he snaps.

"Come in, Control," I say, ignoring him. "Can you do a PNC check on a Citroen? I've got the index." I read from my notebook and then fan my face with it. This action does nothing to cool the heat.

Even with the windows open, it is impossible to escape Matthews's stream of expletives. He jerks the car into reverse and takes off down the road, leaving tread marks on the deep grass verge.

But when Control informs us that the Citroen's registered to Bartholomew Isaac Hedges of 19a Hare Close, Danescott, Penbury, he slows to a snail's pace.

I stay silent for several seconds, savouring Matthews's predicament. Then I explain: "Bartholomew Hedges must be Saul's father. I think the blonde who passed us in the rehab centre was his mother. She must have driven off in the old green Citroen that was parked here when we arrived. Because I'm a plod, I noted down the registration." I look cheerfully out of the window as I say this, unable to meet Matthews's gaze. "I half recognized her from the school car park yesterday. She was the woman having an argument with Mr England and Mrs Howden. I remembered she was driving an old, dark car."

"Well don't just sit there," Matthews says. "Get on the mobile and double-check the address with Cunningham like I asked you to." He presses down the accelerator and doesn't speak again.

I gaze out of the open window and rerun my preferred version of our dialogue in my mind: *Well done, Constable Adams. Excellent observation … Thank you, sarge. It was nothing really. Just doing my job.*

The excited radio voice wavers and crackles. Dr Tarnovski reaches for the tuning dial. In his haste he knocks the transistor off his desk. It crashes against his overflowing wastepaper bin and lands on the floor. He makes no attempt to retrieve it. It was on its last legs before the fall, so this is surely its death throes. Besides, he's unsteady enough in his chair without bending towards the grubby carpet. The wretched cleaner refuses to vacuum until he's cleared enough floor space to make it worth her while. Confounded woman. Science doesn't allow for empty space. Every pile of meticulously collated data represents a significant breakthrough in the development of his system.

The dying hum from the radio makes his head throb. He stabs at the offending noise box with his foot. The kick sends it spinning into a pile of graph paper. He holds his breath and then relaxes. Old computations, defunct, disproved by more recent explorations, discounted by one experiment in particular: the 11.30 a.m. at Lingfield. He retrieves the whisky bottle from his drawer and pours a large measure into his paper cup. Back to the drawing board, and the overdraft. A temporary setback. Until his system kicks in again.

He gets anxious without the radio. He can't even ring to hear the results. The telephone people are working on the line. And he still has evening surgery to do. Another hindrance to be endured. He gulps the whisky and moves towards his computer. He closes the file on the screen. The report on the assault victim can wait another day. He has to prioritize. His system comes first. It isn't as if the report will tell the police anything. She was well and truly beaten up. Even the most illogical of brains would have deduced that from the bruises – in every shade of black and blue, and some were green. And she was threateningly nauseous, no doubt from the shock.

"Blast," he shouts. No phone line, no internet connection. A wave of pain crashes against his skull. Without website access, he'll have to follow up the racing results when he gets home, when Mary isn't watching. It rankles that a scientist of his brilliance has to conceal his investigations from his wife.

He thumps his hand on his desk and knocks a large brown envelope to the floor. Why do they keep sending him chapter and verse on every patient that passes across his examination couch? He kicks the envelope towards the waste bin. Then he has a better idea: he'll send it to CID. It's their investigation. They can pore over the inane minutiae of the victim's life. Just because the law, in its usual ass-like fashion, says medical matters are confidential, it's no concern of his.

Chapter Twenty-Seven

Hare Close is a series of apartment blocks inhabited by people with despair and pride in equal measure. Graffiti-covered walls flank freshly painted doors; boarded-up windows hide behind neatly planted window boxes; and makeshift washing lines attach themselves to state-of-the-art satellite dishes.

"We can say goodbye to our hubcaps," Matthews says, turning off the ignition. He looks at a group of teenagers lounging on a patch of grass by the parking area.

Kirsty Ewell and her friend from the sandwich bar have changed out of their school clothes into ripped jeans and cropped tops revealing bony and pallid midriffs. Kirsty taps furiously into her phone and the other girl nestles against one of the two boys with them.

"Hello, Kirsty," I say warmly.

"Yeah," Kirsty replies, looking nervously around her, aware of her friends.

"And I recognize you from Swan school, too," I say to the other girl who assumes an equally anxious expression. "It's good to see you actually. And to meet your friends." I smile at the boys and watch their bored, indifferent faces grow pink with embarrassment. "You could do me a big favour. Could you keep an eye on the car? We won't be long. I'll make it worth your while."

"How much?" one of the boys pipes up, suddenly interested in talking to the police officer.

"You can have a fiver to share. I know it's not much but it's all I've got with me. It's better than nothing, don't you think? If the car's okay when we get back and you're still here, you can have it."

I take the indistinct shrugging of shoulders as confirmation of the done deal and catch up with Matthews who's already on a flight of steps beside one of the blocks of flats.

The concrete stinks of urine and is peppered with chewing gum and broken glass. Flat number 19a on the first floor is unremarkable in its shabbiness – yellowing net curtains, peeling woodwork. But the glass in the windows is clean.

Mrs Hedges answers our knock almost immediately. Since getting back from Alderley Lodge, she's changed into an old shirt and is carrying a duster. Her face is swollen with recent tears.

"We'd like to come in and talk to you about Saul," Matthews says, after showing his ID card.

"Oh my God. I was with Saul earlier. What's happened?" the woman grips the side of the door.

"It's nothing like that," I say quickly. "We've just left Alderley Lodge and he's absolutely fine."

Mrs Hedges stares at me, as if deciding whether to accept my reassurances. Then she invites us in coldly. An act of resignation.

The front door opens straight into the tiny lounge. A teak wall unit displays biblical textbooks on its open shelves and mismatching crockery behind glass doors. A print of *The Madonna and Child* hangs above an ugly gas fire. We remain standing, choosing to swerve the sagging, brown sofa and a small dining table with chairs pushed under the front window.

"You think he's absolutely fine," Mrs Hedges says, picking up on my words. "I can't remember the last time he was fine. What do you want to know?"

"We are investigating the murder of Carl Brock."

She makes a dismissive noise, then looks away and rubs the duster stiffly over the dining table. "He was Saul's form teacher. We hardly knew him," she says eventually.

"It's possible that Mr Brock was killed by a drug dealer."

"I see." She loosens her grip on the duster and smooths it over the edge of the table.

"We wondered if you knew who supplied Saul."

"I never asked him. I didn't want to know. And neither did my husband," she adds, continuing with the dusting.

"We think Mr Brock may have been killed because he found out about Saul's drug-taking and confronted the supplier."

Mrs Hedges doesn't look up but there's an angry expression on her face when she says, "We don't know anything about the drugs scene."

"Did Saul like Mr Brock?"

The woman folds the duster, considering the question for a moment, and says, "He never mentioned him."

Matthews rocks on his heels, apparently uncomfortable about having to stand for so long. "But Saul went to his homework club. Didn't he tell you about that?"

"Never heard of it."

"Saul went to it for the whole of this school year and he never talked to you about it?" Matthews asks.

Mrs Hedges throws down the cloth. "Saul's not big on talking."

"Did you like Mr Brock?"

"I never met him." Her voice is clear but I note obscurity in her face. I recall what Ms Yardley told us about Carl Brock's angry visitor.

"But you were seen arguing with him in school a few weeks ago."

Mrs Hedges scrunches up the duster and examines it closely

for a moment. She says, "I did go to get some homework for Saul, if that's what you mean. I saw one of the teachers. It could have been Brock."

"But you're not sure."

"Teachers are all the same."

"What was the argument about?"

"There wasn't one. I was upset because of Saul. It screws you up seeing your own son turn into poison." Her dusting goes into overdrive.

"What work did he give you?"

Mrs Hedges shakes her head. I'm not sure she's understood the question.

"For Saul, the homework?"

The woman shrugs. "I can't remember."

"Why did you go to school yesterday?" Matthews asks, shifting his weight again.

She opens her mouth as if to deny it but says, "I wanted to pay my respects."

"To a man you think you've never met," he says with audible suspicion.

"He was Saul's teacher. It seemed the right thing to do." She carries on dusting. "But I was told it was staff and pupils only. No parents."

Matthews watches the yellow cloth move back and forth across the table. A gentle, rhythmic action. But if Mrs Hedges hopes its soothing motion will knock his eye off the ball, she's wrong.

"How did you hear of the memorial service?" he asks. "The pupils didn't know about it until they arrived that morning."

"Some kid phoned me on his mobile before the service started. A friend of Saul's. I don't know his name." The duster takes on a new, haphazard course.

"He had your phone number, but you don't know his name?"

"I think it was John or Joe, something like that. I didn't take much notice. I expect he had our number because he phoned Saul sometimes."

"Was it Joe Walker in Saul's form class?" I ask, trying not to sound excited. "Was it him?"

"It could have been." Another shrug. She dusts the table edges, going over and over the corners.

"Mrs Hedges, I think your table's gleaming," Matthews says. "If I could have your attention for a moment."

She drops the duster as if it's on fire. She faces Matthews and wraps her arms tightly around herself. The gesture reminds me of her son in the music room at Alderley Lodge.

"Perhaps we could sit down?" I suggest. We'll never get her to open up while we stand about like combatants.

Mrs Hedges pulls out a dining chair. We take up positions in either end of the sagging sofa. Matthews resumes the interview.

"Joe Walker told us that Carl Brock supplied Saul with drugs," he says, studying her face.

A smile creeps over her mouth but her eyes remain troubled. "He's having you on. Joe's not a big fan of the police."

"How do you know if you hardly know him?"

She clasps the sides of the chair. "Well none of them like you lot, do they?"

"Does Saul have a problem with the police?"

"What do you think? He's a drug addict. He lies, he cheats, he robs. Why do you think there's no telly in here? He flogged it to get drug money."

I blink and look away. This is the woman's home and her own son has violated it. I don't know what to say next.

Matthews is less moved. "You're telling us that Joe, a friend of Saul's whom you hardly know, has never mentioned to you his suspicions about Brock being a drug dealer. Instead he phoned to tell you that a memorial service for Brock, whom you also hardly know, was about to start. And you rushed straight to school to pay your respects?"

She nods uncertainly.

I have an idea. "Maybe your husband knows Joe better?"

"Absolutely not." She raises her voice. "He doesn't know any of Saul's mates."

"Did he know Carl Brock?" Matthews asks, picking up on my questioning.

"He never went near him." She sits ramrod straight. "I handle school business."

"Where's your husband today?" Matthews asks. Good; I wanted to ask that.

"He can't tell you anything. You'd be wasting your time."

"It's just routine. To close this line of enquiry."

"He's away at the moment. He's a painter and decorator doing up some flats in Swansea. He's been away all week. The contract started at nine on Monday morning."

"When's he due back?"

"It's hard to say." She hesitates. "The job could take a while. A couple of weeks, a month maybe."

Matthews studies the woman for a moment. The same expression on his face as when we interviewed Joe Walker. He doesn't believe a word, but he decides not to press the point. "Here's my card. When your husband gets in touch, please ask him to ring me." He heaves himself out of the sofa. "We may need to speak to you again. Will you be here? You're not off to Swansea yourself?"

"I'll be visiting my son in Alderley Lodge."

"Of course," Matthews says. It sounds like he regrets his sarcasm.

The teenagers, still on the grass when we approach, get to their feet anticipating their reward. "No one's been near it," Kirsty says, adding a matter-of-fact "ta" when I hand over the £5 note.

"There's a pupil at your school called Saul Hedges. Do any of you know his dad?" I ask.

"Yeah. He does decorating. All over the place, I think," the other girl says, watching Kirsty force the money into her waistband.

"Do you know where he is this week?" Matthews says, picking up again on my line of questioning.

"No, but he'll be in church tomorrow. Are you going to arrest him?"

"Church on Saturday?" I ask.

"He goes to that weirdo church by the Co-op. Saul told me he's on the committee or something. He goes every Saturday as well as Sunday. Where is Saul by the way? Have you just been to his house?"

"We're doing routine enquiries in the area. Nothing serious," I say quickly. "Saul's in your form class, isn't he, Kirsty? Did he like Mr Brock's homework club?"

"He went every week. Sometimes twice a week. I suppose if your dad's religious, you're expected to work hard at school. Glad mine's an atheist." The two girls snigger. The boys smile nervously, apparently searching their brains for the word atheist.

We leave the teenagers still laughing at Kirsty's joke.

"It looks like Joe Walker was telling the truth," I say when we get in the car. "If Saul went to the homework club twice a week, he must have spent a lot of time with Brock. But it could have been for school work, not drugs, I suppose."

"How many speed addicts do you know who practise their spelling?" Matthews shuts his door. "There was something going on between Brock and Saul Hedges, and the mother knew about it."

"She was cagey when you asked her about Brock. But why not tell us if she thought he was supplying drugs?"

"She seemed scared to me. But if she was scared of Brock, surely that fear would be over now he's dead," Matthews says.

"Maybe there was more than one supplier," I suggest. "Brock could have had a partner who's still threatening the Hedges family."

"If that were true, I can't see why Walker would risk his neck to tell us about Brock." Matthews starts the engine and reverses past the kids. They're on their phones and don't look up.

"What if Joe Walker's the other dealer? He could have killed Brock, blamed him for Saul's addiction and taken all the drug business for himself."

"Slow down, Agatha. We're talking about a pimply fifteen-year-old not a career criminal like Samuel McKenzie. I don't see Joe Walker as a drugs baron."

I feel my skin redden. "Neither do I really, but I'm trying out all the possibilities. He's probably just a cheeky kid who made up the whole story about Brock. It's more likely that Brock was a good teacher who confronted the dealer. My hunch is on McKenzie for the dealing and the murder. He's certainly cold-blooded and clever enough to get away with it."

"He won't. If he's in the frame, we'll get him." He pulls into the road and changes up to third gear. "We just have to eliminate all the other loose ends first."

"Do we need to see Mr Hedges? If he started a job in Swansea on Monday morning, he wouldn't have been here at the time of Brock's murder."

"We've only the wife's word he's in Swansea. Why did she make a point of mentioning he's been away all week? We didn't ask her. She volunteered the information. And if your faithful band of car minders is right, she lied about him being away until at least next week. They think he'll be at church in Penbury tomorrow. So that's where we'll be too."

Doreen Kenny checks the till for the third time. The day's takings are already in the cash tin and safely hidden behind the kettle in the store cupboard. The coloured gentleman has been in the shop for at least ten minutes already. No one could ever accuse her of being prejudiced, but she's right to be on her guard. She's already told him that she's about to close and if it's men's clothes he's after, they're at the front. He nodded but made no move towards them or the exit. Loitering, Doreen calls it. A shoplifter, no doubt. They get a lot of that. All the charity shops do. People seem to think it isn't stealing if they pinch second-hand stuff. But it is. People make donations to raise money for good causes. And the Cat Rescue Centre is a good cause, whatever Reg says.

She busies herself with rearranging the scent bottles on the counter, but she still has him in her sights. He's pretending to look through a rail of women's stuff. She hopes his game is only shoplifting, but she can't rule out a raid. After what Reg saw the other morning, anything seems possible in Penbury these days. Poor old Reg. He hasn't been the same since. No more bike rides for him. Her porridge is good enough now.

The man pulls something off the rail and approaches her. She stiffens. He proffers a £10 note and lays his would-be purchase on the counter.

"That's £2.50 please," Doreen says in her brightest voice, and adds, "I hope I've got enough change. There's hardly anything in the till. We cashed up earlier. All the money's gone to the bank."

The man stares at her. If anything, the gaze is friendly dog, but Doreen isn't taking any chances. With a deftness of hand she normally reserves for making Reg's breakfast, she keys in the sale, snatches out the change and snaps the drawer shut again.

"Would you like a bag?"

He says nothing but she didn't expect a response. Of course he wants a bag.

"Bye then," she says to the closing door. *Pervert.*

Chapter Twenty-Eight

I perch on the edge of my desk. I daren't look at DS Danny Johnson, standing on the other side of the room, but I'm sure his eyes are still pale and sparkling. He's engaged in a lively discussion with Darren Holtom and Martin Connors. The older detective, Kevin Bradshaw, sits at his desk, reading through paperwork. Matthews is at his computer screen.

I grow oddly cold in the stuffy room as I dwell on being the only female on the team – apart from DI Bagley and Superintendent Chattan – and I can't see either of them as kindred spirits. I shiver. For the first time in three years I feel lonely, but shake off the thought. In those dark days, I went beyond loneliness into despair. I was broken, soul as well as body, spiralling through a gaping chasm that no one else knew existed. Only joining the police force helped me find control, and camaraderie, again. This is nothing in comparison to that, but I wish Matthews hadn't interrupted Danny's body-through-the-window prank. I wouldn't have fallen for it, but I could have played along – a chance to make myself one of the boys.

"Let's get this over with. Fall in now, will you." There's no mistaking that the commanding presence of DCI Hendersen has entered the room. The detectives reach for their jackets, clearly wanting to show respect for the senior officer.

"No need for those, gentlemen. It's Red Sea rig this time of year." Hendersen lumbers to the white board, the hot weather not suiting, and fishes a dog-eared sheet of paper out of his briefcase. "Blast. Left my wretched bins in my office. Blind as the proverbial bat without them." He pads out of the room again.

"Red Sea what?" Danny asks, taking a chair that Darren Holtom passes him.

"He means you don't need to wear that piece of cowhide you call your jacket," Matthews says, laying his own jacket back on his chair and then perching on the desk beside me.

Danny's eyes narrow. "Are you winding me up, Mike?"

"'Red Sea rig' is a military expression," I find myself saying and then realize there are five pairs of quizzical male eyes gazing at me. "My grandfather was in the army. He said it was a Royal Navy term. The only exception to full wardroom dress was in the Red Sea."

"My dad was army," Matthews mutters, but looks away when I try to respond.

"Why is the DCI doing the briefing?" I ask, sensing that it would be better for both of us to change the subject.

"DI Bagley is having her appraisal with the Super."

"At this time of night?"

"All hours are work hours for an A-lister like Superintendent Chattan," Matthews says.

"Remember, I believe in a free and frank exchange of views." Hendersen re-enters the office. "I don't have all the answers, so pitch in with your thoughts. Holtom, would you care to start us off?"

"Yes, sir." The young DC pulls his chair up beside Danny's. "I checked out Reg Kenny, the old guy who found Carl Brock's body on Martle Top. We've got nothing on him. He's a sixty-six-year-old retired caretaker who lives with his wife, Doreen. No convictions, not even a dodgy light on his bike. And I can't find any connection between him and the victim."

"Sounds like we can rule him out then. It's always much easier when the chap who finds the body did the deed but that seems to happen less often these days. We'd better look elsewhere." Hendersen puts on his spectacles to peer at his notes. "What have we found out about the victim? Sergeant Matthews, you visited his employer, didn't you?"

Matthews nods. "Carl Brock was a thirty-six-year old English teacher. He's been at Swan Academy for three years. He met his wife Gaby there when she was a teaching assistant. The official line is that he was well-liked, a hard worker, keen to support the children, especially the lower ability ones. But his teaching methods may not have been entirely traditional. One pupil told us that he let them smoke at his after-school homework club."

"Hardly the crime of the century. My old history master used to hand out cigars, Bolivars no less. Part of our social development," Hendersen says.

"We've also heard a rumour that he gave the kids alcohol and—"

"We had a nip of cherry brandy every now and then. Character building."

"… and drugs," Matthews continues. "Another pupil, Joe Walker, alleges that Brock plied the homework club regulars with beer and cannabis. He also claims that Brock supplied one boy, Saul Hedges, with amphetamines. We know for a fact that Hedges is currently in rehab."

"Good Lord. Did Brock have form?" Hendersen directs his question to DC Holtom.

"Nothing, sir," Holtom answers. "Is this pupil of yours a credible witness, Mike?"

"I have my doubts," Mike Matthews replies. "I've checked with uniform; Joe Walker was picked up for joy riding last year. He's a surly little git. He could well be winding us up. We couldn't put his claims to Saul Hedges because we couldn't get beyond the manager at the rehab centre to interview him. His counsellor thinks it would damage his recovery."

"His counsellor – ha – I might have guessed," Hendersen says. He moves across the front of the room, not so much pacing as marching. "A good dose of National Service would soon bring these youngsters to their senses. It's no good blubbing to a counsellor. Life's not fair, so get on with it. Can you make a connection between Brock and this Hedges boy without an interview, or do I need to apply for a warrant?"

"We haven't found a connection so far, other than teacher/pupil," Matthews says. "DC Adams and I have interviewed the boy's mother. She says the family hardly knew Brock. He was just one of the teachers at Saul's school and she dismisses the idea that Brock was his dealer."

"Either the mother was in the dark about Brock, or your teenage witness's story is bunkum," the DCI says.

"That's certainly what Mrs Hedges is telling us, but we think she's hiding something." Matthews reaches over the desk for his notebook. "A woman fitting her description was seen arguing with Brock in school a few weeks ago. She denies there was an argument. And then DC Adams saw her being turned away from Brock's memorial service. Mrs Hedges says she just wanted to pay her respects, but why bother if she hardly knew Brock? With her son in rehab, you'd think she'd have too much on her plate to turn up uninvited to a service for a distant acquaintance. She's also for some reason cagey about the whereabouts of her husband. We've had a tip-off that he'll be at church tomorrow, so we're going to see what he has to say for himself."

"Which church?" DC Bradshaw asks, for the first time glancing up from the paperwork he's been trying to read.

"All we know is that, according to another Swan pupil, it's 'the weird one near the Co-op.'"

"That'll be the Church of Divine and Eternal Freedom," DC

Bradshaw says. "It's a new denomination that started out in the West Indies but now has a small following here."

"When did you make Archbishop of Canterbury?" Danny Johnson asks, making the other men laugh.

"My wife's studying world religions part-time at Penbury College."

"Jolly good, Bradshaw. Glad to know the dear lady is still trying to improve herself despite being married to you." Hendersen booms out a laugh which drowns the other men's chuckles. "Now, let's move on. Who turned the Hedges woman away from the memorial service?"

"Donald England, Head of English, and his deputy, Mrs Howden." I speak for the first time and glow pink as the men look at me. "The head teacher, Mr Cunningham, says he told them to watch for anyone gate-crashing the service. He didn't want any trouble with the press being there."

"I wonder if they were expecting that particular gate-crasher. I'm not one for the proverbial conspiracy theory, but what if Brock was a dealer and his headmaster and head of department were in on it? It would explain your Mrs Hedges's reluctance to name Brock as a dealer. She'd probably think we wouldn't believe her. Perhaps she intended to make her claim in front of the local press at the school assembly." Hendersen stops pacing. "DC Holtom and DC Connors, find out all you can about England, Howden and Cunningham. Don't wait till Monday to interview them. Track them down at home over the weekend. Interrupt their lawn-mowing or catch them semi-naked on the sun lounger." He lets out another rich belly laugh. "Now, DS Johnson, what have you got for us?"

Danny comes to stand next to Hendersen and replies with an air of easy confidence. "I interviewed Gaby Brock again. She's sticking to her story of two men bursting in and making Brock tie her up before kidnapping him. She also identified the murder weapon as one of her own kitchen knives."

"That's interesting. Wouldn't two organized kidnappers bring weapons with them? Is Gaby Brock to be believed, I wonder? You don't suppose she could have hired the men herself, a proverbial contract killing?"

Danny shakes his head. "I don't think so, sir. We didn't have any forensics to connect the knife with the Brock house. And it's not part of a set. We only know it's her knife because she told us. Why would she do that if she were behind the murder? And remember she was badly beaten and tied up. She's still covered in bruises. She didn't do that to herself and I can't see her paying someone else to do it."

"Fair point, Johnson. I'm just trying to make sure you chaps keep an open mind. What else is she saying?"

"Carl Brock bought the Ford Mondeo about three weeks ago, so that's bad news for Liz Bagley's case against McKenzie. The villain might be telling the truth about not knowing Brock. He could have been in the car with the previous owner."

"Gaby Brock identified him as one of her attackers from police photographs. He's in it up to his neck," Kevin Bradshaw says gruffly.

"Steady on." Hendersen raises his hand towards Bradshaw. "Samuel McKenzie wouldn't know the truth if it jumped up and bit him in the proverbials, but he's a slippery customer. Get on to the DVLA. I want the full ownership history of Brock's Mondeo. Maybe we'll get lucky and find out that the car's been owned by a string of drug dealers who are willing to implicate McKenzie. Then we'll look out for the proverbial flying pigs."

"What sort of car did Brock have before the Mondeo?" Matthews asks, looking at Danny Johnson.

"How should I know? Is that relevant?" Danny rolls his pretty eyes.

Matthews ignores him to address Hendersen. "I was thinking that if we could find his old car and *that* had McKenzie's prints in it, we'd still have a connection between them."

Hendersen rubs his hands over his considerable midriff. "A bit of a long shot and expensive on the old forensics, but to hell with the budget, we need to try every angle to get McKenzie. See what you can find out," he says. "Anything else, Johnson?"

"Forensics say there are no prints on the back door at the Brocks' house. The glass was definitely broken from the outside. The lock wasn't forced. Someone put a hand through the broken glass and turned the key. The only DNA in the area was Mr Brock's."

"What about the tissue and the cotton thread found on the lounge carpet?" Matthews asks.

"We asked Gaby Brock. She was mortified." Danny laughs. "She's a proper little housewife."

"And the clothing found in the washing machine?" I find my voice.

"There were traces of Brock's blood on one of his shirts, probably from his hand injury," Danny replies, eyes twinkling.

"What's this about training shoes found in the car?" Hendersen squints at his notes.

"Mrs Brock confirmed they belonged to her husband. Forensics found traces of soil on them from the field where his body was discovered. As the trainers were still in the car and not with the body, it looks as if Brock got the soil on them at a different time. He must have been to Martle Top before, although Gaby Brock can't confirm this. She doesn't know whether he'd ever been up there or not."

"Has *she* ever been up there?" I ask.

"She says not and there was no soil or pollen on her bare feet or on any of her shoes at home," Danny says. He continues to look at me and I feel the blush rising.

"How is Gaby?" I ask, masking my embarrassment with the only question I can think of.

Danny smiles. "A pretty little thing, or at least she will be when the black eyes have gone."

"I meant how is she coping."

"Oh, I see. She doesn't say much. Still waters and all that. Despite looking like bone china, I think she's coping."

"I wish I'd known you were going to interview her. You could have taken the flowers from the staff at Swan school. They're in my sink at home."

"You girls and your flowers," he smoulders.

The heat in my face is scorching. "It's just a little posy of roses … but it's nice … I mean … "

"Perhaps we could leave the floristry discussion till later. We're on murder at the moment," DCI Hendersen barks. "Does anyone else have anything relevant to say?"

"Yes, sir," DC Bradshaw says. "I've been round all the DIY and sex shops, but I can't get a trace on the chains and handcuffs."

"But you had fun trying," Danny Johnson says. The room dissolves into laughter again.

When it subsides, DC Holtom says, "I did a PNC check on Linda Parry, Carl Brock's sister. She used to be married to an Edward John Parry who has a string of convictions for robbery and receiving stolen goods."

"Eddie Parry. I remember him," DC Bradshaw says, clasping his hands behind his head. "It must be going back ten years or more now. Petty criminal. Small time stuff and disastrously incompetent. He was always getting nicked. Then one time we arrested him for attempted kidnap, but we had to release him when the victim withdrew the allegation."

"Who was the victim?" Matthews asks.

"A young woman who turned out to be a totally unreliable witness. We wasted a lot of time on that."

"Attempted kidnap. Is it possible that he was behind the attack on the Brocks? Maybe with his wife, Linda, as an accomplice?" Hendersen asks.

"Doubtful," Holtom says, glancing at his notebook. "He and Linda divorced eight years ago and he's currently doing three years in the Scrubs."

There's a collective sigh of frustration; another line of enquiry squashed.

"Probably the proverbial dead end then. Bradshaw, have a chat with Linda Parry. Check her alibi for Sunday night. Maybe some of her ex-husband's ways have rubbed off on her." Hendersen stuffs his notes into his briefcase. "DI Bagley will be back with you tomorrow, so jump to it if you want to impress the dear lady. Now, DS Matthews, Mike," his voice softens, "I want you here first thing in the morning. I've almost finished the departmental annual report, but I would like you to cast your trained eye over some of the figures."

"Of course, sir, but I'm supposed to be interviewing Saul Hedges's father, if we can find him. And I'll have DC Adams with me. I'm her supervisor. Maybe DS Johnson could help with the report."

"Come on, Mike," Danny says quickly. "You and DC Adams aren't joined at the hip. It'd do her good to get a different perspective. I'll take care of her."

I sit on my hands. Can the others see I'm trembling?

"But you hate supervising," Matthews protests. "You told me."

"I was joking. I'd love to work with her."

"Well, DC Adams, you've managed to get the chaps fighting over you already," Hendersen says. "You don't mind working with DS Johnson tomorrow, do you?"

"No, sir," My voice sounds matter-of-fact, although my stomach turns cartwheels.

"That's settled then. The lady has the last word. DS Johnson will do the Hedges interview and DS Matthews will do the Annual Report." He clears his throat. "Or rather, I mean, help me complete it."

Chapter Twenty-Nine

"Your clear-up rate is outstanding," Superintendent Naomi Chattan says. "No unsolved murders since you were made DI. When was that?" She glances down at Liz Bagley's file. "Oh, quite recently."

Liz follows Chattan's long fingers and reads the text upside down. "I went into the real world after A levels. I wasn't fast-tracked like some university people." She winces; everyone knows Chattan has letters after her name: B.Lib. MSc. MA.

"That may be so," Chattan says, ignoring the challenge. "In the last twelve months you've demonstrated the first-class detection skills I'd expect. From what I've seen, the Brigghamshire Force only appoints worthy candidates to its key posts."

"Thank you, ma'am," Liz says. The new Super obviously hasn't met Dr Tarnovski, resident prat surgeon.

"How is the Carl Brock case progressing?"

"We are pursuing several lines of enquiry," Liz says, unable to resist aping the words she heard Chattan say when she listened to the press conference on Radio Brigghamshire. If Liz had taken her rightful place on the panel, she'd have come up with something more dynamic. "I'll get the breakthrough we need very soon," she says, voicing her thoughts.

"I have every confidence that you will."

"Thank you, ma'am," Liz says. *Even though your press appeal turned up nothing.*

"How do you explain your magnificent detection rate?" Chattan asks, clasping her hands together over her notes.

I've worked my arse off for it. "I've been lucky," she says. "I'm glad I'm not at Briggham nick. The Easter Day shooting is a bugger's muddle." She gives a smirk but adds, "ma'am" to dilute the swearing.

Chattan fixes her with her dark, feline eyes. "Every outcome is part of the winning process. I'm sure that particular investigation is a fruitful learning experience for the whole team."

"Of course, we all relish the challenge." Liz does her utmost to match the music of Chattan's voice with charm of her own. Chattan's a big-picture person, talking up the whole constabulary. For her, there was no "them and us" between Briggham and Penbury. But Bagley knows otherwise. It comes down to watching your own backside and beggar the rest.

Chattan bestows a warm smile on her. "As I was saying, I have every confidence in your abilities as a police officer."

Liz replies with a mechanical grin of her own. Never has she heard the word "police officer" sound so damming. She waits for the "But".

"However, I'd like us to spend time looking at your methods. How would you feel about a People Skills refresher course?" Chattan adopts the same soft, lilting tone she employed when praising Liz earlier in the interview.

"Do I need it?" Liz does her best not to snap.

"We could all do with a reminder now and again – even assertive people like you and I. Occasionally assertiveness can spill over into aggression," Chattan says sweetly.

"I make points, that's all."

"And sometimes making those points leads to confrontation."

"I get things done." Liz shifts her weight in her seat. "It's not like I enjoy conflict."

"A senior detective needs to inspire her people. If we don't show that we appreciate what they do, they won't rise to the challenges we expect of them. The more responsibilities you take on, the more it's about achieving results through others. You may wish to try for DCI one day."

"Yes, ma'am." *One day? Sooner than you think. I've got friends in higher places than you, superintendent. I'll catch you yet.*

"I'm also going to put you down for a two-week residential course in February. It's on Modern Leadership. It should give you the basics."

Liz daren't speak in case she spits bile. She watches Chattan retrieve a glossy course brochure from her filing cabinet. Lean – all neck and no tits. According to Clockwise Chisholm, the font of station gossip, her husband lives in Surrey, keeping the marital home ticking over until his wife's next career move. He isn't missing out on much. No curves to cuddle up to.

What Chattan lacks in upholstery she makes up for in the art of formal informality. She comes round the front of her desk and sits on the spare chair next to Liz. "Tell me what your thoughts are," she says.

Liz sits straight. "With respect, ma'am, courses are all very well, but they don't compare with the benefits of front-line experience. Ticking the right boxes won't make me catch more villains."

"Are you worried about spending time away from your duties? I notice that you've been to a number of seminars and conferences already this year."

Heat invades Liz's face, but she keeps her voice cool. "John Wise thought they were important for my professional development." He whispered as much across many a hotel pillow.

"Assistant Chief Wise has authorized me to assign appropriate candidates to the Modern Leadership course. Detective inspectors must lead by example. It's vital to successful policing. The course touches on aspects of good team management like listening to advice, gathering information, keeping on top of all the loose ends, giving praise and—"

"Not pulling rank," Liz interrupts.

"I'm sorry?"

"You know, good leadership. It's not about pulling the rug out from under a junior colleague, especially when the boss sees a PR opportunity." *Like a press conference.* She watches a brief cloud settle on Chattan's normally sunny mouth. But not for long. Chattan blows the storm in Liz's direction.

"There's a section of the course on Dressing to Impress," she purrs. "It may seem trite, but clothes do maketh man or woman."

Liz glares. How dare she? At that moment she hates Chattan so much her throat hurts. "I thought that was manners," she croaks.

"Manners are in here too. It's the course for you." Chattan sports a beatific smile as she hands Liz the brochure.

Chapter Thirty

A fitful night. Hot and sticky in the flat. And the thought of working with DS Danny Johnson makes me stew. I kick off the sheet and lie motionless on my back, but my brain refuses to rest, awash with stupid plans of what to wear and what to say.

What type of clothes would Danny find attractive on a woman? A skirt, perhaps. Something like the skirt of my new suit, a bit shorter maybe. Shame I don't have any high heels … I sit bolt upright, shocked at the direction my thoughts have taken. What am I thinking? I don't do attractive. Not anymore. I turn onto my side and slam my fist into the pillow.

My mind fills with the script for the next morning:

Hi, Pippa. Good to be working with a promising new officer.

Thank you, sergeant.

Call me, Danny.

Thank you, Danny.

My heart rate slows as I imagine Danny's easy companionability – no rebukes, no "Agathas" – just friendly professionalism. I reach across to Tuppence, pulling the soft teddy fur to my cheek and wait patiently for sleep to come. A fierce jolt in my stomach forces me wide wake again.

Danny Johnson and I are going into a church. I'd rather face an armed gang on the Danescott than a church full of worshippers. It'll bring me too close to something I've ignored for three years.

Religion was effortless for me as a child. My grandfather sent me to a good Catholic school. My father mostly kept his agnostic views to himself, no doubt not wanting to interfere with an education paid for by his father-in-law. At least the school featured music and Catholicism might give his daughter some values. Everyone needed values. It wouldn't have mattered to him what those values were, as long as I had some.

School religion was good to me. Morning Prayer, grace before meals and Mass on Sundays – easy rituals which preceded other routine pleasures like choir practice and buttered toast. Yes, religion had been fun – until Dad left Mum and my world got a whole lot less snug.

When Dad went, I turned to my grandfather, expecting the staunch Catholic in him to give me the spiritual reassurance I craved. Unlike other army officers, his first priority on arrival at a new posting was not to set up his mess account. Instead, he headed to the nearest RC church to meet his new priest. But his reaction to daughter Isabel's separation shocked me almost as much as the split itself. He'd urged Mum to divorce her husband. For years afterwards, I didn't understand how he could circumvent his own beliefs at the first sign of trouble. Then, three years ago, I came to know the aching desolation of having my own faith ripped away.

When I finally fall asleep, the dark music room of Alderley Lodge replaces my usual dream of the warmly lit dance studio. On my back in a straitjacket, trying to lift my legs, but they cling to the floor as if made of iron on a magnetic surface. DS Matthews, in a white medical coat, strides across the floor, seemingly unaware of my presence. He stops in front of an old-fashioned tape recorder with a peeling label marked: *Property of Swan Academy* and twists the volume knob. A rumbling funeral march grows too loud. My muscles tense and pools of sweat form inside the tight sleeves that bind my arms across my body. Suddenly Danny Johnson is kneeling behind me, rubbing my shoulders. An intense feeling of harmony spreads through my body. I sleep soundly after that, but wake early with a knot in my stomach.

Can't remember the last time I was inside a church, apart from my grandfather's funeral, and that seemed more like a state occasion than a spiritual farewell, attended by many of his former comrades. After my parents' divorce I boycotted church, but years of passive indoctrination were hard to shake off and I continued to believe in a divine force for good, even if I kept it at arm's length.

I toyed with Buddhism, enthralled by the idea of being reincarnated as something better in the next life. At the time I couldn't imagine how any life could be better than the one I already had. Two loving parents, albeit divorced, a caring mentor, Zelda, about to introduce me to the successful producer, Barry Marcos, with every chance of securing my first professional contract.

But there was no divine force for good. If He had existed, He would have intervened and stopped what happened next. Everything that happened was my own doing, not God's. I joined the police and vowed to control my destiny. Religion has played no part in my life for three years. But I'm going to church today.

Chapter Thirty-One

Danny is sitting in a pool car with the engine running when I arrive in the car park. He leans across to open the passenger door. "Jump in, girl," he says with a smile.

"Thank you, sergeant." I clamber in, glad I've chosen a long cotton skirt that hides my ungainly entry.

"Call me, Danny."

"Thank you, Danny." The dialogue's going exactly as I composed it. I fumble with the seatbelt but have to let it slip back inside its reel as Danny accelerates out of the car park. When his speed finally becomes constant, I stretch the strap across and stab the metal prong in the vicinity of the socket until it clicks into place.

Danny overtakes an elderly driver, giving a cursory wave to the oncoming car, which has to slow down to let him complete the manoeuvre.

"I think this is a complete waste of time. This guy, Hedges, is probably where his wife says he is – halfway up a ladder, slapping on the magnolia in South Wales. But I'd rather be doing this than the Annual."

"The Annual?" I ask.

"The Annual Report. That's what Matthews has got lumbered

with. Hendersen fingered him for it last year as well. I told Matthews he shouldn't have done such a good job. He's going to start looking like an accountant soon. He already acts like one." He flashes a cheeky grin and the corners of my mouth turn up in response.

"I was worried Hendersen might ask me to do it this year," Danny says. "That's why I volunteered for this. No offence to you, but I can't stand babysitting probationers. I'd rather that than the Annual though." He casts another twinkling glance my way. I beam back, ignoring how far he's deviated from my imagined script. I'm not a probationer, just a new transfer to CID. But I only notice his dancing eyes and the fact that I don't have to brace myself for every sentence to end with a scornful "Agatha".

I've driven past the Church of Divine and Eternal Freedom lots of times. One of the landmarks on my route to the motorway. It always puts me in mind of an Alpine cottage. My grandfather once bought a novelty barometer in Germany – a miniature wooden house with two front doors. In warm weather a freckly cowgirl would appear out of one of them. When the pressure dropped, a shepherd in lederhosen would come out of the other. The church has the same long wooden roof sloping down to the ground and two small glass doors. Whenever I travel past, one or both of them seem to be open, as they are today.

Danny drives beyond the half-empty car park by a parade of shops and pulls up on double yellow lines in front of the church. He slaps a *Police On Duty* sticker on the dashboard.

We head for one of the open doors. Taking a deep breath, I prepare for reverence and gloom. But to my surprise, the atmosphere inside is light and busy. A radio plays gentle pop music while groups of people, all elegantly dressed, engage in various tasks – flower arranging, polishing the altar rail, dusting the pews, replacing candles. A young black woman kneels inside the entrance with her back to us, tidying a shelf of hymn books. Close by, a toddler in a smart blue and white shirt and matching shorts pushes a toy train along the tiles. Danny, on his way towards three grey-haired white men in the back pew, says "Hello, mate" to the child. The boy lets out a howl and the young woman turns round to comfort him. I kneel beside her, apologize for the disturbance and ask whether she knows Bartholomew Hedges.

"He always here. Never misses his turn on the rota," she says and pops a dummy into the child's mouth.

"Where is he?"

"Haven't seen him today. Not yet."

I thank her and reach Danny in time to hear him say to one of the men, "I can get a warrant if I have to. Is Hedges here or not?"

I suggest we check the vestry and give the three stony faces a conciliatory smile.

"Never know where you stand with God-botherers. Give me an honest scrote any day," Danny mutters as we walk down the central aisle. Perhaps he's joking. Just his way. I look around anxiously, but apart from a couple of impassive glances, most people concentrate harder on their work, pretending not to notice us.

Danny strides towards a heavy humming sound coming from an open door to the right of the altar. The vestry beyond is a small room. A rail of ceremonial robes fills one wall and there's a writing bureau lined with prayer books along another. The source of the noise is a vacuum cleaner being dragged over the thin carpet by a heavy black woman in a headscarf and floral overall. She wears white trainers and trousers showing below the overall. Although she's the only person suitably dressed for cleaning work, her scruffiness sets her apart from the elegance of the other workers.

The second cleaner in the room is a thin white woman wearing rubber gloves and a plastic apron over a neat beige dress. She's cleaning a small washbasin. When she sees us approaching, she puts down her cloth. Danny's about to shout to her above the noise of the vacuum but changes his mind. He draws his hand across his neck and points at the machine, mouthing, "Cut". For a moment she looks as if she's going to pretend not to understand but seeing the determined expression on Danny's face, taps the other woman on the arm. The woman kills the noise, picks up a feather duster from the bureau and flicks it over the books.

"Thank you," I say. "We're looking for Bartholomew Hedges. We were told he'd be here."

"We are the only ones cleaning the vestry today," the small woman says in clear, clipped tones. "Isn't that right, Vi?"

The woman nods and continues dusting.

"What's through there?" Danny points at a door beyond the washbasin.

"Those are the lavatories. We've already cleaned them today," the small woman replies proudly.

"What about outside? Is anyone doing gardening?"

"We don't have a garden yet. We're still fundraising." She points to a plastic charity box on the bureau. "Perhaps you'd like to contribute?"

I reach into my bag but, before I find my loose change, Danny orders me to check the female toilet while he inspects the gents. Afterwards, he bundles me back into the main church, thwarting my attempts to say goodbye to the two cleaners.

"It's a waste of time." He heads for the door.

Something's not right, but Danny's moving too fast for me to ponder what. I resent being bulldozed and make a point of locating some coins at the bottom of my bag. I tell Danny I'm popping back to the vestry. The heavy woman is vacuuming under the bureau and she doesn't hear me approach. As I drop the coins into the tin, I briefly meet her startled eyes. She snaps her head back towards the carpet and presses the vacuum hose into the skirting board. I make my way out of the church as a cloudy picture tugs at my memory but refuses to clear.

"Did you see that cleaning woman again?" Danny asks when I return to the car.

"Yes, did you recognize her?" My recent doubts about Danny's professionalism vanish. His tough cop routine was an act and he's now going to enlighten me.

"The girls I know don't look that rough," he laughs and runs his hand through his hair. "Talking of which, Bagley wants us back. She's got some new information."

I don't try to make conversation on the way and mentally shred my script. Suddenly, working with DS Matthews who calls me Agatha doesn't seem so bad.

Mike Matthews surveys the motley pile of papers which DCI Hendersen thrust into his arms. If he stares at it until his retirement, he won't make himself believe it resembles in any way a near-completed Annual Report. He can picture how it came into being. The report deadline looming, Hendersen would have gone on a hasty memo cull and thrown together a folder. It's now landed on Mike from a great height, as it did at the same time last year. He tried to burrow his way out of the rubble this time by suggesting Johnson for the task, but Danny Johnson dug faster. And that rankles more than being lumbered with the paperwork. Admin he can handle, arrogant arseholes are another matter. If Johnson were any cooler, he'd freeze his cobblers off. Some hope. He'd better keep his tricks to himself while he's supervising Agatha.

Agatha. There he is again, thinking about her. Why should he need to protect her? She must have come across her fair share of Danny Johnsons. She's been a copper for three years. And she's blonde. Her sort always lands on their neat little feet, inside their neat little Gucci sandals.

He switches on his computer terminal. He had the good sense to save a copy of the Annual Report he wrote last year. Providing Hendersen has salvaged the budget and crime figures from the heap in his office, all Mike has to do is input the new numbers into the old report. If Hendersen had given him the job in April, when it was first due, he could have updated the text too, but now there isn't time.

Agatha. Did he really just think about her hair? Shame on him. His mother told him he shouldn't go on about blondes. *Some people know what it's like to be judged by the colour of their hair.* Did Mum mean herself? A Jamaican woman arriving in 1970s Penbury? Mike's grateful for the changing times. Prejudice is now a shrinking cancer, but still capable of deadly resurgences, especially since the Brexit vote.

Are blondes at risk from his own prejudice? He hasn't always felt that way. He once welcomed a blonde, Kate – with open arms – and an open wallet. She soon emptied that and more besides. He's steered clear of the type ever since. But now he's supervising a walking, talking (definitely talking), blue-eyed, peaches-and-cream blonde.

He flicks through the DCI's scrapbook and finds the staff returns. Kate was a slick chick who would never have worn any of Agatha's dodgy T-shirts – unless they had a designer label inside. And he can't see Agatha teetering about on Kate's strappy sandals. Agatha's more of a jolly hockey pumps kind of a girl. Mike suspects a posher accent lurking below her evenly modulated tones. He's good at accents. He's played a few in his time.

He hunts through the papers for the crime statistics, but can't find the sheet for October to December. He knocks aside his computer mouse in frustration. The report will take longer than expected, and he's anxious to get back on the Brock case. The only lead has been provided by Joe Walker, a fifteen-year-old joy rider. Everyone else claims Carl Brock was God's gift to teaching. It just takes one snivelling no-mark pupil to bad-mouth him, even after death, and his reputation could be shot to pieces. Who'd be a teacher? Mike has asked his mother the same question often enough. Rewarding, she says.

But some things about Brock don't add up. Why was there soil on his trainers when he left them in the car before he was murdered? Had he been to Martle Top another time? Was it a regular meeting place? Why? Dodgy deals and blackmail seem unlikely given the conservative state of Brock's bank account. A lover perhaps? His mind wanders to Swan school and the heavily pregnant Mrs Ferris. Possible. They wouldn't be the first work colleagues to play away, and to get caught out.

Or perhaps the child was planned. The wife, Gaby, lost a baby. Maybe she couldn't have any more. Were Carl Brock and La Ferris planning on playing happy families? It would have given Gaby Brock the perfect motive. The theory has legs, except for the part about Mrs Ferris. Mike chatted to her in school. She seemed like any expectant mum, looking forward to the new arrival, not a mistress mourning her murdered lover. She had nothing more on her mind than swollen ankles.

So was it drugs then? He hopes not. He'd like nothing better than to charge Joe Walker with wasting police time. And yet Samuel McKenzie, Penbury's own happy pill pharmacist, has been in Brock's car. A coincidence? Only when it snows in July. The car belongs to a corpse, which is starting to smell high – McKenzie's kind of high. Hopefully the search into the car's previous owners will turn up a major player in McKenzie's drug league.

Suddenly he remembers his intention to find out what Brock was driving before he bought the Mondeo. He picks up the phone. "DVLA? Can you put me through to archives, please?"

Chapter Thirty-Two

"Hope you're wearing your flak jacket, Danny boy," Darren Holtom says as we enter the main office to join the other detectives. "The DI's taking no prisoners today."

"I thought she'd had a breakthrough she wanted to tell us about," Danny says.

"She does, but she's seething after her appraisal, isn't she? Imagine that: savaged by a librarian."

There's a salvo of chuckles before Kevin Bradshaw enlightens me.

"Superintendent Naomi Chattan has a dark secret. Before she joined the police and got fast-tracked to the top, she used to be a librarian. But she prefers the term 'knowledge manager'. Apparently they don't use the 'l' world anymore."

"Twin set or not, I reckon she hung Bagley out to dry," Darren says, rubbing his hand through his red hair.

"I wouldn't have minded being a fly on that particular executive wall. It would have been good to see Shagley squirm," Danny says.

"I thought you already had," Martin Connors leers.

The men, including Danny, laugh crudely but I hardly notice. As I take my seat with the others, I'm absorbed in trying to fit together a crazy jigsaw I've created in my mind.

"Listen up, everyone. We've got some new evidence." Bagley enters, holding a small buff file above her head. Beneath her heavy make-up her face looks like thunder.

"We've finally got Carl Brock's medical records. Shame we couldn't have been given them sooner. But that's the level of incompetence I have to work with."

The men look at each other nervously, no doubt wondering if she intends to attribute the blame to one of them as well as the National Health Service.

"Six years ago Brock was treated for a cocaine addiction."

A wave of excitement sweeps through the room.

"So Joe Walker at Swan Academy was telling us the truth. Brock was into drugs," I say, unable to keep quiet.

"Hold on a minute, DC Adams." Bagley flashes a dark look. "There is no mention of drugs in his medical records since that time." Sensing the new despondency in the ranks, she adds, "However, there isn't a mention of anything else either. He hasn't been to see a doctor since then. His medical history prior to his addiction problem was the usual." She opened the file. "Ingrown toenail, backache and laryngitis. But for the last six years he's been completely ailment free."

"Where was he treated for the addiction?" Danny asks.

When Bagley's voice softens, I wonder whether it's down to the questioner as much as to the question. "Well, Danny, it appears that the GP treated Brock himself. Over a six-month period, Brock had consultations every week. Then he stopped visiting the doctor altogether," she says.

"It sounds to me like he never kicked the habit," Danny says. "He stays away from the doctor's when he's fed up of trying treatment."

"You might be right, Danny." She's almost smiling. "I've told Dr Spicer to speed up his tests on the body and check for evidence of drug abuse." Her face hardens again. "He's getting as bad as Tarnovski. It's a pity he didn't suspect drug abuse when he noted the nerve damage. Simple hair analysis would have revealed any drug use. It's situations like this when my department gets blasted for other people's mistakes."

I wonder whether she's talking about a specific "blast". Her appraisal? It would explain her apparent wish to boil us alive. But Bagley's conveniently overlooked the fact that at a previous briefing, she dismissed the nerve damage as irrelevant.

"This puts McKenzie right back in centre frame." Bagley's barking again. "McKenzie's had a finger in the drugs pie for years. Whether Brock was clean for the last five years or not, they must have crossed paths before that. And we've already got his prints in Brock's car. It's time you lot got digging on this one. We've let McKenzie make idiots of us for long enough."

"Do you have Gaby Brock's medical records?" My question is out before I've time to consider the likelihood of Bagley's fiery response, which duly comes.

"Why the hell would I have the medical records of the living, breathing wife of a murder victim?"

"I thought that if she were an addict, too, she might know more than she is letting on."

"No court in the land would give me an order to see her records, nor would I want it to. Gaby Brock is no more an addict than you are. Don't waste time. Reading up on her chicken pox is a wild goose chase."

The corners of her mouth turn up to acknowledge her own pun, but her jaw sets again when Danny says, "There's a problem with the prints in the car. I checked with the DVLA. Brock bought that car three weeks ago. There were four previous owners, all local."

"Well do what DCI Hendersen told you to. Dig the dirt on the previous owners. There's more than one way to skin a dog like McKenzie."

"I did, ma'am." Danny pauses. He shoves his hands in his pockets and won't meet Bagley's eye. Eventually he continues:

"Brock bought the car from a second-hand dealer in Danescott." He hesitates again before adding, "It was Morgan McKenzie Motors."

Danny has lit the touch paper and we feel the full force of Bagley's explosion. "You're telling me Brock bought his Ford Mondeo from our prime suspect's brother? Well that's the end of that then. It doesn't matter that Samuel McKenzie is a blackmailer, a drug dealer, a pimp and that an assault victim has picked out his mugshot, he'll walk for murder. His oily solicitor will argue that McKenzie's prints got there when the car belonged to his car dealer brother, Morgan." She hurls the file at one of the desks. As it lands, it sends several other sheets of paper skidding to the floor. "I might as well pack up now. Spend what's left of the weekend topping up my tan. Can anyone give me some good news? Bradshaw, make my day."

"Sorry, ma'am, it's nothing you want to hear." Kevin Bradshaw bends down to pick up the fallen papers. His scalp reddens through his thinning hair. "We interviewed Linda Parry, Brock's sister. She hasn't had any contact with her husband, Eddie, since they divorced years ago. She didn't even know he was in prison. Her boyfriend, Dean Rogers, swears that she and her kids were with him at his place at the time of Brock's murder."

My colleagues' faces are impassive. Is the parallel lost on them? Linda's boyfriend and her children vouched for her. Estelle Gittens and her son spoke for Samuel McKenzie. Is it the truth or does partner loyalty extend to providing alibis for murder?

"Yet another line of enquiry dead in the water," Bagley says. "Connors, what illuminating evidence have you got for us?"

Martin Connors sits up, his bulk making his chair look tiny. "Forensics say the pyjamas Gaby Brock was wearing when uniform found her are clean as a whistle. Brand new, in fact. No trace of Brock's blood. Her DNA was found on the thread of cotton and the piece of tissue by the chair on which she was tied, but they're not time specific and probably predate the crime."

"So this in-depth investigation has so far turned up a wife without blood on her pyjamas, a sister who's not now married to a criminal, a victim who may no longer have been a coke addict and a villain with a cast-iron alibi. Can't any of you cut through this crap?"

She turns her head towards the door as DS Matthews opens it. "Nice of you to join us," she says. "I'll forgive you, if you tell us you've got concrete evidence against McKenzie and we can all go home."

"Sorry I'm late, ma'am. I was writing the DCI's Annual Report. I've got nothing on McKenzie but I'm having doubts about Carl Brock."

"If you'd been here earlier, you'd have heard me say that we now suspect him of having a cocaine addiction."

"That makes sense, then," Matthews says, smiling. "It turns out that his previous car was a Mercedes. He had it for about six months."

"Unless it's covered in McKenzie's DNA, is this relevant?"

"The Merc is a quality car. It's not the sort of thing you suddenly trade in for a Ford Mondeo."

"Unless you're short of money," Bradshaw says.

"Exactly. But I've looked into Brock's finances over the last five years and there's nothing out of the ordinary. Mortgage and living expenses out, teacher's pay in. But what did he do with the money he would have made on the sale of the Mercedes? And where did he get the money for the Mercedes in the first place? Neither transaction appears in his accounts."

"Drugs money," Danny says, standing up to address the room. "He bought the Mercedes out of the proceeds of his dealing and then had to sell it to pay off debts or to buy in bulk."

"Which brings us right back to Samuel McKenzie," Bagley says, not acknowledging Matthews's research. "If Brock was dealing, McKenzie was either his wholesaler or his business rival. Whatever way, he's in it up to his neck. Someone, somewhere knows it. Danny, did you get anything out of Bartholomew Hedges?"

"We couldn't find him." Danny shrugs and sits down. "A couple of kids told Matthews and Adams that he'd be in the Church of Clappy Happiness, but they were having them on. There was no sign of him. I can go round and work on the wife if you like. See if she's still saying he's in Swansea like she told Matthews. I could try a bit of a charm offensive. It's worked before."

Connors and Holtom chuckle but a flash of anger crosses Bagley's face and she seems lost for words. I'm annoyed too at the way Danny insinuated that Matthews and I were to blame for not finding Hedges. Suddenly I'm immune to Danny's glittering eyes. For reasons that I can't explain, I want to defend DS Matthews.

"The kids we saw outside the Hedges's apartment block seemed sure Mr Hedges would be at church this weekend," I say. "I don't know why he wasn't there this morning. I could go back there tomorrow, meet the worshippers coming out of their morning service. I'd be bound to find him then."

"Don't waste your time." Danny folds his arms. "I doubt he's ever been a member of the congregation. How many young or middle-aged white blokes did you see in there? It's not cool to be a God-botherer."

"Is Bartholomew Hedges white?" I say, surprised. "Is he Saul's stepfather? In that case you're probably right. I've misunderstood." I study the crack in the carpet tiles, feeling foolish as I realize the absurdity of the theory that's been taking shape in my mind.

"What are you on about, Agatha?" DS Matthews asks.

"I'm sorry. I haven't checked my facts properly. I should have asked. But the boy I saw with Sonia Hedges at Alderley Lodge was mixed race. I assumed that it was her son, Saul. I thought we were looking for a black man."

"Is Saul Hedges black?" Bagley fires the question at Matthews, as if his own skin colour makes him responsible for knowing.

He gives an embarrassed shrug. Bagley demands to know whether anyone has bothered to get a description of Saul's father. There's a general, painful shaking of heads.

"Bradshaw!" The older officer jumps as Bagley shouts his name. "Get on to the head at Swan school. We need descriptions of Saul and Bartholomew Hedges immediately."

"Johnson and Adams, get back in that church. Get a full list of worshippers from the vicar. Confirm that Hedges's name is on it and then question them all. Someone will know where he is even if he turns out to be in Swansea as his wife says. Don't any of you make an error like this again. If DC Adams hadn't caught sight of Saul Hedges at Alderley Lodge, we would have lost even more time."

I should have seen enough of DI Bagley in my first week to know that a compliment like that would be followed by a searing insult if I let my tongue run away. Haven't I done that already with babble about Gaby Brock's pet cockatiel? Some people learn from their mistakes, but not me. What I say next will haunt me for some time to come.

"Ma'am. I know this sounds silly.' Heat consumes my face and I grip the chair tighter.

"Well? Get on with it," Bagley says.

Here goes. "I think Hedges was at the church when we went there this morning. I recognized the eyes. They were like Saul's. I mean the boy I thought was Saul at Alderley Lodge. Everyone else in the church was smartly dressed, even though they were doing the cleaning. But the headscarf and overall were scruffy and I think she – he – had a man's suit on underneath. It was the trainers that gave him away. He must have swapped out of his best shoes to look less conspicuous. But they were at least size tens. I always notice women's feet. I'm a bit self-conscious, being an eight myself. I don't see many women's feet bigger than mine."

Bagley looks as if she is going to be sick. The three DCs study their own shoes in confused discomfort. DS Matthews stares at me. Only Danny registers any sense in my ramblings.

"Are you seriously telling us that cleaning woman was a bloke? That would explain why she was do damned ugly."

My voice is almost inaudible. "Mr Hedges never misses a turn on the church rota, someone told me that. He was determined to do his duty but didn't want us to find him there. Hence the disguise."

"Why the hell didn't you tell me?" Danny snarls. The usual glint in his eye has turned to fire. "We could have arrested him immediately, and the posh, skinny woman for being in on it. I take it that the other cleaner was a woman or were they all in drag?"

I shake my head. "I didn't see how he could be involved in Brock's murder. He's a devout Christian not a drug dealer. His own son is in rehab."

I wait for Danny Johnson's counter-argument but it doesn't come. He stares intently at DI Bagley. All the men in the room look at the DI. I can almost taste their nervy expectation. They don't have long to wait.

"What did you say, Adams?" Bagley shrieks, her thick dark curls shaking with fury. "You recognized a suspect in a murder inquiry and you let him get away. Didn't it occur to you that if Brock had been a dealer – and we now have circumstantial evidence that says he was – it would give Bartholomew Hedges a powerful motive for murder? Revenge for the damage Brock did to his son. Have you completely forgotten that Forensics found hair from an unknown black male in Brock's house? We know it's not McKenzie's but it could be Hedges's.

"Johnson, Bradshaw, take some uniforms to the Hedges' flat and to the church. Find Hedges and bring him in. See if Gaby Brock can pick him out of a line-up.

"As for you, Adams. Go home. Take the rest of the weekend to have a long hard look at your conduct. You need to think whether you're cut out for CID. I have serious doubts."

Chapter Thirty-Three

The stainless-steel sink is hard against my hip. I lift the posy and pull the plug to release the greenish water. I turn on the tap and splash my face with tepid water. The stifling summer heat streaming into the flat has nothing on the furnace in my head. I should return to uniform. Sergeant Conway would have me back. His bouncy bobby with a smile on her lips, a winner with the public and a match for the drunk and disorderlies.

Although it still isn't running cold, I rub more water into my eyes and across my forehead. What a mess. DI Bagley thinks I'm utterly incompetent. To DCI Hendersen I'll forever be the Boogie Babe. DS Danny Johnson looked ready to hit me when I piped up about recognizing Hedges. Dashing Danny shed his skin. I should have seen through him when he played the sick prank in the office.

And Matthews. His look of disappointment hurts the most.

I splash my face again and place my wrists under the running tap. I notice the red and white flowers I've put on the draining board. The posy for Gaby Brock from the teachers at Swan Academy. Can't believe I've forgotten to deliver them. I'm losing it. I'll ring Sergeant Conway on Monday and ask for my old job back. They can draft someone else into CID. Someone who can cope. My eyes water and I do nothing to fight back the tears.

Sudden, excruciating pain burns my wrist. I snatch my arms away from the steaming flow of hot water. I can't even manage to get the right tap. I plunge my sore skin under the cold.

The shock brings me to my senses. "Blast the lot of them," I shout. If it wasn't for me, none of them would have identified Hedges. Just because Bagley had a poor appraisal, she doesn't have the right to use me as a scapegoat. It was DS Johnson who rushed us through the church before I'd time to register the likeness between Saul Hedges and the cleaner. What's more, it was before we knew about Carl Brock's drug history. We went into the church to find a potential witness not a murder suspect.

I've as much right to be in CID as anyone else. I don't need the rest of the weekend to consider my position. I'll be in work on Monday. At least now I have Sunday free to spend with Jamie and get back in Joanne's good books. I'll ring later and tell her that I can take Jamie to Magica after all. Right after I've dropped off the posy with Gaby Brock. Because it's been in the sink, the petals still look fresh despite the heat.

Linda Parry lives in an end-of-terrace house in a new estate on the edge of Grape Fields. Unlike her brother, Carl Brock, she hasn't made it to the leafy avenues of Southside, but the communal gardens are well cared for and all door and window frames are gleaming uPVC white. A good few rungs up from the Danescott estate inhabited by the Hedges family.

She shows me into the small lounge where Gaby Brock's curled up on the sofa, leafing through a magazine. When she sees me, she puts the magazine to one side and places her bare feet on the floor, a purple bruise by her ankle. The red weals around her wrists have paled but still conjure up an image of her handcuffed to the kitchen chair in her lounge. The sleeves of her dress are rolled up to below her elbows, revealing fading bruises on her mottled arms. My hand goes to my own bruised cheek. Gaby's physical scars are healing faster than mine, but as to progress on the mental wounds, a look into the tiny face still discoloured from the pummelling it's taken, provides the likely answer.

A large television set on top of a DVD cabinet, crammed with Disney classics and American teen movies, dominates the small, homely room. A Welsh dresser displays a dozen or more framed pictures, ranging from baby photos to a school portrait of two blond children in navy sweatshirts. Linda motions me to the armchair nearest Gaby and plonks herself in the other one. My foot nestles against a plastic tub, containing Lego and a collection of Barbie dolls in various stages of undress.

I place the posy on the coffee table beside a small plate of dry cream crackers and two mugs. One full of a rich brown liquid, which smells alcoholic, the other a half-finished herbal tea.

Gaby sniffs the flowers for a few moments and then whispers, "Red and white. Blood and bandages. How apt." But adds, "It was kind of the teachers."

"They thought highly of your husband." My voice sounds bright. Gaby stares back with an impassive gaze. "They thought well of you, too. They told me what a good teaching assistant you were."

"Really? They said that about me?" For the first time her face opens up and takes on expression.

"Ms Yardley said you had a good rapport with the children, and Mr England was sorry when you left."

The face closes again. "I had a home to run."

"Have you thought about what you'll do now? I bet they'd have you back at school when there's a vacancy."

"Give the girl a chance," Linda interrupts. "We haven't even had Carl's funeral yet."

"It's OK, Linda. I don't mind talking about it," Gaby says. "I'm going to sell the house and look for somewhere new, away from Penbury."

"I've told her she can stay here with us," Linda says, "but she insists on getting her own place. Perhaps you can talk some sense into her. I don't think she should be on her own. Don't you agree, constable?"

"Are you sure you want to sell your house? You must have some happy memories there as well as …" I falter, unsure how to complete the sentence.

Gaby seems to retreat into her thoughts.

"Are you forgetting what happened to her in there?" Linda talks to me as if Gaby isn't there. "How could she sleep at night? That's the good thing about her being here with me and Dean, when he stays over. She's sleeping better than I am. She feels safe here." She eases herself out of the armchair. "You tell her there's no rush for her to move out. I'll get us some orange squash. Are you all right with your camomile, Gaby? Or do you want something else? I wish you'd try my brandy toddy." She points at the mug of brown liquid. "It's a great pickmeup."

"I'm fine with this, thanks." Gaby reaches for the other mug, the camomile. She takes a sip, flinches at the taste and picks up one of the cream crackers.

"Are you sure? I can soon heat up the toddy again."

"I'm sure."

When Linda has left the room, Gaby and I sit in silence. She nibbles painfully at the cracker, seems to have trouble swallowing. Tears threaten my eyes as it dawns on me when Joanne had the same difficulty years ago. If I'm right, Gaby will have to contend not only with her husband's murder and her own assault, but also with an uncertain future as a single parent. I toy with keeping quiet – maybe I've misread the signs. Even if it's true, it's no one's business but Gaby's. The poor woman has been robbed of so much of her dignity, surely she has the right to keep this to herself. But I'm a police officer who's vowed to uphold the truth. Secrets, however well meant, fester into lies.

"How many weeks are you?"

The biscuit falls into her lap. "What makes you think—?"

"Dry cream crackers and camomile tea. Remedies for morning sickness? And after your … ordeal you refused a sedative from the police doctor and you haven't drunk that brandy."

"You look too young to know about things like that," Gaby says softly.

"When my stepmother was pregnant, she had a horrendous time. Tried every natural cure and wouldn't take any kind of medicine or alcohol. Lived on crackers and camomile tea." I stop talking and put the same question to her again. Gaby reluctantly confirms that she's ten weeks pregnant.

"You should have told the police doctor. You might need a check-up after what happened. Does Linda know?"

"The police doctor was in a hurry. There was something on the radio he wanted to hear. I'll get Linda to take me to my doctor in a few days. I think she suspects."

"Did you have a chance to tell Carl?"

Her voice cracks. "I wanted to be sure."

"I can understand that. I know what happened last year."

Gaby flinches and peers up through her fringe, blinking back tears.

"Losing a much-wanted child must have been a terrible shock for you both."

Her shoulders relax. Before I get a chance to make sense of her body language, Linda returns with two glasses.

"For the record, constable, I don't make drinks for every police officer that comes to call," she says, handing one drink to me and taking the other to her seat. "Those two who came yesterday certainly didn't get any. They tried to make out I'd murdered my own brother with the help of my good-for-nothing ex-husband."

"You didn't tell me," Gaby says, sitting up and for the first time showing an interest in something Linda's saying.

"You were upstairs having a nap. They didn't stay long once they realized they were barking up the wrong tree. I haven't seen

Eddie for years, thank God. That Sue did me a hell of a favour. I owe her big time."

"Sue?" I ask.

"The tart he went off with. I worry about her sometimes, but I'm sure she can handle him. She certainly started as she meant to go on."

"Did she?" I ask, half hoping that Linda's chatter might reveal something new. My peace offering to the DI.

"Sue told the police that Eddie had kidnapped her. Showed them the rope marks on her wrists. It was going to go to court and everything. Then out of the blue she withdrew the charges. She'd kept Eddie dangling for weeks, not knowing how long he'd stay banged up. He was so grateful to her after she dropped it that she had him eating out of her hand. He couldn't do enough for her, bought her presents when it wasn't her birthday, and flowers every week. I never saw as much as a bunch of dandelions when he was with me. And he agreed to keep his fists off her from then on. They scarpered to Brighton together soon after."

"Keep his fists off her?" I talk into my glass, trying to sound casual. If I play this right, there's more information to come.

"He liked it rough. He used to tie her up sometimes. I think she enjoyed it. But she called in the police when he went too far. That got him back in line."

I swallow a mouthful of sweet squash, my mind racing. Could this be important? Bradshaw and Connors didn't mention any of it at the briefing. *Keep cool, Pippa*. "Did he treat you like that, too?" I ask, looking up from my glass.

"There was never any of that kinky stuff with ropes. He used me as a punch bag now and again, not all the time." Her voice is matter-of-fact, but there's pain in her eyes.

"What?" Gaby gasps, her sudden animation startling us both.

"I'm sorry, love," Linda says, landing beside her on the sofa. "I never told anyone that Eddie knocked me about. Not even Carl. I couldn't talk about it at the time and after Eddie cleared off there didn't seem any point. I'd only myself to blame anyway."

"Don't say that," Gaby says. "I wish you could have told me." The hurt expression, which has been building while Linda spoke, gives way to tears.

Linda squeezes the tiny body against her flabby arm. "It was years ago, before I met you. And it wasn't that bad – nothing like the beating those thugs gave you. It was only when Eddie had a few too many down the pub. Most of the time he'd grab me a bit rough or push me about a bit. The best thing to do was keep out of his way until he sobered up."

Gaby sniffs. Linda pats her arm. "He managed to kick his foot through the kitchen door once but most times he just stood there, banging and yelling. I'd be by the back door, stuffing myself with biscuits to calm my nerves. That's how I put on all the weight. I never have managed to lose it again. I should've had the guts to leave him." Her arms pull tighter around Gaby. "Don't cry on my account. You've got enough on your plate."

"I still wish you'd told me." Gaby sobs into her shoulder.

"It's all in the past." Linda cradles her quivering sister-in-law in her arms for several minutes. Eventually Gaby wipes her eyes, excuses herself for her outburst and heads upstairs for a lie-down.

I'm still holding my breath as I picture Eddie Parry pushing, hurting and controlling. I slip into darkness as my memories come with physical pain and bruises. And with the absolute knowledge that I'm powerless.

"Are you all right, love?" Linda asks.

I peer at her with dizzy eyes. My whirring thoughts come to a screaming halt and I remember where I am. I snap out of the past.

Linda is saying it's good to see Gaby finally opening the floodgates. "I expect it was the mention of Sue and the rope marks that triggered it. After what she's been through, I'm surprised she can even get up in the morning."

"It sounds like you had a tough time, too," I say, being a police officer once more but thinking of Linda as a victim rather than potential line of enquiry.

"It's ancient history now. At least I always knew how far Eddie would go. He never hit me in the face and he never murdered anyone. It was nothing compared to what those two monsters did to Gaby … and to Carl." Her voice cracks.

My turn to move on to the sofa and offer consolation. I place my arm around the older woman's shoulders. "It's awful to think that if Carl and Gaby hadn't left the key in their back door, the intruders wouldn't have got in so easily. They might have heard them breaking in and had time to escape."

"Carl left the key in the door?" Linda says and begins to cry. "After all he said to me." She eases a tissue out of the front pocket of her tight shorts and blows her nose hard. "Before Dean and I got together, Carl was always on at me to leave night lights on and shut windows, and not to keep keys in locks. If he'd practised what he preached, he might still be alive."

I hold her as the soggy tissue fails to stem the flow from her eyes and nose. I long to tell her about Gaby's new baby. There'll be tough times ahead but maybe also a ray of sunshine for them both. But it's not my place. Gaby must tell her in her own time.

Chapter Thirty-Four

"Are you watching, Pip?" Jamie says in a whisper, but loud enough for the theatre to hear. Eyes wide with excitement, face flushed with recent exertions and T-shirt stained with dried raspberry ripple. "You're not looking at the ring girl."

Reluctantly my eyes drift back to the stage. The girl in a silver leotard stretches out her arm, spinning three large metal rings on her wrist while lying on her stomach. The circus show's always the highlight of the day at Magica for Jamie, but I'd rather be outside, delighting in his unsuccessful attempts at juggling bean bags and walking on stilts.

I watch the girl. Her tiny, childlike body is supremely supple but her face is aged and hard. I think of old films of Soviet gymnasts starved of puberty. The thought of the girl's selfimposed deprivation in the name of performance makes me squirm. I shift in my seat as she pushes herself off the ground with her free arm, her face fixed in a grimace.

It's too much for me. "Stay here," I say. "I'll get you a candy-floss."

With relief I emerge from the theatre into bright sunshine and join the long queue for refreshments. It's going to take a good ten minutes to reach the front. I'll miss the rest of the hoop girl and most of the fire-eater who usually follows. With a bit of luck it might take even longer to get served depending on who's behind the kiosk counter. I look down the line. Good, it's the older, chatty assistant. From the back of the queue, I hear her recounting a childhood memory.

"Mind you, my dad didn't hit me much as a child. I was the youngest, see. He was fortytwo when I was born so I could run faster." Her hair's a brighter shade of orange than any of the lollipops that hang above her kiosk. Even from this distance, I can see her long diamante earrings moving with the same frantic animation as her jaw. "He was quite religious. So when I thought he was getting near the mark, I'd jump up on the window ledge and say, 'Call yourself a Christian'. That would stop him."

As the queue slowly moves forward, I become anecdotally acquainted with the woman's long-suffering father, as well as her poor dead and inappropriately named cat, Lucky; her husband Ken's prize-winning dahlias; and her own recent bout of flu. "It kept coming and going in my throat. Then Ken got his cold and passed it on. Right at the back of my throat it was, until Ken's cold put the tin lid on it. I was in bed for a week. I could hardly speak."

Gradually the line of queuing visitors shuffles forward. Close up, the woman's curls look brittle, beaten into submission by years of orange dye. When I reach the kiosk, I place the order and feel disappointed as the woman tips the sugar into the pan without a word. I try to get her talking.

"I came here with my parents once as a special treat. I think I remember you from then. Have you been at Magica a long time?"

Works like a charm. "I've been here longer than Magica," she says proudly, "I was here when it was Giovanni's".

"The circus?"

"Ahead of his time he was. He stopped using animals long before it was fashionable to care." She lets out a throaty chuckle.

In full flow, she doesn't notice that the candyfloss has reached maturity. I try a few polite gesticulations but soon give up.

"A regular Harry Houdini he was. Then there was his little son. Much better than that lass who's on today." She nods her head, causing her earrings to swing in the direction of the theatre. "A body like rubber, could bend himself in half, tie himself in knots. And his three nephews had a human juggling and balancing act. Fit lads they were. That's £1 please, love." She continues her monologue on the Giovanni family as I hunt through my bag for cash. "But there was no money in circus. People stopped coming. The son moved to America. Became some sort of yoga guru. Such a waste of talent." She hands over the outsized pink ball.

Back in the theatre, the fire-eater is swallowing a series of burning torches. Jamie thanks me for the candyfloss and eats it messily with his gaze fixed on the stage. He's the one good thing to come out of my parents' divorce and Dad's remarriage. The precious gift of a brother – a sunny boy who's somehow avoided inheriting his mother's nervy petulance and his father's earnest superiority. In many ways, although there was no genetic connection, Jamie reminds me of my mum, but I know better than to tell her. Jamie is a closed, painful subject for Isabel.

As the fire-eater consumes ever-larger quantities of flames, my head chases a thought I can't catch. When he takes his final bow, I applaud with the twenty or so other people in the audience and then groan when I see the stagehands wheel out a large black box for the hapless magician we saw last time we came. Jamie loved him, of course. He became genuinely concerned when the man had to ask for assistance to free himself from handcuffs after his escape trick went "wrong". His inane commentary was in the kind of slow patronizing voice that some adults reserve for small children. When the act starts, my eyes follow the magician's antics but my mind keeps returning to the candyfloss seller and I can't work out why.

"Look, Pip, he's stuck again. They'll have to help him like last time." Jamie bounces in his seat.

Pulling at the handcuffs, the man trips grandly and begins rolling back and forth across the stage. If it's anything like before, this part of the performance will go on for several painful minutes. The desire to make my own escape becomes overwhelming. Now seems a good time for another candyfloss.

"Another one? I don't think Mummy would like it."

"I'm sure Mummy wouldn't mind," I lie. "Stay here I'll be right back."

It's a good fifteen minutes before I return to the theatre. I hold the candyfloss aloft like a trophy yet I don't feel triumphant. My second chat with the candyfloss seller has troubled me. I'm a jumble of disjointed thoughts, but that's preferable to what will happen if I join them together. My eyes adjust to the gloom as I ease into my seat but it's the wrong row. Jamie isn't there. I stand up and look to the rows in front and behind. He isn't anywhere.

Chapter Thirty-Five

"Jamie," I call out.

A loud "shush" hits back from across the darkened room.

Blood pounding in my cheeks, I run to the exit and find a block of switches on the wall. The first two don't do anything. I hit the third and fourth. A row of fluorescent tubes illuminates the front of the stage.

"What the flaming hell?" the magician says, abandoning his children's TV presenter patter.

The last four switches light the room. I run back down the aisle, looking left and right, and bending down to see under the seats. "Has anyone seen the young boy I was sitting with?"

"Who the hell are you?" the magician bellows.

"Police," I fumble for my ID card with one hand, still holding the stupid candyfloss in the other. "Has anyone seen an eight-year-old boy wearing a Star Wars T-shirt and trainers?"

"That description covers half the kids who come in here," the voice on the stage hisses.

I search the faces of the audience. Most stare at me blankly or shake their heads. My heart races. Jamie isn't here and no one can remember him. I dash for the exit.

"Turn the bloody lights off before you go," the voice shouts on the stage.

I hesitate by the block of switches and stab at two of them before running outside. People everywhere, milling about by the different attractions. Jamie is now a needle in several haystacks. There's no sign of him in the refreshment queue. I consider asking the candyfloss seller, but she's engaged in another reminiscence and not easy to interrupt. I'll lose even more time.

Jamie must have got bored and gone back to the pogo sticks. The only logical explanation. I race to the circus skills area where families are grappling with stilts and Rollerblades. I dart among them, holding the candyfloss up like a tour guide's umbrella. A beacon for straggling tourists and, please God, for lost boys. My head fills with every missing persons enquiry I've ever been involved in – the painstaking and fruitless house-to-house, the tear-stained relatives on the evening news, the unhappy endings … All my anxious enquiries meet with embarrassed shaking of heads. One man, carrying a toddler on his shoulders, suggests I try the Punch and Judy show that's started on the grass behind the theatre.

I run round the building and meet a sea of faces all looking in the direction of a blue and white puppet tent. Heads of tussled hair, mucky T-shirts and grass-stained knees move in and out of focus, all so like Jamie and yet so alien at the same time.

I'm about to retrace my steps when I register a hand waving. A cross-legged Jamie grinning in the back row. My relief turns to anger. I beckon him. Jamie, unused to seeing a stern expression on his sister's face, duly obliges. As he picks his way through the rows of other children, I rehearse my words in my mind. I don't recall the last time I was cross with him and I'm sure how to handle it. However, the decision on what to say is taken from me.

A starchy voice says, "So you've come to look for him at last, have you?"

I spin round into my stepmother, her face like thunder.

"Joanne, where did you spring from?"

"Never mind that. You left Jamie on his own. Anything could have happened to him."

Unable to look her in the eye, I hang my head. "I was only gone for a few minutes. I could see the door from the queue."

"But you didn't see him leave, did you?" Joanne says, dark reproach hammered into every word.

"But Mum, you made us creep out when she wasn't looking," Jamie says when he reaches us.

Joanne colours but continues to claim the moral high ground. "He was free to roam all over the place before you even realized he was missing. I'll have to think twice before letting you bring him here again. And you let him have candyfloss." She points at the stick that I'm still holding.

"This is for me." I sink my teeth into the sickly fibre.

"From the state of him, I'd say he's already had his helping and look at his T-shirt. Ice cream is a nightmare to wash out. Not to mention the E numbers. He'll be high as a kite tonight and I'll get no peace. It's all right for you. You don't have to get him to bed."

I scrub my teeth, removing every trace of the sugary red stain. I scoop a couple of palmfuls of water over the toothpaste blobs on my top but don't care. What a difference a week makes. Don't give a damn if I'm covered in toothpaste. Past trying to create a good impression with my clothes, or with anything else. I've been relieved of duties twice in as many days. First at work and then with Jamie. I'm beginning to see the similarities between DI Bagley and Joanne. Both bossy, demanding and with an unerring knack of making everything seem like my fault. Bagley didn't instruct me to apprehend a murder suspect at the church. Johnson took me with him to talk to a minor witness. And Joanne didn't agree to let me take Jamie to Magica. She forced me into it. It turns out that Joanne found a free voucher in one of the parenting magazines she always reads but never applies. Typical Joanne to get me to pay for Jamie's ticket and then come later with her free ticket and take over.

Surely it was just as irresponsible to encourage Jamie to sneak out of the theatre past me as it was for me to leave him alone in the first place. And why shouldn't I buy him an ice cream? I never have trouble getting him to bed on the Saturday nights he stays over.

But I'm fogging my mind with trivia to stave off other, darker thoughts. Suddenly, they come crowding into my head and I can only think of Carl Brock's murder.

I shudder at the far-reaching power of a single act. One turn of the knife and there's a widow, a fatherless unborn child, a brotherless sister, a teacherless classroom. One drug deal puts a boy into rehab, a mother in despair and a father in hiding. One botched arrest bruises a constable's face and a sergeant's ego. But which is the cruellest act? Who is the greatest victim?

When I've finally accepted my own answers, I'll have to present them to Bagley. At best the DI will laugh, at worst … who knows. I could keep quiet. I've no evidence and only a hazy idea of the motive. But I stayed quiet yesterday and a vital witness got away. I know the danger of silence. I joined the police to get victims heard, justice done. I have to trust my instincts whatever the personal cost. And the cost to others.

Chapter Thirty-Six

After a deep breath, I prepare to run the gauntlet. I force my head up high as I stalk along the corridor past the CID office. I don't look through the glass panelling but am aware of movement inside. My new colleagues will be staring, faces fixed in open derision.

An angry shove to the double doors at the end of the corridor. One door bangs against the wall and adds another chip to its shabby paintwork. I hesitate as I look beyond the stairwell to the senior officers' corridor. Just after 9 a.m. Perhaps the DI won't be in yet. Of course she'll be there, like any self-respecting Rottweiler with a keen work ethic.

Time to march right in, but my carefully rehearsed speech deserts me. Can't remember a single one of the well-chosen words which would tell Bagley not only that I intend to stay in CID but also what I now know about the case. Coward. I walk into the general office. Might as well fight the warm-up match first.

Kevin Bradshaw's at his desk, chair pushed back, legs stretched out and hands tucked behind his head. Martin Connors and Darren Holtom hover near him, drinking from polystyrene cups. Danny Johnson's looking out of the window, deep in conversation with his mobile phone. I give quiet thanks that there's no sign of DS Matthews.

Connors sees me. "Morning, Agatha. You missed a good night last night but it's nice to see you back."

I wait for the punchline to go with the catching nickname but none comes.

Then it's Holtom's turn. "The boss wants to see you but come over here first."

This's more like it. They intend to marinade me before sending me to Bagley for spitroasting. I brace myself.

"She's brought in the champagne. Her idea of team building. We know she's taken all the credit from the rest of us but at least it's decent plonk." Holtom raises the white cup to his mouth. "Hair of the dog stuff after last night. Cheers."

My first thought is that they've concocted another prank, this time with nice Kevin Bradshaw playing along too, but there does seem to be a sweet alcoholic smell in the air.

"Is DI Bagley celebrating something?" I ask cautiously.

"Haven't you heard?" Connors says. "We've cracked the case. We started our celebrations at the boozer last night."

"And you're back on the payroll," Bradshaw says, taking up his cup from the desk. "The boss reckons we got a confession thanks to you."

"Me?"

"She actually reckons it's down to the sergeant over there," he says, looking at Danny Johnson who's putting his mobile in his back pocket, "and no doubt she'll be offering him the *proper* thank you again later." Throaty chuckles from Connors and Holtom. "But as you were with him at the church, you can have some of the credit, too."

"That's right," Danny says, approaching the group, his gait cocky. "She reckons he only confessed because we went in there on Saturday and rattled his cage. We gave him time to chew things over. If we'd arrested him there and then, he'd have been a tougher nut to crack. But he'd bottled it by Sunday."

The precariously constructed jigsaw in my head, the one I

intended to pluck up the courage to present to Bagley and the one held together by shaky instinct, start to pull apart. "Are you saying Bartholomew Hedges has confessed?" I can hardly get the words out.

"Cool as a cucumber he was," Bradshaw says. "Danny and I went to the church yesterday and there he was up at the lectern, reading a lesson. He'd ditched the frock and dressed himself in his Sunday best. He saw us, and calm as you like he finished reading. Genesis 38: 14, appropriate in the circumstances: 'So she changed from the widow's clothes she had been wearing'. Then he walked straight up to us, leaving the congregation warbling, 'Fight the Good Fight'."

"I interviewed him with Bagley," Danny says. "He coughed straightaway."

"But what was his motive?" I'm bewildered, and fervently hope that I'm a victim of another joke. This can't be true.

"A pretty good one. He found out Carl Brock had introduced his son, Saul, to drugs."

"This can't be right."

"You're not going to start that 'he's a devout Christian' crap again, are you?" Danny says. "The guy's confessed and Forensics reckon the hair found in Brock's hallway is a class match."

"The hair could be Bartholomew's? He was in the Brocks' house?"

"Of course he was. He told us everything. He trussed up Brock's wife and dragged Brock out of the house, took him to Martle Top and stabbed him to death. The only thing he won't tell us is who his accomplice was. He's adamant he acted alone despite Gaby Brock's statement that there were two attackers in the house that night."

"This is awful," I say, more to myself than to Danny Johnson.

"This is a result. Come on let's go and see Bagley, and get you your champagne," he says. "You need to loosen up."

"I don't want any."

"You don't have any choice, girl." There's no sign of the twinkle in his eye. "If the boss wants you to have a drink in her office, that's what you do."

"Give me a minute." I head for my desk.

"Don't be long," Danny says, waving his cup. "I'm off for a refill now."

"That's what you call it, is it?" Holtom leers. "Let's all go and tap her for more booze." His red face says he's already had plenty.

As they reach the office door, Connors turns back to me. "There's a large brown envelope on your desk. It's addressed to the Brock case detectives. None of us fancied it so we thought you could do the honours. It looks like Dr Tarnovski's scribble. It must have been quite a change for him to write on anything other than a betting slip."

I slump into my chair, sending it wheeling backwards. I sigh and lift the envelope to push my finger under its gummed edge. Of all the scenarios I've pictured for this morning, I couldn't force this one into my worst nightmare. I will the scene to rewind and restart as it should have done. I long for the abuse I expected from Bagley. And I'd have welcomed an earful from Danny Johnson, too. And what about Matthews? Dour and angry, "Read any good books, lately, Agatha?" Even that would be preferable to what's really happening.

I force the scrappy-looking form out of the envelope and make out the words *Medical Report* but refuse to focus on anything else. Something's very wrong. I try to concentrate. I jump when Danny Johnson sticks his head round the door again.

"The boss wants you now."

"I've got to go out," I say, standing up as I come to my senses with a jolt. "Get Gaby Brock in to pick Bartholomew Hedges out of a VIPER line-up."

"Who made you chief inspector? Bagley's prepared to forget Saturday if you go to her now."

"It's important. Make sure Gaby Brock views the line-up. I have to go."

"Don't get on the wrong side of Bagley," Danny shouts to the closing door.

I run on. I have a script to rewrite.

Chapter Thirty-Seven

Fifteen minutes to wait at the bus stop outside the police station, but it seems like an age. I squint at Tarnovski's form, my hand hovering above the page to reduce the glare of the sun. As I decipher the contents, I feel a desperate need to act. The sensation grows more intense with every sentence I read. It coils itself in my chest like an urgent, nagging indigestion.

I fall into the bus, launch my bus fare at the driver's hand and have to scramble about the floor to retrieve it. I leap out again at the stop in Danescott and hit the ground running. But the heat soon slows me to a half walk.

Hare Close is as drab on a warm Monday morning as it was on a balmy Friday evening. Just as well I haven't driven. No teenagers to guard the hubcaps. Perhaps they're in school or playing truant at the Dynamite. A cold shudder runs through me as I force my sticky body up the concrete steps. I shake off the memory of McKenzie's squalid nightclub and knock on the door of 19a. I listen for movement inside but hear nothing.

Knock again. Silence. The coil of unrest within me threatens to unravel. I raise my hand to give one final dispirited knock. I hear the door catch move.

"You bitch!" Sonia Hedges screeches. She's wearing the same

old shirt and her lank hair's pinned behind her ears, which are devoid of their usual hoop earrings. Her face is peppered with blotches. Her lips and nose are sore.

"Have you come to arrest me, too?" she screams. "You might as well. This family's ruined."

"I just want to talk."

"Talk. That's all you lot ever do. That's all anyone does. That's what they do with Saul, but talk isn't going to make him better."

"I want to listen more than talk. Can I come in?"

Sonia steps back, leaving the front door open for me to follow. There's a large holdall on the dining table. Untidy piles of women's clothing surround it.

"Are you going away?"

"I'm not doing a runner if that's what you mean," Sonia snaps. "I'm going to Alderley Lodge. Kyle Stewart, the care manager, says it's better for Saul if I stay there. He'll be on suicide watch when he finds out you've arrested his father." Loud sobs cover most of her words and she busies herself with the piles of clothing.

I place a hand on her arm.

She shakes it off. "If you want to talk, make it quick. My son needs me."

"I'm sorry," I say.

"Sorry for what? For getting my husband arrested for murder?"

"He's confessed."

"He didn't do it."

"So why did he confess?"

Sonia doesn't answer but begins throwing the clothes into the bag.

"He had a good motive," I venture.

"He didn't kill anyone. When we realized that Saul was taking drugs, Bartholomew's first reaction was to go to church and pray."

"How did you find out?"

"Saul was puking in his bedroom, in agony and terrified. It panicked him into telling us he'd taken heroin. He said it was his second time, but he'd been taking speed for months. Suddenly everything made sense. His extreme mood swings, from not eating and lounging in bed all day to stuffing himself stupid and staying up all night. He had a thing about his clock radio, always taking it to bits and putting it back together. Obsessive.

"How could we have been so blind? We thought it was teenage stroppiness. I even thought the squares of paper I found in his trainer were to plug a hole." She breaks off from the packing to wipe her eyes. "Things had gone missing and I thought I was going mad. But it wasn't me. Saul had taken them for drugs money. He even flogged his father's steam wallpaper stripper for a fiver. Bartholomew needed it for work. It was worth far more."

So Saul Hedges moved from amphetamines to heroin in a few short months. A drug career like that normally takes years to establish. But when the pusher is a teacher, someone kind who Saul saw every day, the downward spiral can be rapid.

"Did Saul tell you that Brock was his supplier?" I try to catch her eye but Sonia won't meet my gaze and continues to pack. I put my hand over her wrist. "Did he tell you?"

"Do you really want to know?" Sonia says, her voice cracking. "My husband had never lifted a finger to that boy but we needed to know who was responsible. Bartholomew beat the shit out of him." Tears drip onto the holdall.

"And Saul admitted that his teacher, Carl Brock, had introduced him to drugs?" I ask gently.

Sonia nods.

"Did your husband confront Brock?"

"I went. Bartholomew was too fired up. He didn't trust himself. I phoned the school. Told them we needed to get some homework off Brock."

"You didn't tell Mr Cunningham the truth?"

"What was the point? It was Saul's word against his teacher."

"What happened when you met Brock?"

"He laughed in my face." She chokes on her words. "He said it was Saul's choice. He was just meeting demand."

"He admitted it?"

"He boasted about it. Said we needed him. Reckoned it could be four months before Saul got a place in Alderley Lodge. Said we'd have to keep him in speed until then."

I wince. If only they'd gone to the police or their GP, they'd have known about the range of help available, not just at Alderley. But, too afraid, too ashamed, their only source of information was the pusher.

"We became a drug family. We had to sell everything: the microwave, my one decent coat, the silver bracelet Bartholomew gave me when Saul was born." Sonia rubs her bare wrist. "We didn't get anything like what they were worth. Bartholomew had to flog his old radio for two quid and he even tried to sell his gold-embossed St John's Gospel but no beggar round here wanted it. Carl Brock bled the life out of us and the worst part was having to keep going to that filthy man's house to get the stuff Saul needed." She wraps her arms around her body. "It broke Bartholomew. It was worse than finding out his son was a junkie."

"Why did you go to the memorial service for Brock?"

"Joe Walker knew what Brock had done to Saul. When he heard that Mr Cunningham was going to hold an assembly to tell everyone how marvellous Brock was, he phoned me. He told me there'd be TV cameras. We decided to disrupt the service, make a noise, shout about what sort of low-life Brock really was. I knew I'd be carted off and Joe would get suspended, but it would be worth it. Cunningham wouldn't be able to cover it up.

"But Cunningham was ready for me. He might not have known about Brock but he didn't want the mother of his junkie pupil turning up. He got two teachers to meet me in the car park and send me away." Her shoulders drop and she clutches one of the piles of clothes. She speaks again, gasping for air. "Why should he keep his precious school reputation intact while my son becomes a drug addict?"

I'm at a loss to reply. How can I reassure this wreck of a woman? Even now I can see Cunningham charming his way around the school governors, ensuring that nothing sticks to his Teflon suit. But who could Sonia Hedges charm? Who would believe that a respectable teacher like Carl Brock peddled drugs to his most vulnerable pupils? Sonia didn't even trust me when Matthews and I asked her to confirm Joe Walker's story. She could have told us everything then. But, no, her only hope was a humiliating public protest and even that was denied her.

I was powerless once and vowed never again. Yet here I am, overwhelmed by Sonia's misery and wanting to leave. Something stirs in my mind and I remember why I'm here, defying DI Bagley and risking my career. Self-pity isn't the answer. I resume my questioning. "Was Brock always alone when you went to his house?"

"I never saw Brock again. Meeting him at the school sapped the life out of me. I couldn't be near him. Bartholomew said he'd do it. I always stayed in the car outside." Her face hardens. "I sat and looked at Brock's neat little house in his neat little street while my poor husband had to go in and do business with the most odious piece of scum to crawl the Earth."

"Did your husband see anyone else there?"

"He never talked about what went on, and I never asked."

"Please, Mrs Hedges, this is very important. Did he ever see other people there?"

"One night when we went round, we could hear Brock shouting. It sounded like furniture being turned over. We figured he was rowing with another dealer. We went back home and called on Brock the next day."

"When did your husband last see Brock?"

"We visited on the Friday before he died. He was alive and

slimy when Bartholomew left him." She breaks off from the packing and looks straight at me. "He didn't kill him."

I take a breath. "I know he didn't. Brock was killed on Sunday night but Bartholomew wouldn't have murdered him then. As abhorrent as it was, you still needed Brock's drugs. You were expecting to need him for several more weeks. Saul was unexpectedly offered a rehab place on Wednesday. Two days *after* Brock's murder."

"That's right." Excitement sounds through her sobs. "That's it. We needed that vulture. He told us it would be weeks before Saul would get a rehab place. And he put his prices up. It was me who sold our television to pay Brock. We couldn't kill him, even though we longed to pulverize every vile bone in his body. You can see that, too." She grabs my arm. "You've got to help us."

I smile but then check my rising enthusiasm. There'll be no happy ending yet.

"Why did he confess? I can help you, but you have to tell me."

"I've nothing to tell you." She takes her hand away. She presses down the packed holdall and forces up the zip.

"It's the same reason he disguised himself at the church, isn't it?" I say softly. "He's an honest man, a Christian. He didn't want to miss his cleaning duty and he didn't want to lie to the police. If we'd found and questioned him that day, he'd have felt compelled to tell us the truth." I seek eye contact with Sonia. "That truth is why he hid from us and it's what's made him confess now, isn't it?"

Sonia clasps the holdall to her chest and looks away.

I sigh, knowing that what I say next will break the broken woman into even smaller, sharper pieces. "You and your husband knew you had to maintain a relationship with Brock to make sure Saul got his fix. But, given his condition, Saul might not have been so rational in his thinking."

Sonia puts down the holdall and faces me, sheer terror in her eyes.

I wish I could stop and save the woman's anguish, but everything has to be said. "There is only one reason a man would confess to a murder he didn't commit. To protect someone else. To protect his son."

Chapter Thirty-Eight

Steve Chisholm sits at his desk in Forensics, sipping his coffee and scratching his chin. He should have shaved before he came in, but there wasn't time. Still it was worth oversleeping after a good night out with the CID lads. A bit of a rarity for him. The coppers don't always want Clockwise Chisholm along to celebrate a case result. He knows they all think of him as the resident anorak, but he doesn't care. While they're playing cops and robbers, his forensic evidence solves most of their cases for them.

He showed them last night that he knew how to party, and they enjoyed his anecdotes. He likes to inject his stories with a touch of science and technology every now and then. Most other people don't.

After Liz Bagley went home, the evening really got going. She'd been doing one of her "Look how many lagers I can drink" routines. Steve grunts into his cup. Trollop. He hates senior officers who join the DCs in the pub. All fake. They happily get them bladdered in the evening and then bollock them for being five minutes late the next morning. Women officers like DI Shagley are the worst, using their sexuality to manipulate men and then pulling rank when they've got what they want.

Rumour has it she's even got her claws into the assistant chief constable, but ACC John Wise must have been out of town last night because she was slumming it with the underlings. She hung around Danny like a bad smell. He did well to avoid getting two black eyes, the way she was thrusting her tits in his face. Steve has to hand it to Danny. Somehow he gave her just the right amount of attention, so she didn't feel brushed off but knew she'd be going home without him. She got the message in the end and left, but not before giving Danny a look that said she'd drop her knickers for him another time.

Steve looks at his desk. He'll have to get this lot tidied up. The murder's solved and it's up to the Crown Prosecution Service to make a credible case. Just as well the Hedges guy confessed. This one could have dragged on for weeks, like the Easter Day business at Briggham. He sounds a right nutcase, going to church in stockings and suspenders, according to the rumour Steve heard. The prison chaplain better watch his back.

When the office door bursts open, Steve manages to retain his grip on his coffee. It's Mike Matthews's new girl, breathing heavily and her cheeks flushed a brighter shade of pink than her T-shirt.

"Easy does it, Agatha," he says.

"Where are the forensics for the Brock case?" she gasps.

"It's all here." He points at his desk. "I'm still sorting it. What do you want to know?"

She comes towards the desk. He straightens up in his chair but she still towers over him. The word statuesque crosses his mind.

But then again, statuesque women don't trip over chair legs and land with their full weight against the side of desks.

"Ouch! Sorry!" she yelps.

"Mind how you go, love," he says.

Shame really. That body could be sexy on someone else. Her eyes dart over his piles of papers and plastic bags.

"If you tell me what you're after, I might be able to help," he says.

"I just need … these." She snatches two small evidence bags and heads for the door.

"You can't take those. There's such a thing as continuity of evidence," Steve shouts, awake for the first time that morning.

"I won't break the seals."

"You'll have to sign for them."

She returns to the desk and holds out her hand impatiently. Steve retrieves the appropriate form from his top drawer, her sense of urgency rubbing off on him in spite of himself. She seizes it out of his hand and makes a grab for his pen. It's attached to its holder by a short chain. She leans across him so that the pen will reach the form. Seconds later she's gone.

Statuesque after all. He looks at the form. And barking mad. Just right for CID. She's signed it "Agatha Adams".

My footsteps thud down the tiled staircase. No going back. People will get hurt, destroyed, but I have to see it through. Panic threatens. How will I ever get DI Bagley to listen? The woman has cracked open champagne. Case closed as far as she cares. I'll have to try my luck with DCI Hendersen. No incriminating logos on my T-shirt and he's my best hope.

I crash onto the stairwell and through the chipped doors, my feet becoming quiet on the carpeted floor. I slow to a brisk walk. Decorum needed now. Decorum and professionalism. I don't look at the first door and pray it doesn't open. The last thing I need is to bump into DI Bagley. As I pass the second office, a door opens further along. DS Matthews leads Gaby Brock into the corridor, and DCI Hendersen follows them out, drinking from a coffee mug.

"Ah, DC Adams," he calls. "You can drive Mrs Brock home."

I come to a halt but my insides carry on for several inches in front of me. No chance now of laying my case before him in the confines of his office. Time to go for broke, in front of Gaby Brock and Matthews. I'm not sure where decorum fits in, but I'll do my best.

"Of course, sir," I say, mentally keeping my pounding heart inside my chest. "But can I just ask Mrs Brock why the key was in the back door?"

"You what, Agatha?" Matthews asks.

"No more questions," Hendersen says and sups his coffee. "Mrs Brock has given us enough answers for the time being. She's just picked Hedges out of a line-up. Luckily for you the VIPER identification video was set up before we got his confession. Not sure why you insisted on it, but it's another nail in the proverbial coffin for the accused."

"It was unusual, wasn't it, Gaby?" I keep my tone soft.

Gaby looks back blankly. Her face still carries the grey hue that's masked it since I first met her, but the bruises around her eyes have turned green like badly applied eye shadow.

I try again. "Carl's sister, Linda, said Carl never left keys in door locks. He knew it was an invitation to burglars."

"He must have forgotten," Gaby says and looks at Matthews as if appealing to him to support her.

"Let's get you home," he says.

"What clothes were you washing in your machine that night?" I ask.

"What?" Exasperation in her weak voice.

"Agatha, you know as well as I do that it was men's shirts," Matthews says.

"Carl's shirts?" I put my question to Gaby who doesn't reply. I ask another. "Why were you wearing winter pyjamas in the middle of June?"

Gaby Brock opens her mouth to speak, but Hendersen steps in.

"Will one of you please take this lady home?"

I'm getting nowhere. "Sir, Bartholomew Hedges didn't kill Carl Brock."

Gaby lets out a soft, shocked sob.

"Not now, Adams." Hendersen's angry baritone voice reverberates along the line of doors.

The doors are all closed, ganging up on me, not listening, not believing. I take a shaky breath. "Bartholomew Hedges wouldn't have killed Brock on Sunday night. He still needed him to supply drugs for Saul. The family didn't hear from Alderley Lodge until Wednesday – more than two days after the murder."

"The man has confessed, and Mrs Brock has identified him at an ID parade." Hendersen speaks slowly, as if explaining something to a child. He drains his mug and smacks his lips. End of discussion.

Matthews, who's begun to move Mrs Brock along the corridor, turns back. "Why did he confess, if he didn't do it?"

"To protect Saul."

"You're saying that Hedges junior committed the murder and Dad took the fall for him?" he says, rubbing his chin and apparently forgetting Gaby and Hendersen are there. "It's possible. Saul could have been off his head enough to do it, and his father wouldn't be the first parent to cover for a son."

"Stop it now, you two," Hendersen says. "Take Mrs Brock back to her sister-in-law's. Make sure Linda Parry is there. Mrs Brock shouldn't be alone at a time like this."

"Will you grieve now, Gaby?" I ask, my tone soft again.

Gaby Brock stops sobbing for a second.

"I mean grieve for the baby you lost last year."

Gaby seems to crumple in on herself and her sobs become louder.

"What happened, Gaby?" I ask. "Did you fall down those stairs last year or did Carl push you?"

Gaby freezes in mid-sob and her shoulders shake.

"That's enough." Hendersen again.

"Sir, Carl Brock was a violent wife-beater. Ask the police doctor to have another look at her injuries. There are older fading bruises on her arms, as well as the fresh ones from when we found her. I'm sure a full examination will confirm this and the fact that she's pregnant again."

"I want to go home," Gaby sobs, her eyes beseeching Hendersen.

Before he has chance to come to her aid, I fish the brown envelope out of my bag. "I have Mrs Brock's medical records. At the time of her miscarriage, she also suffered a broken ankle, a badly strained wrist and—"

"Injuries entirely consistent with a fall down stairs," Hendersen interrupts. "Stop crossexamining Mrs Brock. Has it completely slipped your mind that she's just lost her husband and was herself the victim of a kidnapping? Where did you get that file?"

"… and a scald mark on the side of her mouth, consistent with being struck by something hot," I continue, not answering the question. I force the envelope back in my bag. We both know it's illegal for me to have the file. But does Gaby know?

Apparently not. Her doe eyes are on Hendersen. "I fell down the stairs and lost my baby."

I press on before he intervenes. "Your medical records also say you've been treated on four separate occasions for injuries to your knuckles."

"My knuckles are prone to dislocation," she says. Her voice is calm but tears stream down her face.

"A witness heard Carl arguing and fighting with someone at your home three weeks ago. Was he beating you?"

"What witness?" DS. Matthews asks.

"Mrs Hedges."

"Have you completely lost the plot, Agatha? Sonia Hedges is the wife of the man who's confessed to murder. It's hardly rock-solid evidence, is it?" Matthews says, his earlier interest vanished.

"Get Mrs Brock out of here," Hendersen tells him and then to me: "You, my office, now."

His voice echoes around my head, like a gong that can't be silenced. I'll disappear inside the noise unless I act swiftly.

Matthews leads Gaby Brock almost to the double doors before I find my words again.

"Why are you still making excuses for him?" I call out. "He can't hurt you anymore. Tell us what kind of a man he really was."

Gaby stares blankly at me, then turns to go.

"You've had a dislocated shoulder, a fractured cheekbone, two broken ankles, severe bruising to the chest. And all in the last two years. How long were you and Carl married?"

Gaby looks at the floor, silent.

"How long, Gaby? I already know the answer. Shall you tell the chief inspector or shall I? How long were you married?"

She turns round and gives a sigh, letting go. "Two years," she whispers.

Matthews and Hendersen exchange a glance. I blunder on.

"You know we might not pursue the drugs issue. We've only got Hedges's word that was why your husband was killed. Carl's dead anyway, so we'll probably drop it."

"You're back in uniform, Adams." Hendersen's jowls are red with rage.

I falter. The corridor zooms in and out of focus. Adrenaline pounds in my ears but I've heard what he said. Slippery ground. I've no right to predict the course of the case however good my background research might be. But there's no going back. I catch up with Matthews as he holds the door for Gaby.

"He's probably died with his reputation intact. Is that what you want?" I clasp the door edge, my fingers shaking as I struggle to keep hold.

But Gaby doesn't step through the door. She hangs back and loses all semblance of composure. Her tears become wild and she drops to her knees.

Squatting beside her, I pull a clean tissue from my bag. "Did you ever try to leave him?"

She dabs her eyes with the tissue. "He said he was going to

leave me once," she sniffs. "I remember clinging to his legs, begging him to stay. I bumped along the pavement as he dragged himself away."

"Why didn't you want him to go?"

"I was nothing without him. I couldn't manage on my own – too stupid, too useless." She slides to the floor, arms wrapped around her knees.

"Is that what he told you?"

Gaby nods. "He chipped away at me for so long, I shrank and shrivelled as a person."

"Mrs Brock, I'm sorry to hear of your difficult domestic situation, but we have a confession from the killer." Hendersen sounds like a kindly uncle. "We'll take a statement from you when you've calmed … when things are calmer."

But Matthews doesn't move, turning to me in anticipation of my next question.

"Couldn't you have told someone?" I ask.

Gaby wipes her eyes again. "Who would have believed me? Everyone thought he was the sweetest guy. Whenever he opened his mouth honey came out. Dedicated teacher, loving husband."

"I think Linda would have believed you," I say.

"Carl would sit me down on Linda's sofa and take my hand. Linda thought he was playing with it, a sign of affection." Gaby gives a weak smile, then her eyes narrow. "But he was crushing my fingers, daring me to call out in pain. That's why the knuckles dislocated. I never cried out." She swallows a sob.

"So you had to kill him," I say.

Gaby shakes her head. "I didn't know what to do. I decided the solution was to kill myself."

"Why didn't you?" Matthews says, leaning against the wall with his arms folded.

"First I couldn't leave Pipkin and then I was pregnant again."

"Who the devil's Pipkin?" Hendersen asks.

"She means her pet cockatiel," I explain. "We found his old

cage at the house. Linda Parry said his feathers went black and he died."

Gaby sobs again. "Carl did it. He knew I loved that bird. I'd do whatever he wanted to protect him. One day he brought a man into the house and told me to be … nice to him. Carl was trying to make some big deal, but I couldn't do it. After the man had gone, Carl set fire to Pipkin's tail to teach me a lesson. The shock killed him a few days later." She swallows her words.

"And that was the final straw, was it?" I suggest.

Gaby doesn't reply, her fingers rubbing furiously over her crossed arms.

"What's all this got to do with Saul Hedges killing Carl Brock?" DS Matthews says, stepping away from the wall.

I shake my head. "I didn't say that Saul killed him, just that his father thought he did it."

Matthews rolls his eyes. He helps Gaby to her feet and pushes open the swing doors again.

"How's your yoga these days, Gaby?" I say.

Gaby Brock freezes.

Chapter Thirty-Nine

"Linda told me you're good at yoga. It must make you very supple."

Gaby still doesn't move.

"I went to Magica yesterday," I go on. "Have you ever been? My little brother loves it. The candyfloss seller told me a story that got me thinking. It was about the Giovanni clan, the people who owned Magica when it was still a circus. Apparently Giovanni's son became a yoga guru in the States. But he didn't start off with yoga. He used to be in the circus, a contortionist."

"What are you on about, Agatha?" Matthews asks. It's his turn to grip the door. He rocks it angrily back and forth.

I continue. "If he could use his contortionist skills to become a yoga master, maybe a yoga expert like you could use those skills to chain yourself up in a fake assault. I wonder how difficult it would be to move from yoga to contortionism and escapology."

"If I'm an escapologist, why did I have to wait to be rescued?" Gaby says, suddenly defiant.

"You stopped the act halfway through. You only had to lock the shackles and wait."

"That's impossible. Carl locked the chains and put the keys in my pocket."

"That's right," Matthews snaps. "Only Carl Brock's prints were found on the chains and keys. How do you explain that?"

DCI Hendersen takes command again. "I can't see how even the world's greatest contortionist could snap shut padlocks and get the keys into a breast pocket. You can go now, Mrs Brock. I'll send a couple of my people along later to take a statement from you about your husband." He taps his empty coffee mug on his curled fist.

Matthews leads Gaby out to the stairwell. I rush past them and block their path. I hold up the two exhibit bags I snatched from Steve Chisholm. The colour drains from Gaby's face.

I know then that I've guessed their significance but unless Gaby admits what they are, the evidence is too flimsy. Time for a different approach.

"Bartholomew Hedges, that man you've trapped, wasn't a dealer," I say, bending my knees to bring my eyes directly into line with hers. "He was a poor, proud man, trying to save his son from your husband. When he's convicted of his murder – and he will be convicted – he'll go to prison for years. But he's a victim just like you –– with a child to protect."

My words hit home.

"Oh, God. I didn't know," she cries and falls against Matthews. He has to hold her to keep her on her feet. "It seemed the easiest way …." Her whole body's shaking. "I had to think of my baby. I thought I was framing a criminal."

Hendersen drops his mug. It shatters across the floor.

I begin the caution. "Gabrielle Brock, I'm arresting you for …" The words stick in my throat.

"The murder of Carl Edward Brock." DCI Hendersen continues it with resumed authority.

Chapter Forty

The interview room is a functional, nondescript space with a plain table and four chairs, all fixed to the floor. It often rings out with the not-so-innocent protests of angry, drunken suspects, but the current, sombre atmosphere reminds me of the mortuary where I took Gaby to see Carl's body. The woman sits opposite me now.

Chief Inspector Hendersen speaks the introductions into the recorder and adds that Mrs Brock has declined legal representation.

"Right, Mrs Brock, shall we get on with this?" he says, shuffling his paperwork. He switches to a more conciliatory tone, no doubt hopeful of charming her into a quick confession for the tape. "Please take your time and tell us about Carl. Perhaps you could start with how the two of you met."

"I met him when I started work at Swan Academy." Her voice is monotone, no nostalgia in recounting this story. "We just clicked. He was like a breath of fresh air in that school. He used to go out of his way to help the low achievers. The ones who were neglected at home, you know."

"You mean he sought out the company of children with low self-esteem, vulnerable children," I say.

"I didn't see it like that then. It was much later that I realized he might be cultivating them as customers for his drugs business."

"You said he changed after your marriage?" Hendersen says.

"When we met, he was charming. He tried hard to woo me. Flowers every day and expensive meals. He even wrote love poems. He was an English teacher after all. I fell head over heels for him. And we married within a few months.

"The first time his mask slipped was on our honeymoon. I got friendly with another couple in the hotel and suggested we join them for a meal. He went mad." Gaby wipes away tears with her fingers. "I didn't know what I'd done wrong. He held me down on the bed and bent my fingers back. He made me promise I only wanted to dine with him."

The vision of a powerful Carl Brock bearing down on his fragile bride fills my mind. I hand her a tissue. "And after the honeymoon?"

"He could be charismatic and loving one minute, aggressive and abusive the next. He made me give up work. And he'd throw terrible rages if he thought I wanted to spend time with other people. I wasn't allowed to go out, except with his sister, Linda, and he wasn't even keen on that. He wanted to control every aspect of my life. He told me what to wear, how to do my hair and wouldn't let me wear make-up except to cover up the bruises." She rubs the green bruise in her eye socket." I remember the tidy bathroom cabinet stocked with heavy foundation and concealer. I twig why we didn't find any lipstick. Brock didn't allow it in the house.

"After you gave up work, what did you do all day?"

"Cleaning. Carl liked the house to be tidy."

I think of the pristine house – a terrible legacy. "What about your yoga?" I ask.

"He stopped me going to evening classes but he let me keep my books and videos. He didn't see them as a threat."

I see deep into the empty brown eyes. If only Carl Brock had known the role yoga would play in his wife's alibi for his murder. Is Gaby thinking the same thing?

"Didn't you try to leave him?"

"He'd phone me from school at breaks and lunchtimes to make sure I was at home. He took my purse, my car keys. He said that if I ever left him, he'd find me and kill me. No matter how long it took, he'd get me. Once he told me that if I left, he'd kill himself and I'd have to explain it to Linda and her children. But he knew I'd never leave. He'd spent so long telling me I was useless, I believed it. He said I was nothing without him and I couldn't make it on my own."

"Why didn't you tell someone?" I ask.

Gaby spreads her hands, palms up, on the table. "Who would have believed me? Carl was everybody's favourite teacher, devoted to his pupils, adored by them all. Everyone thought he was a loving husband. He was good at keeping up appearances."

"Didn't Linda suspect anything?" I ask.

"Why would she, his own sister? Maybe if I'd known about her ex-husband. There might have been a chance."

I think back to Gaby's uncharacteristic outburst when Linda Parry recounted her abusive relationship with husband Eddie. If only Gaby had known sooner, Linda might have been sympathetic to her plight and she might not now be facing a murder charge.

"You could have come to us," I say. "I've seen your medical file. There was enough physical evidence to prosecute Carl."

"The physical abuse wasn't as bad as the mental. It was the anticipation of fear as much as the fear itself. His drug-taking increased. The cocaine made him more unpredictable."

"Did he cause your miscarriage last year?" Hendersen asks gently.

Gaby squeezes hard on the tissue. "Things were better at first. He was excited about the baby. He kept his fists off me for nearly two months, just the occasional slap in the face." Her matter-of-fact tone sends a shudder through me." Then one day I was suffering with terrible morning sickness. Carl didn't like me to go to the supermarket on my own. But I couldn't face cooking what he'd bought. He always left a £10 note in the house for emergencies, but I wasn't supposed to use it. I didn't think; I wasn't feeling well. I should have known better."

"Tell us what happened," I say, resting my hands over Gaby's.

"I ordered Carl a take-away meal. I paid the delivery boy with the £10 and put the food in the oven to keep warm until Carl came home. Then I went to bed. I woke up when I heard him shouting. He met me at the top of the stairs." She shreds the tissue.

"The medical report said your face got burned," I say.

"He pressed a hot chicken leg from the take-away into my face. I fell."

The interview room's silent for a moment; the three of us lost in our private thoughts.

Gaby Brock speaks first. "Things were much better again for a while. I thought we'd be okay. He was sorry about the baby. He knew it was partly his fault."

Partly. I squeeze her hand again. Even after everything she's been through, she still only "partly" blames Carl Brock for her baby's death.

"But eventually he went back to his old ways?" I prompt.

"The usual. I broke a couple of bones."

I note again her failure to blame Brock – surely *he* was the one who broke her bones. "And how did you feel when he started up again?"

"It was like the baby had left a hole in me. I didn't know what to do. The only solution was to kill myself."

"But you didn't," Hendersen says with less sympathy than I expected.

"I found out I was pregnant again. If I killed myself, I'd be killing the baby, too. I'd already lost one."

I look at the tiny figure sitting opposite me. Never has the word pathetic seemed more apt. I formulate my next question in my head but am reluctant to ask it. It will be the beginning of the end for Gaby Brock.

"Was it then that you saw another way out?"

"The only person who was going to rescue me was myself," she whispers.

I cast my mind back to the rows of romantic paperbacks nestling among the yoga manuals on the Brocks' bookcase. How long did she wait for a knight on a white charger to rescue her?

"It was after he set fire to Pipkin," Gaby continues. "I knew then that he would target anything I loved in order to control me. If I managed to dodge the punches long enough to carry this baby full-term, it would only be a matter of time before he turned on our child to get at me. I might be too weak and stupid to stop him using me as a punch bag, but I couldn't let him do that to my son or daughter."

"I must remind you that you are entitled to a solicitor," the DCI interrupts. He's taken the words from my mouth. I'm comforted he recognizes the victim in Gaby Brock, not just the crime she's committed. To the disappointment of us both, Gaby once again declines a lawyer.

"Please tell us what happened on the night of Sunday, the 17th of June."

"He'd given me a beating that morning."

The older bruises on her arms and legs make sense. The vase of roses in the Brocks' lounge must have been Carl's last peace offering. He found a garage forecourt or a roadside stall doing decent flowers on a Sunday. Perhaps he didn't have to search; he knew where to go from previous experience.

"I made sure I didn't fall asleep that night," Gaby explains. "At about two a.m., I got up and put the key in the back door. I woke Carl and suggested a drive out. We used to go to Martle Top for midnight picnics before we married. He'd been a gentle lover then." She hesitates for a moment as if recalling an older, happy memory.

"He couldn't believe his luck. I hadn't initiated anything romantic for months. Normally he had to force me to … He practically dragged me out of bed and into the car – which was what I wanted; the more bruises I picked up the better. As we stopped in the lay-by, I told him I'd changed my mind. That gave me two black eyes. I jumped out of the car and ran into the field on the other side of the ditch. I'd hidden a kitchen knife there earlier. As he climbed up the ditch towards me, I stabbed him."

"Why didn't we find any blood traces on your pyjamas?"

"Carl cut his hand on Saturday morning when he tried to hit me. I can't remember why. It hardly matters now. His punch missed and he caught his knuckles on the table edge. He wiped his bleeding hand on his shirt, so on Sunday night I put on the bloodied shirt before I woke him up. He didn't notice; it was dark and he was eager to get out to Martle Top. The sleeves were too long, so I grasped the knife over the material. I did the same when I smashed the back door window and turned the key after I got home. That's how you found his blood there. I wanted it to look like a break-in. I put the shirt in the washing machine with several other shirts. I figured that if the blood didn't wash out completely and you decided to analyse it, you'd think that the blood came from his earlier cut."

I'm at a loss for words. I didn't expect this level of planning.

"How did you get home from Martle Top?" Hendersen asks.

"A few days before, I took a bicycle from a garden in the next avenue and rode up there. I hid it in the ditch with the knife, out of sight of anyone who might park in the lay-by. It only took an hour to walk home. I was home in plenty of time, before Carl got in from school. I rode the bike back on Sunday night after I'd killed him and dumped it outside the house I'd taken it from."

Mrs Perkins and her incredible vanishing bicycle. It hardly registered at the time.

"We didn't find soil or pollen on any of your shoes."

"I was wearing Carl's trainers when I took the bike up there. I was barefoot when I went back with Carl. I had a shower when I got home."

"Then you set about faking your own assault," Hendersen says.

"I knew you'd find out about Carl's involvement in drugs sooner or later, so I made it look as if Carl had been taken by drug dealers and that they'd made Carl tie me up."

"And you helped us along with the 'You need a lesson of your own, teacher' quote, drawing us straight into an investigation at Swan Academy. You could have just let us find drugs at your house. That would have speeded us along," Hendersen says.

"There weren't any in the house. Carl brought in what he needed for a deal or his own hit. He kept the rest at his allotment."

Brock's allotment. Another thing Mrs Perkins mentioned and I failed to follow up. She told me that Brock had an untidy allotment near her husband's. I pray the DCI doesn't notice the omission.

He says nothing and I fill the silence. "How did you get Carl's prints on the chains and the key?"

"They were his chains and handcuffs," she whispers. "He used them on me sometimes."

I put my head in my hands, trying to shake off a vision of Gaby's suffering.

"I see." Hendersen coughs. "Why didn't we find your prints? And how in Hades did you place the key in your own pocket?"

Gaby reaches forward and touches the two exhibit packets on the table. They're the ones I took from Steve Chisholm and contain the toilet tissue and the fragment of cotton thread found on the Brocks' lounge carpet. Danny Johnson joked that they were signs of a sloppy housewife. But it was the immaculate carpet below that spoke volumes about Gaby's housekeeping. The carpet she cleaned as if her life depended on it. Perhaps it did.

"I placed tissues over my hands and drew the keys up to my pocket on two threads of cotton. I swallowed most of the thread and one of the tissues. The rest fell on the floor."

I picture the preparation she must have done, the winter pyjamas she wore because they had the appropriately positioned pocket. How long has she been waiting to do this? The pyjamas are brand new – I imagine Gaby somehow saved the money and bought them while Carl was at work – but heavy nightwear like that would not have been available in the shops for several months. Gaby must have bought them long ago. I harden my heart.

"And you planned to frame Bartholomew Hedges?"

"At first I didn't mean to frame anyone. I'd seen two different men at our house with Carl. One was the man Carl wanted me to be nice to and the other was the one you've arrested. I thought they must both be dealers. I had no idea what Carl had done to Bartholomew Hedges's son. When you showed me the police photos and I did the video ID parade just now, I recognized them and assumed I was right about them being dealers. Dealers are killers anyway so what did it matter if they were arrested for the wrong murder."

I see her logic, although she's only half-right. Hedges is innocent, but for the other man, the one she had to be "nice" to, she picked out Samuel McKenzie's mugshot. A creeping, cold memory works its way up my spine. *Be nice to me, why not, you want it too* … I clench my fists. My feelings for McKenzie and all men like him go beyond loathing. If only Gaby had just framed McKenzie and not dragged Hedges in to it.

"Why didn't you come to us?" I ask. "We could have helped you. Couldn't we, sir?"

Hendersen coughs again and ignores the question. "Mrs Brock, you need to get yourself a decent lawyer. You will stand trial for your husband's murder and like as not will go to prison."

Mrs Brock looks up into his face. "Carl's already been my judge, jury and executioner. My life ended two years ago."

Step, shuffle, ball change, stamp.

It's ten p.m. I almost stamp through the floor of the dimly lit studio, making my ankles ache. I repeat the steps over and over with increasing ferocity. In my mind I go through DCI Hendersen's lengthy debrief.

Well, constable. Your hunch was right this time, but don't rely on Agatha Christie to help you again. CID is about asking questions, putting together pieces of information, and gathering evidence.

And don't mislead witnesses by saying we wouldn't pursue cases where the suspected perpetrator is dead. You practically tricked a confession out of her.

You'd better brief DI Bagley about McKenzie being Brock's dealer, but I doubt she'll get anywhere. McKenzie's slippery lawyer will make mincemeat of Gaby Brock's evidence. The statement of a killer carries little weight.

And get the dear lady to bring me the head of Dr Tarnovski, our so-called police surgeon. Only a third-rate medical student would fail to spot Gaby Brock's pregnancy and previous beatings. And what possessed him to send you her medical records? He needs to get out in the field more. He's spending far too much time in the office. Can't imagine what he finds so fascinating. To hell with the paperwork, that's what I say.

And I wouldn't go having too much sympathy for Gaby Brock. We've only her word about their relationship. She killed her husband in cold blood. Planned it in the finest detail, right down to her getaway bicycle – And I want to talk to you about how we came to overlook that piece of evidence – It wouldn't surprise me if she hadn't goaded Brock into swinging a punch and cutting his hand so that she had the bloodied shirt.

Besides, you shouldn't promise what we can't deliver. It was pointless telling her everything would have been all right if she'd reported the abuse. Only one in one hundred domestic violence incidents we attended last year resulted in a prosecution.

Step, shuffle, ball change, stamp.

One in one hundred, stamp.

So this is what getting a CID result feels like. Bagley grudgingly offered to crack open more champagne, when I told her the news, but I declined it. Detection work had left a foul taste in my mouth.

Matthews wasn't in the mood for celebrating either. Although he acknowledged my success with a surprisingly hearty thumbs-up across the desk, he spent the rest of the day sulking behind his computer. He's about as content with the result as I am.

Step, shuffle, ball change, stamp.

One in one hundred, stamp.

"Philippa, you'll damage the floor."

I wheel round to see my father with Jamie.

"Dad, what are you doing here? And out with Jamie this late."

"Your chief inspector phoned me. Said you'd had a hard day and needed some company."

"Hendersen said that?"

"He's old school, your chief inspector. I like him," Edward says. "What happened? Did he give you a …?" He puts his hands over Jamie's ears before mouthing the end of the sentence, "bollocking?"

"No. Well, yes. But I solved a case, a murder." I pick up my towel and head for the studio door.

"Really? You solved a murder in your first week," Edward says. "I knew you had a brain."

"You mean you put a baddie in jail, Pip?" Jamie runs excitedly behind me.

I pat his head before pushing through the door. "If only, Jamie."

Acknowledgements

Thank you for reading *The Good Teacher*. I hope you enjoyed it.

I wrote the book a few years ago. I'd like to thank my editor Finn Cotton at HarperCollins for helping me rewrite and update it, and my agent Marilia Savvides at PFD for seeing something in the original version and making sure the story saw the light of day again. I'm also grateful to eagle-eyed copy editor Janette Currie.

I'd like to give a big shout out to all the book bloggers who promote books for the sheer joy of it. Their support helps bring unknown authors like me to a wider audience. Thank you also to everyone who has taken the trouble to post a review of my writing.

Not long ago I took a course in Creative Writing at Lancaster University. Meeting fellow MA students Fergus Smith, Peter Garrett and Gillian Walker changed my writing life. We continue to support each other and I'm grateful for their wise advice on this book.

As always the biggest thank you is for my husband Nigel for his boundless encouragement and his practical help in PR and proofreading.

If you'd like to know more about my writing and reading, please visit my website at:

www.rachelsargeant.co.uk

I'm also on Twitter:

@RachelSargeant3

If you'd be willing to write a short review of *The Good Teacher*, I would love to read it on Amazon.